Love Begins

Tender Blessings: Book 1

by

Teresa Slack

Thank you for buying this book. To get to know me and my other titles better, I'd like to gift you with a free download of *A Promise for Josie: A Willow Wood Prequel*. Simply follow the link and sign up for my newsletter to get the free download of the story that started the best-rated *Willow Wood Series*.

Click here to pick up your free novella.

Also by Teresa Slack

Tender Blessings Series

Love Begins
A Little Goodbye

Stand Alone Novels

The Ultimate Guide to Darcy Carter
Runaway Heart
Joy Redefined
Cheater, Cheater

Nine Brides for Cowboy Creek

Rennie
Eliza
Carrie
Bridget
Katie
Marianne
Scarlett
Rachael
Amelia

Willow Wood Brides Series

A Promise for Josie: Willow Wood Prequel

Story Behind the Story

The Tender Blessings Series was originally published as a trade paperback entitled A Tender Reed. The story was a huge success with readers and reviewers alike, but they wanted more. I received emails, calls and questions at events about when to expect Book Two. Readers also let me know they wanted more romance. Don't we all!

I went to work enlarging the story and spending more time on Michelle's lackluster love life. It didn't take long to realize there were two books here—hence the Tender Blessings series.

The original book, A Tender Reed, is still available for purchase through Amazon and other online booksellers. I would love to know what you think. If you've read any of the books, including the original, please consider posting a review online. We authors live to hear what readers think and what they want to see more of. Your input and advice matter. What means the most to me are your encouragement and support. Thanks so much for reading.

The Tender Blessings Series

"Infused with humor and practical insights, (Tender Blessings) and its characters will capture the hearts of readers who love children, understand their challenges, and appreciate the many definitions of family." —Aspiring Retail Magazine

"...Slack's feel for her Ozarks setting and her knack for drawing minor characters turns this romance into a fine realistic novel."
---Booklist

"Teresa Slack has done it again! She created a great cast of true-to-life characters that have captured my heart with pathos and with humor. I am rooting for Michelle and can't wait to see what the next installment holds in store for her." ---Reader review

"In this series Slack puts into perspective real life troubles that we see in our world and sometimes our own lives. If you have children or irresponsible siblings, you can connect with this story for sure." ----Reader review

"YES! A funny, clean romance. Believable and loveable characters keep the reader engaged while the plot plays out many hilarious scenes." ----Reader review

"...A perfect blend of humor and humanity as (the author) reveals the story of a young woman's struggle with in herself. She also addresses the feelings of men and their relationship with a woman who is already established in a career, something often not covered in the Christian writing world." ----Reader review

Dedication

Every writer has a friend or family member who thinks all her books are about them. For me, that friend is Tammy Osborne. I must admit I've gotten piles of ideas from our almost-daily phone calls through the years. While much of the inspiration for my Tender Blessings Series came from my years as a preschool teacher at Noah's Ark Preschool, the rest came from Tammy. This book is dedicated with love & deep thanks to her and her thoroughly messed up life.

Couldn't do it without you, girlfriend.

Chapter One

I awoke to the sound of Gypsy barking like a wild thing. She had spent the night on the front porch like she often did when the weather was nice. Leaving her outside overnight was not a problem. The farmhouse was two miles down a back road, off another back road, off a minor highway. The nearest neighbors on either side were kin to both of us and didn't seem to mind Gypsy's late night comings and goings or her howling at the moon.

Sometimes I woke to Gypsy competing with another dog a couple of miles away in one of those bark/howl sequences, depending on how put out she was, to let the other dog know she was on duty and not to go getting any ideas. Normally I rolled over and went back to sleep. Gypsy wasn't much of a watchdog. Not a lot happened on our end of the road worth losing a night's sleep. Unless someone was standing over me with a chainsaw, she didn't raise her hackles. Even then, sometimes I wondered.

I looked at the clock on the nightstand beside my bed. Six-fifteen. On my weekend off, no less. I had planned to sleep in, which for me was around seven. I stuffed the pillow around my ears and tried to ignore her.

The barking continued. It wasn't her usual "there's-a-squirrel-in-the-tree" or "here-comes-the-meter-reader-and-I-haven't-got-anything-better-to-do" barking. She wasn't stopping. I could either stay where I was as the racket wore on my every nerve or get out of bed to see what had her stirred up.

That dog. One of these days…

I threw the sheet off my damp body. For a moment the change in temperature, or maybe the breeze from the sheet, cooled my skin. But then I was hot again. It was going to be another scorcher like every other August day in northern Arkansas.

I sat up and swung my legs over the edge of the queen-sized bed, the linoleum cool and delicious under my bare feet. I went to the window and hit the pane with the heel of my hand to loosen the swollen wood. Someday I would install vinyl windows. It would be nice to have windows that slid smoothly up and down and didn't have to be propped open with a stick. I had dialed the flashing number at the bottom of the TV screen during one of those infomercials last fall. The guy on the other end offered me a steep discount if I agreed to replace every window in the old farmhouse. Even with the discount it was more than I wanted to pay. This house had thirty windows if it had one, and I didn't know how much money I wanted to sink into it. I was only thirty-three. Free and unattached except for Gypsy. I might wake up tomorrow and decide to go off and find a new life somewhere else.

It wasn't likely, but I still didn't want to sink my taking-off money into replacement windows.

I stuck my head out the screen-less window in hopes of seeing or hearing the cause behind Gypsy's tumult. She was on the front porch directly below me. I couldn't see her through the porch roof, but I could tell she was at her usual post next to the left roof support with her paws dangling over the edge of the top step. I cocked an ear to listen for what she heard. It could be another dog barking, Uncle DeWitt tinkering on a project down the road, or a masked gunman breaking through the front door. All was quiet except for Gypsy.

"Gypsy!" I hollered in my usual early morning croak. "Knock off that barking,"

The dog paused for a half breath before going right back at it. She wasn't going to listen to any commands from me as long as she knew I wasn't serious enough to come downstairs to correct her.

With an aggravated huff, I left the window. I stepped into the pair of cotton shorts I'd stepped out of last night, pulled them up over the tail of my thin nightgown and padded down the stairs in my bare feet.

If Gypsy was carrying on over a dead snake she'd dragged onto the porch, I was going to let her have it. The other night she'd dug a mole out of the yard and then barked at the blind, confused creature and knocked it around every time it tried to get back underground. She wouldn't kill it. She just tortured it for her own sadistic pleasure. My sweet natured Australian Shepard-Beagle-Collie mix was a Nazi.

I finally had to kill the mole with a shovel and throw its remains over the fence. If I had to get that up close and personal with a snake, Gypsy was going to be in hot water.

I yanked the front door open with enough force to demonstrate my irritation at getting woken up so early on a Saturday morning. I stepped onto the porch and set my fists on my hips to drive home my point. Gypsy stopped barking long enough to glance at me over her shoulder before turning back toward the road and starting in again.

The posturing hadn't worked. It was time to get serious. "Gypsy, for crying out loud. Is this necessary? Do you think the neighbors appreciate hearing your mouth at six o'clock on a Saturday morning?"

Gypsy and I lived alone on what remained of the family farm. From the day I brought her home, I had talked to her like she was a person instead of a dog. I enjoyed her company above any other living creature on the earth so I figured she deserved the respect. I also believed she understood more that came out of my mouth than the usual "Sit" and "Stay". In fact, those were the commands she chose to not understand.

Rather than heed the irritation in my voice and stance, Gypsy leaped off the porch, bypassing the steps in one bound, and landed deftly on the worn dirt path. She headed to the opening in the white picket fence some fifty feet away. She dashed through the opening where a gate once stood and made a right turn toward the mailbox on the other side of a thirty-year-old lilac bush. The white gate I passed through every day on my way to and from the school bus had been missing for years. Even back then the gate was loose, one hinge rusted and squeaky and the other completely gone. I couldn't remember when the gate disappeared for good. Probably around the time I started applying for scholarships and had a personal reason for checking the mail. I still painted the wooden fence every other year so it remained white and crisp against the lilac and forsythia bushes, but I never gave a thought to the missing gate, until now.

I could see Gypsy's hindquarters sticking out from behind the lilac bush. Her fluffy tail was erect, the tip twitching slightly. She barked once more for effect before going silent. While she still felt it prudent to proceed with caution to whatever was on the other side of the fence, she was no longer threatened. I could dismiss the notion of someone waiting for me with a chainsaw—I hoped.

I wished now I'd taken the time to slip on a pair of flip flops before hurrying out the door. The dirt under my feet was cold and damp with dew. I'd track mud into the house when I went back inside if I didn't first spray them off with the garden hose around back. I winced as a pebble dug into the ball of my foot. That blasted dog. One of these days I was going to wring her hairy neck. Whatever she was carrying on about had better be worth all this trouble.

I stepped through the opening in the fence and turned right. The dirt path ended. Gooseflesh rose on my bare legs as the wet grass brushed my ankles. "Gypsy, what's all the..." I began as I rounded the lilac bush.

Gypsy looked at me over her shoulder and then sat back on her haunches, barely missing my foot. She turned back to her discovery.

I followed her gaze. My breath caught in my throat. Gypsy sensed my reaction and jumped forward, I suppose to assure me there was no cause for alarm.

She put her nose against the trembling little boy, circled him and the little girl huddled next to him in the cold grass, and then looked back at me. *"I told you it was a big deal,"* her reproving gaze scolded. *"Now what are you going to do about it?"*

I snapped out of my trance and moved gingerly forward so not to startle the wide-eyed children staring up at me.

That's when I recognized them.

"Jonah? Emma?"

Neither child's expression changed.

Gypsy nudged closer, apparently satisfied all was well. She put her nose against the little boy's neck and sniffed. He turned toward her, and his lips twitched into a smile. A tiny hand disappeared into her thick, dark red coat. It was all the encouragement she needed. She shoved against him and nuzzled his neck. Then she reached across him to inspect his sister, knocking him over with her broad body in the process.

I stepped forward. "Gypsy, stop."

I heard a muffled giggle.

I took hold of Gypsy's collar and pulled her back. The little boy lay on his back in the grass, his knees against his chest where Gypsy had upended him. At the sight of me towering over him, the giggling stopped and his face sobered.

"Are you okay?" I asked.

He stared up at me. After a moment, he pulled himself upright and asked in a tiny voice, "Are you my Aunt Shell?"

Shell. I hadn't been called that in years. Not since before my kid sister Nicole learned to correctly pronounce Michelle. Someone must have told the boy whose yard he was in. He never would've recognized me on his own. He'd been a fat, slobbering, happy baby the last time I saw him two years ago. I wouldn't have recognized him either had I seen him somewhere else under different circumstances, though I did see a lot of Nicole around his eyes.

At the sound of the little boy's voice, Gypsy lunged free from my grasp on her collar. She loved everyone, but children were her favorite. She inspected his face with her wet nose before straddling him to get to his sister again. The little girl, who was around four if my memory served me correctly and more recognizable than her brother, shrank away from the big dog's face, apparently not as sure of Gypsy's intent as Jonah.

I took hold of the dog's collar again. "Gypsy, that's enough."

I gave the collar a firm jerk. She reluctantly complied and sat down at my feet, keeping her eyes on the children.

"Yes, I'm your Aunt Michelle. You must be Jonah and Emma." I leaned forward and stretched my arms out to the little boy. He paused only a moment before reaching for me. Regardless of how shy he might normally be around a practical stranger, the wet grass and fear of spending who knew how long out here by the gate, drove him into my arms.

Gypsy whimpered and looked close to pouncing again. A growled "stay" from me held her in place.

I took Jonah in my arms and straightened. He wrapped his legs around me for balance and warmth. His bare feet chilled my ribs through my nightgown. How long had he and Emma been sitting here? Not long since Gypsy had just started barking, but long enough that he shivered in the morning air.

I shifted Jonah to my right hip and reached out my free hand to Emma. She looked from my hand to Jonah and back again. I resisted the urge to hurry her. Her brother was getting heavy, and I didn't want to stand here in the wet grass all morning. But I could be patient when I had to be. I was a nurse in a cardio-care unit where I dealt with scared, hurting, cranky patients every day. Emma didn't know me. She was probably wondering as much as me what she and Jonah were doing on the road like something left for the garbage truck to haul away. Surely I could exercise some professional compassion with my own niece and nephew.

After a long moment of staring at my hand, Emma rose onto her knees and took it. She stood up on shaky legs. Her feet were also bare. She was dressed in a pair of cotton shorts and a baggy tee shirt that looked like she'd been wearing it for several days. Her curly blond hair was a tangled mess, and she had a dollop of what looked like dried spaghetti sauce on her chin. She eyed Gypsy warily. Gypsy stood up and returned the stare, eager and expectant. Cautiously, Emma took hold of Gypsy's collar with her free hand.

When our bedraggled group stepped away from the lilac bush, I noticed a frayed book bag in the grass. It probably contained their belongings. I'd come back for it later after I got the kids into the house, into something warm and dry and put some food in their bellies. It looked like they could use it. I headed up the dirt path no longer worried about the mud that would get tracked across my relatively clean floors.

Jonah bounced on my hip, his cold feet snuggling intentionally into my warmth. Emma's hand trembled in mine. I still hadn't heard a peep out of her. Gypsy, who wasn't that big of a dog, came nearly to the little girl's shoulder. She strode beside Emma, her head and tail erect, the only one among us happy with the circumstances.

I was trained to take care of a situation first, fix what was wrong, make everyone as comfortable as possible, and then ask questions. At this moment I didn't need to worry about how the kids came to be under my lilac bush. I wouldn't think of them just inches from the road where anyone could have come by in the early morning light and run them over.

And I certainly didn't want to worry about Nicole. As my mind conjured up questions about my missing sister, I resolutely pushed them aside. I couldn't think about what tragedy must have befallen her to make her leave her two young children in my front yard without a word of explanation. Or worse, that nothing had happened and she simply abandoned them.

Chapter Two

I was nearly ten years old and happily relegated to the status of only child when my parents saw fit to present me with a little sister. It turned out they were full of surprises. When I was eleven and Nicole fifteen-months, Dad took off. One day he was coming home from work and spinning Nicole in the air and asking me about school, and the next he was gone. Mom never told us where he went, what possessed him to go, or even if she saw it coming. The whole situation makes no more sense to me now then it did twenty-two years ago.

Mom, Nicole, and me held out as long as we could in our little apartment in Memphis, Tennessee, but Mom wasn't one of those 'step-up-to-the-plate, when-life-gives-you-lemons-make-lemonade' type of people. She was a good woman, but she lacked the fortitude to raise us on her own.

We packed everything we had that the bank didn't own into our battered Chevy Cavalier and moved back to the family farm where Mom and her sisters and brothers had been raised. Grandma Catherine still lived in the big farmhouse. Grandpa was nearly twenty years older than Grandma and had been dead for a number of years. By then the farm had been divided into several portions to accommodate members of the family who felt no inclination to move away. Mom's oldest brother, DeWitt, a crusty old bachelor, lived in a simple shotgun house he'd built in the late seventies. It was a half-mile east of the original farmhouse, and he farmed eighty acres there. No improvements had been made in the ensuing forty-plus years. The trees he planted in the yard had grown into massive, looming pines, successfully concealing the house from the road, which was his intent. No one saw much of Uncle DeWitt.

Aunt Wanda and her husband Jeb Rowe, a retired state highway worker, farmed and raised cattle on the forty acres to the west of my house. The rest of the family used the sense God gave them and high tailed it out of the county as soon as they were able. Uncle Jeb tore down the little house on his portion of the property and built Aunt Wanda a modern brick tri-level about the same time Nicole, Mom and I were moving in on Grandma. I was often envious of Aunt Wanda's modern kitchen, ample closet space and finished basement that didn't flood after every spring rain but not enough to sink any real money into Grandma's house.

Aunt Wanda and Uncle Jeb had one child, a fair-haired, whiny, spoiled girl named Violet who looked a lot like me. She was nearly a year older than me, but we were in the same grade at Jessup Elementary in Winona, the tiny town five miles east of the farm. Since the small school only had three homerooms per grade, I spent a lot of time in Violet's company.

I hated the school, the depressingly outdated farmhouse, and most of all, simpering Violet who got off the bus every day at the farm with me. Even after Mom moved us to the farm, Aunt Wanda finished her housework every morning by ten and came over to spend the rest of the day with Grandma. Supposedly it was to help out. According to Grandma, she couldn't get along without Wanda. It seemed to me Grandma just liked a sympathetic ear for her constant complaining, and Wanda liked to remind Mom her own husband hadn't taken off, leaving her high and dry with two kids to raise alone.

Considering Uncle Jeb's options, I never understood what kept him around.

Whatever Aunt Wanda's motivation, much of my afternoons were spent entertaining Violet when I would rather have been reading, walking in the woods behind the house, playing with Baby Nicole or composing tearful letters to my missing father, begging him to come home—letters I would never send since Mom wouldn't, or couldn't, tell me where he'd gone.

I missed Dad and could think of little else. My grades had always been at the top of my class. After moving to Winona, about a hundred miles east of Memphis, my grades plummeted and continued their downward spiral well into high school. I couldn't get over Dad's leaving. I thought our family was happy and stable. I didn't know of such things as other women or disenchantment with life. Even if I had, I never would have thought they applied to my father. He was my rock, and I loved him more than anything. I thought he loved me back.

Had I been able to see past my own misery, I might've noticed the toll our new circumstances were taking on Mom. I should've known she couldn't last. Grandma Catherine was a faultfinder—in me, Mom, Nicole, Uncle Jeb, even Grandpa Walt who had the foresight to die early.

Mom didn't have it in her to stand up to anyone, least of all someone as headstrong as Grandma. She took a job she hated in town because Grandma insisted she do so. She stood quietly and nodded and swallowed her resentment at Aunt Wanda's unwelcome advice on every subject from motherhood to growing cucumbers. She wasn't strong enough to tell them to mind their own business. How could she when she needed them so badly?

I didn't pay much attention the first time I saw her take a sip from the narrow bottle she kept in her underwear drawer. Mom and Dad had always been what they called 'social drinkers'. It didn't take long to realize there was nothing social about her behavior. I did her share of the housework when she was hung over. I shushed Nicole and tried to keep her out from underfoot when Mom was sleeping in. I didn't want to give Grandma another reason to scold Mom like a child. I was secretly pleased to know I wasn't the only one suffering from Dad's absence. Our pain became a badge we shared.

It shouldn't have come as a big surprise when she left.

Instantly, it was Nicole and me facing the rest of them. The ones here, not by invitation, but because of a curse sent by God to punish Grandma for some sin she had unknowingly committed. At least that's the impression I got. I was fourteen when Mom left. Nicole was nearly four. No longer a baby whose behavior could be overlooked. She was precocious, darling and too energetic to be tolerated by Grandma. Nicole had no recollection of Dad, whom I was also beginning to forget, and her memories of Mom soon became blurred.

"Does your dog bite?"

The sound of Jonah's voice snapped me out of my reverie. I climbed the three porch steps and opened the front door. "No, she loves everybody." I let go of Emma's hand to trip the latch on the screen door, and held it open with my hip while Gypsy led Emma in ahead of Jonah and me.

"She barked at us," Jonah told me.

"I heard her. I hope she didn't scare you."

"She scared Emma. A little."

I stepped inside and lowered Jonah to the floor. The screen door banged shut behind us. I looked at Emma. She had apparently gotten over her initial fright of Gypsy. Her hand still clung to the dog's collar.

"I'm sorry she scared you, Emma."

Emma patted Gypsy's head with her free hand. A tiny smile curved the corners of her mouth as she looked into Gypsy's unique Australian Shepard eyes. She reminded me of Nicole at that age—sunny blonde hair cascading down her back in long, loose curls, delicate features, an upturned nose, and the bluest eyes this side of heaven fringed by long blond lashes.

I arched my back to work out the kinks. For such a little guy, Jonah sure got heavy between the lilac bushes and the front door. His blond hair was several shades darker than Emma's, the kind that some people would already call brown. His eyes were brown as well, and the shape of his face was angular where Emma's was soft. If I didn't know Emma was the oldest, it would be hard to know for sure. They were almost the same height and build, and Jonah was definitely the more outgoing of the two. I counted backwards in my head. He'd been born three years ago in the spring. The last day of March I thought, though I'd have to ask Aunt Wanda to be sure. That made him three and a half. Emma's birthday was easier to remember. February fourteenth, the year before Jonah came. A sweetheart baby. That's what Nicole called her. Too bad the sweetheart who helped produce her didn't hang around after the stick from the drugstore test turned blue.

What in the world was I going to do with two preschoolers? Today was the start of one of my rare weekends off, but I had to go to work on Monday. I worked long hours at a stressful job. I didn't have time to baby-sit two tiny children while my irresponsible kid sister was finding herself or sleeping one off.

When I got my hands on her…

Emma and Jonah stared expectantly up at me.

"You must be starving," I said belatedly.

Jonah nodded. Emma laid her head on Gypsy's back and hugged her neck. I mentally went over the contents of my pantry. Slim pickings if I remembered correctly. I didn't cook.

When I wasn't working, which wasn't often, I grabbed whatever was easy and convenient—low fat yogurt, Lean Cuisine, fast food take-out or a bag of microwave popcorn. I relied on multi-vitamins to balance out my irregular diet.

"Do you like pancakes?" I asked in as cheery a voice as I could muster. Surely I had the necessary ingredients to whip up a batch as long as I remembered how.

Jonah nodded again. Emma tightened her arms around Gypsy and buried her face in the dog's long hair.

"Emma likes pancakes too," Jonah said, ever the helpful one.

"Great." I took Jonah's hand in mine and reached for Emma's with the other. As soon as I made contact, she let out a wail that nearly stopped my heart. She let go of Gypsy's neck and dropped to the floor on her hands and knees. She buried her face in her hands and bent forward until her forehead rested against the cool wood floor.

I jumped back like I'd been scalded. Now what? I was good at handling emergencies with my adult patients with grace and a cool head. This was different. I avoided children at all costs, especially screaming ones.

Jonah slipped his hand out of mine and squatted on the floor beside his big sister. "It's okay, Emmy," he soothed. "She'll come back. She always does." He patted her back and pulled her tangled curls away from her face.

Even Gypsy seemed to know what to do. With a loud sigh she slumped on the floor next to the crying child and laid her head in her paws. Emma rose up enough to wrap one arm around Gypsy and the other around Jonah as she continued to cry onto the floor.

I stood there just inside the door of the old farmhouse and watched the drama at my feet. In my thirteen years of nursing, I'd seen families weep as I explained a Do Not Resuscitate Order for their terminally ill parents. I stood within reach to provide a comforting shoulder or someone to scream at when parents received the news their child had died from head trauma sustained in a traffic accident. My entire adult life had been spent taking care of people at the absolute lowest points in their lives.

Now as my own niece and nephew sat on my floor and bawled their eyes out over their missing mother, I was helpless. Even if I could think of an appropriate platitude that would explain to a child why she and her little brother had been abandoned in a stranger's yard in the middle of the night, the words wouldn't have gotten past my thickened throat.

"It's okay, Emmy. She'll come back. She always does."

What did that mean? What had these kids been through during their short time on earth? More importantly, where was Nicole? What was she thinking?

How could she have done this to me?

Chapter Three

I couldn't remember the last time I made pancakes. Since Grandma passed away six years ago, I'd become a stranger to the kitchen. It turned out I hadn't lost my touch, at least not with pancakes. They turned out perfectly. Neither Emma nor Jonah had much appetite.

Emma stopped crying long enough to move the pancakes around on her plate in a puddle of syrup. Jonah ate a little better. He also had better luck at keeping his tears in check, but just barely. Neither one looked up or spoke to me while they ate. I stayed close to the stove, fearful of saying too much or intruding on their suffering, lest the tears start flowing again.

After they finished breakfast, I ushered them into the living room, sat them in front of my miserable twenty-seven-inch pre-Plasma television, and flipped around for cartoons or something that might interest them. I didn't have cable. The set was a throw back from Grandma Catherine's days. I didn't have time or the inclination for television and got by just fine with an occasional dose of evening news.

I found something animated though it didn't look anything like the Bugs or Daffy cartoons of my childhood. Emma and Jonah stared at the low-definition picture and exchanged glances. I backed out of the room and fled to the telephone in the hallway. I took the handset from the base and retreated to a secluded corner where I wouldn't be overheard.

It was nearly eight a.m. I knew Aunt Wanda and Uncle Jeb would be up and working on their second pot of coffee by now. Aunt Wanda answered on the second ring.

"Can you come over?" I asked without pretense. "It's Nicole. She's gone and done it this time, and I don't know what to do."

"Oh, dear," Aunt Wanda said. "Is she all right?"

"I'm not sure. I woke up this morning and found the kids outside under the lilac bushes."

"Emma and Jonah? You're kidding. You don't suppose something happened to Nicole, do you?"

"I don't think so. At least I hope not. Jonah told Emma not to cry, that she always comes back."

"Oh, dear," Aunt Wanda said again. "Those poor babies. I'll be right over."

It was sad that I didn't need to convince her I was telling the truth and not over-reacting. The family was accustomed to Nicole and her antics by now. By the time she was sixteen, embroiled in her third or fourth serious love affair—with a married man this time—we realized there was no scandalous behavior beneath her.

Aunt Wanda burst through the back door five minutes later. I was waiting, perched on a kitchen stool, relieved someone more up to the task was available to take charge of the situation. Her garishly unnatural blonde hair stood out from her head in a fuzzy mess. Years of overuse of harsh hair coloring products and home perms, coupled with an incredibly dated hairstyle, added years to her appearance. I had never seen her outside the house, even to go to the mailbox, without that hair teased and sprayed within an inch of its life. Uncle Jeb always said her car didn't need air bags. Her hair would save her in the event of a crash.

The messy condition of her hair today spoke volumes about the interruption in her usual morning routine.

"Where are they?"

I jabbed my thumb toward the kitchen doorway. "Watching TV."

"What did Nicole say?"

"Nothing. I didn't see her. Gypsy woke me up barking. When I went out to see what was going on, I found them huddled outside the gate next to the road."

"Oh, this is rich," Aunt Wanda fumed, "even for Nicole."

She crept to the doorway and peered into the living room. She looked back at me. "Did she leave a note or anything? Did the kids say where she is?"

I shook my head. "I don't think they know more than I do. They're upset of course, but I don't think they're terribly surprised."

She shook her head and clicked her tongue.

I remembered the book bag under the lilac bush. "They had a bag with them. Maybe there's something in it." I stepped into the mudroom and took a pair of garden shoes out of the wicker basket by the door. "I'll be right back."

When I got back, the battered book bag in tow, Aunt Wanda was no longer in the kitchen. I looked into the living room and saw her sitting in Grandma Catherine's easy chair, watching the kids watch TV. Only they weren't watching anymore. They cowered together in the center of the sofa with Gypsy leaning protectively against their legs. All three were staring at Aunt Wanda.

Everyone looked up when I walked in.

I held up the book bag and smiled. "Look what I found. Does this belong to anyone?"

"That's ours," Jonah offered. "Dean brought it."

Dean. I vaguely remembered the name from a previous telephone conversation with Nicole. It was during one of our typical, "Can you send me a few bucks. I'm in a real bind?" conversations.

Without going into particulars, Dean had apparently messed up her face in a drunken fight and forced her to lose her hostess job at Denny's. When I tried to talk her into coming home until she got her life together, we ended up having a fight of our own.

She didn't come home. I transferred some money to her local Walmart.

"Is Dean the one who brought you here?" Aunt Wanda asked.

Emma and Jonah exchanged glances. I wondered if they'd been warned against telling anyone how they ended up outside my gate.

"May I look in here and see what you brought?" I asked.

They exchanged glances again, but the panic in their eyes had subsided. Jonah nodded. Emma had yet to speak or even maintain eye contact with me.

I sat down on the chair opposite them and set the bag on my knees. "What a nice book bag. It's so big and heavy. You must have lots of cool stuff in here."

Jonah gave me a half-smile. Emma wrapped her arms around Gypsy's neck and stared into space.

I had the bag halfway unzipped before I wondered if this was a good idea. What if there was something inside the children shouldn't see? Jonah said Dean was the one who brought the bag. It occurred to me Dean could've done something to Nicole. My stomach lurched. What if Nicole was hurt somewhere and totally unaware of what Dean had done with her kids? Even if she had left the kids before, it didn't necessarily mean she had willingly done so this time.

I scooped the bag into my arms and stood up. "Oh, my, I think I forgot to turn off the stove."

Aunt Wanda gave me a strange look and jumped out of her chair. She followed me into the kitchen. I deposited the bag on the table and turned to look at her.

"What's going on?" She knew I hadn't left the stove on. She stared at me and then the bag as if it might be ticking.

I glanced toward the door to make sure no little ears were within hearing distance before I finished unzipping the bag. "I was afraid this might contain something the kids shouldn't see."

Aunt Wanda sucked air between her teeth. "You're right." She pulled out a chair and sat down in front of the bag.

I reached inside and pulled out a sheaf of papers. Underneath were hastily packed clothes—tee shirts, shorts, two pairs of jeans, a pair each of boys' jockeys and girls' panties. No socks, no shoes, no jackets or sweaters.

I exhaled with relief. "They apparently aren't going to be here long. This is only enough stuff to last a day or two."

"Or it could've been packed by a man who wouldn't know what children needed."

Aunt Wanda reached for the sheaf of papers. Her brow furrowed as her eyes scanned a few pages. "What is all this about?" She held the papers up for me to see. "Here's both the kids' birth certificates and their shot records."

My stomach plummeted. "Why in the world…" I snatched the papers out of her hand and scanned over them. "Why would Nicole think to send shot records and birth certificates but not a simple pair of shoes? What is she thinking?"

Aunt Wanda stood up and peered at the papers over my shoulder. "I don't know, Michelle, but I doubt this Dean, whoever he is, would include a birth certificate if Nicole didn't know what he was doing."

My head began to pound. I forgot to be relieved Dean apparently hadn't hurt my sister. "So you think Nicole is planning to leave the kids here…indefinitely."

I gazed at Aunt Wanda hopefully, silently begging her to tell me I was wrong. Nicole wouldn't do that. She just needed my help for a few days. She was probably between jobs and in a bind. I'd keep an eye on the kids for a couple of days, a few weeks max, and then she'd come get them and my life would go back to normal.

"She knows you go to work every day. If you have her kids, you're going to need daycare. You can't put a kid anywhere these days without this stuff. She's apparently put some thought into it."

I refused to accept what seemed to be happening. I sank into a kitchen chair and stared despondently at the papers. "This doesn't make sense. Nicole is a piece of work, but she loves her kids. I know she does. She wouldn't just leave them here, especially without telling me what she's doing."

Aunt Wanda continued to stare at the rumpled pile of clothes on the table, neither confirming nor denying my rambling thoughts.

I told myself not to panic. Sure, Nicole was flighty. She wasn't even a great mom. She lived here on the farm until Emma was a few months old. Barely out of high school and between boyfriends and jobs, she had no patience for a needy, demanding baby when she was practically one herself. Her hairpin temper snapped frequently over colic, messy diaper changes and Emma just being a baby.

I found myself getting up in the middle of the night more and more often for feedings. I couldn't stand listening to Nicole's cussing and grumbling through the thin walls as she demanded Emma to hurry up and eat so she could go back to bed. Or worse, when she ignored her altogether.

When she decided to move with Emma to the city where she could look for work, I refused to dwell on what life would be like for the baby. I didn't offer to take Emma or help Nicole find childcare or a job. The situation was Nicole's problem, not mine. Mollycoddling and taking over responsibility would only enable her to continue making poor choices. At least that's what I told myself every time I started to worry about Emma.

I didn't hear anything about the next boyfriend, some long-haired loser named Bones who played in a band, until after Nicole called and said she was pregnant again. It didn't take much math skills on my part to realize she had become pregnant while living with me. I didn't think Bones was a local boy, so I was pretty sure he was off the hook should he ever face a paternity suit.

For the life of me, I couldn't imagine how Nicole had let another unplanned pregnancy occur when Emma was still waking her up in the night. She went out a few times to a club in town with a couple of girlfriends while living here, leaving me home to baby sit. She never mentioned meeting someone. I couldn't believe she was the type of woman who could meet a guy in a club and get pregnant, practically on the same night. Apparently, that was exactly what happened.

"Nicole has been on her own for almost four years," I said to Aunt Wanda. "She works most of the time and every time I talk to her, she seems to have things worked out. I can't believe she would leave her kids without a word of explanation."

Aunt Wanda gave me the same long suffering look I'd seen on Grandma's face too many times over the years. "We can only pray Nicole is planning on this being a temporary arrangement."

I wondered if she was thinking of the way Mom disappeared and left Nicole and me here with no explanation for Grandma. At the time we thought she'd come back any day. She didn't call for two and a half years.

I couldn't think of Mom right now, and I wouldn't let Aunt Wanda think about her either.

"Of course this is a temporary arrangement. Nicole will call any minute and straighten this whole thing out."

"When was the last time you talked to her?"

"It's been awhile. I sent the kids some stuff for Christmas."

"Goodness, Michelle. That was eight months ago."

Like I needed her reminding me. I had a calendar.

"She was living in Memphis," I said, "but I think she moved since then. Her cell number stopped working months ago."

If I didn't shut up, I'd start bawling like Emma.

We sat at the table and stared at the papers in front of us. My mind was whirling. I didn't want to think about how this would affect my life. I didn't have time for children. Besides putting in forty hours a week in the I.C.U. unit at a major hospital in Jonesboro, I worked weekends on contingency in the surgery prep unit at the local county hospital. It was a rare thing for me to take a weekend off. I had planned to do some chores around the farm while the weather cooperated. What was I supposed to do with Emma and Jonah when I went to work on Monday? There weren't enough clothes in the bag to last through the weekend, and I certainly didn't have anything around here they could wear. I didn't even have food in the house to appeal to a preschooler's palate.

Aunt Wanda must have been thinking the same thing. She got up and went to the refrigerator. She looked inside and sighed in dismay at the meager contents. She slammed the door with her elbow. "I see I need to go to the store if you plan on feeding those two anything besides pancakes."

"That's what I was thinking."

She crossed her arms over her chest and leaned against the refrigerator. "So, what are you going to do with them?"

I rested my chin in my hand. "I have no idea. At least I have the weekend to figure it out."

"They haven't said a word about where Nicole might've took off to, or when she's coming to get them?"

I shook my head. "I can't get more than a word or two at a time out of Jonah, and Emma's not talking at all. Since Dean brought the bag, it means Nicole isn't alone. I don't know if that's good or bad."

"That girl's never been without a man for more than a week at a stretch. I've never seen anything like it." Aunt Wanda returned to her chair. "What a mess. What an absolute mess. Leave it to Nicole to act without even thinking of the consequences. How typical. She has no more business with two kids than a submarine has with a screen door."

The last thing I wanted to hear was a list of my sister's shortcomings, especially with her two abandoned children comforting one another less then twenty feet away. "She surely wasn't thinking," I agreed. "But regardless of what Nicole's done, I don't want those two in there thinking it's their fault."

I thought of Grandma and how she reminded me every day of my life how she never asked to be saddled with me or Nicole. Regardless of how irritated I was by Emma's crying or the money I'd have to spend to get her and Jonah through the weekend, I didn't want them to feel the way I did whenever Grandma went off on one of her rants about my missing parents.

Aunt Wanda smoothed at a wayward curl. "What would Nicole have done if you hadn't been home this weekend? Wouldn't that have been a sight if she left the kids here and they weren't found for three or four days?" She clicked her tongue again. "No decent mother would do that."

"She knows I never go anywhere," I said in Nicole's defense, though she certainly didn't deserve it.

"How does she know anything? She hasn't been home in over a year."

"When I see her again, I'll personally wring her neck. In the meantime, I've got to decide what to do about Emma and Jonah."

Aunt Wanda crossed her arms over her ample bosom and sat back in her chair. "From where I sit, the decision's been made for you. Nicole's made a mess of things, but she is family."

Her earlier irritation seemed to have softened into resignation. "You do for family. And even if they weren't kin, Michelle, it's plain Christian charity. You're duty bound."

My jaw tightened. I'd heard enough about Christian charity from Grandma. The only reason she allowed Mom to move in with Nicole and me after Dad left, and the only reason she kept us after Mom disappeared, was Christian charity.

She never let us forget we were living under her roof, eating her food and sleeping under her warm blankets because she was a good Christian. If not for her generous spirit, the Lord only knew what would become of us.

I had enough Christian charity to last me a lifetime.

"Maybe this is for the best," Aunt Wanda went on.

"How can it be for the best?" I snapped.

We both jerked our heads toward the door that led to the living room. I lowered my voice and resumed talking. "I'm sorry, Aunt Wanda, but this is not for the best. I work sixty hours a week. I'm barely home long enough to take care of Gypsy, let alone two kids I didn't bring into the world."

Aunt Wanda covered my hand with hers. "None of us know a thing about kids until we become parents. It's something you figure out as you go."

I leaned toward Aunt Wanda and whispered, "But I don't to figure it out. I don't want kids. Not now, not ever. I don't particularly like them. I don't want a husband. I don't like those either. I'm perfectly happy here with Gypsy. I don't need or want anything else."

Aunt Wanda actually had the nerve to laugh. If she kept it up, she was going to find herself on the receiving end of the wrath I felt for Nicole.

She got up and pulled open a cabinet drawer. "Have you got any paper in here? We'll make a grocery list and I'll go shopping for you."

As usual she wasn't paying attention to anything I said. She thought I was making a joke. What did I have to do for someone to take me seriously?

I jumped to my feet. "I'll do the shopping." I took the paper and stub of a pencil out of her hand. I needed to get out of this house, at least for a few minutes. And I sure didn't want Aunt Wanda spouting Nicole's and my business all over town. "It would really help me out if you stayed here with the kids."

She sighed. "I suppose I could. I'll make lunch with something out of these cabinets." She opened one door and then another, working her way down the wall. "You don't have much, do you?"

"I'll take care of it."

"Michelle."

I looked up from the paper.

"It will all work out. You may find this is the best thing that's ever happened to you."

Now who was the one making a joke? I tried to smile like I thought she could be right, but my lips stuck to my teeth. This was not the best thing that ever happened to me. I didn't want my life to change. I wanted to go to work Monday like always and not worry about two little people who were suddenly dependent on me.

Chapter Four

When I got home two hours later with enough frozen and pre-packaged food for an army of little people, Emma and Jonah were fast asleep on the living room rug, their arms around Gypsy. Gypsy raised her head off the floor and looked at me but didn't get up. That was a first. I guess I'd been replaced in her eyes. I wouldn't take it personally. Gypsy sensed who needed her most. Still, I couldn't help wondering what the kids' presence in the house would rob me of next.

I followed the sound of pots and pans rattling in the kitchen and found Aunt Wanda on her hands and knees rearranging the bottom cabinet shelves.

She paused in her rattling long enough to explain it was no wonder I didn't cook with the lack of organization in my kitchen. "Now that you've got little ones," her voice rang out from the dark recesses of the cabinets, "you're going to have to start running a tighter ship."

I didn't want to run a tight ship. I wanted everything to stay exactly the way it was. I earned a decent wage doing something I loved. I kept the farmhouse's old roof from caving in on my head. Gypsy's shots were up to date. I didn't owe anyone money I couldn't pay back in an acceptable amount of time. No tighter ship could anyone expect of me.

I turned and left the kitchen without a word and went back to the car for the next load of groceries. This was the first time since Grandma Catherine died that I couldn't carry all my groceries into the house in one trip. Things were already changing, and I didn't like it.

I had run into Sandy Cline while I was at Winn Dixie. She eyed my grocery cart suspiciously and asked if I was expecting company. In a town the size of Winona anyone with the slightest observation skills can figure out their neighbor's business by looking at what they bought at the grocery store. You couldn't develop diabetes, adopt a kitten or confirm a suspected pregnancy in private unless you shopped in the next county.

I had smiled at Sandy and said I was expecting my sister any day, which I was…sort of. When she asked where Nicole was keeping herself since she hadn't been seen around here in a month of Sundays, I smiled brightly and pushed my cart toward produce. I called out to Sandy over my shoulder that I would tell Nicole she had asked about her.

The joys of small town life.

I started putting away groceries as Aunt Wanda backed out of the cabinet and slowly got to her feet. She slapped at the knees of her slacks. I braced myself for the lecture on the condition of my floors and tried to recall what possessed me to buy yogurt in a tube. Couldn't kids eat yogurt with a spoon anymore? Did everything have to come out of a squeezable, convenient, overpriced tube these days?

"Did you stop by Children's Services?" Aunt Wanda asked in lieu of the lecture.

I stared. "Children's Services? Why would I do that?"

"Michelle," Aunt Wanda said, in that mildly irritating, condescending way of hers I'd learned to ignore over the past twenty years, "Nicole has disappeared. The police aren't going to go looking for her since technically she isn't missing. Personally I don't think anything happened that a swift kick in the rear wouldn't cure. But in the meantime, you've got her kids. What if she isn't coming back—ever? Does your insurance cover them if they get sick? Do you have the authority to have them treated? What are you going to do about childcare? A birth certificate may not be enough to enroll them in daycare. They barely have more than the clothes on their backs. All this is going to cost money. Who's going to pay for it? You?"

I closed my eyes and massaged my temple. She had obviously done a lot of thinking while I was out. This was adding up to more than a simple weekend's worth of inconvenience.

I opened my eyes. "There's no need to bring the county authorities into our business."

The last thing I wanted was for everyone in Harrison County to know my irresponsible sister had abandoned her kids in my front yard. "Emma and Jonah might not be here that long. Besides, it's Saturday. All the public offices are closed."

Aunt Wanda ignored that minor setback. "You don't have a choice, missy. Things like this aren't as simple as they used to be."

Do you mean like they were when Mom walked away and left Nicole and me for Grandma to take care of? I wanted to ask.

"I'm sure Nicole thought about all those things. That's why she left the backpack."

Aunt Wanda arched her eyebrows. "You're kidding, right? This is Nicole we're talking about. If she was only leaving them for a week or two, she wouldn't have done a single thing to make things easier on you. She wouldn't have thought far enough ahead to consider one of them getting sick. She would've assumed you could use a few vacation days you've got stored up to baby sit while she did whatever it is she's doing."

She was right. Nicole never put herself out if she could avoid it. But I wasn't ready to accept the fact her kids were here and I was the one responsible for them. I had a full-time, very demanding job. I drove a sports car the dealer ordered especially for me the week the new model was launched. I never cooked and sometimes forgot to change the sheets on my bed. To suddenly be responsible for two kids for an indefinite period of time—no, that couldn't happen!

I loved my niece and nephew. Or at least I thought I did considering I didn't really know them. But I had no room in my life for children.

"If I don't hear from Nicole over the weekend, I'll call Children's Services first thing Monday morning and see what this means."

That gave my sister thirty-six hours to remember she had two small children who needed her.

Just as I was getting the kids out of the bathtub that evening Uncle Jeb came over to see how we were getting along. I heard his heavy tread on the stairs long before he appeared in the bathroom doorway. I was sopping up water off the floor with a towel, and Emma and Jonah were struggling to slide their still-damp bodies into nightclothes. The nightclothes consisted of old tee shirts of mine since neither Nicole nor Dean had thought to pack pajamas.

"Well, would you lookie here?" Uncle Jeb's amiable voice boomed. He grinned at Emma. "If I didn't know better, I'd think little Nicole was back in the flesh. You're the spittin' image of your mama, little lady."

Emma stuck her finger in her mouth and took a half step behind me. I smiled reassuringly at her and got to my feet with the wet towels in my hands.

"She's a beauty, isn't she?" I said to Uncle Jeb. I dropped the towels on the floor and put one hand on her shoulder and the other on Jonah's. "Kids, this is your Uncle Jeb. He's married to Aunt Wanda, the lady who fixed you lunch. He lives on the next farm."

"Yep," Uncle Jeb said to the silent, staring children, "Got a real nice pond on my farm just perfect for fishin'." He focused on Jonah. "Don't guess you know anybody who'd be interested in fishin', now do you?"

Jonah's eyes grew wide with delight, and a smile crept across his features. He nodded. "I'd be interested."

Uncle Jeb jerked his head back in mock surprise. "You? You like to fish? Well, if that don't beat all."

Jonah nodded faster. "I do. I like to fish."

"Now ain't that something? I was just telling Wanda the other night. 'Wanda', I said, 'what I need me is a fishin' buddy. Somebody to sit on the bank with me and drink soda pop and tell me stories to keep me from fallin' asleep and fallin' into the water.'"

Jonah's face flushed with excitement. "I will. I can do it. I love to fish."

"He ain't never been fishing."

I jerked my head around to stare at Emma. She was still partially concealed behind me. It was the first words I'd heard out of her mouth.

"Have to," Jonah countered.

Emma realized Uncle Jeb and I were staring at her. "Nuh-uh," she said with less assurance, then stuck her finger back in her mouth and focused on the floor.

Uncle Jeb recovered first. "Well, now, ain't this just dandy? I bet I could get me two fishin' buddies. What do you say, Michelle? I came here lookin' for one and I might've found two. Ain't that the best news you heard all day?"

Jonah stepped over the wet towel and stood in front of Uncle Jeb. "I can go fishing anytime, whenever you want."

"Now, that's good to hear." Uncle Jeb took Jonah's hand and reached for Emma's. "Why don't the three of us go downstairs and find something to eat while Aunt Michelle finishes straightening up the bathroom."

Emma studied his calloused outstretched hand for a moment before deciding it was okay to take it. As the three of them started out of the bathroom, Gypsy jumped up from her position between the tub and commode and crowded in close. Emma took hold of Gypsy's collar with her free hand and followed Uncle Jeb and Jonah down the staircase.

Uncle Jeb introduced himself again on the way downstairs in case the kids hadn't been listening when I'd done it. Jonah offered his name eagerly. After a moment of waiting for Emma to do the same, I heard him introduce his sister.

I rinsed out the bathtub and laid the wet towels over the side to dry. I washed the toothpaste out of the sink. Jonah and Emma had shared an extra toothbrush from my last trip to the dentist. Toothbrushes were one more thing I forgot to buy while I was out, and there weren't any to be found in the bottom of the frayed backpack. I had no business taking care of children. I didn't have the usual items people kept on hand when small children were around; chewable aspirin, underwear, pajamas, band-aids, coloring books, socks, and most importantly, shoes.

Didn't Nicole know how dangerous it was to let children run around without shoes? Especially on a farm which contained all sorts of hazards for bare feet, from sharp rocks and rusty nails to bees.

I added toothbrushes to my mental list. We were definitely taking a trip to Walmart tomorrow.

Downstairs I found Jonah perched atop Uncle Jeb's knobby knees on the couch, a place I'd seen Nicole many times in years gone by. Violet and I were too big for lap sitting by the time we moved to the farm, but Uncle Jeb attracted children like moths to a flame. He was always carrying somebody's baby or toddler around the church before and after services. With his booming voice and infectious laugh, they automatically went to him. Even the shyest ones sensed his loving, patient spirit. It didn't hurt that his pockets were always full of candy and gum. While Grandma and Aunt Wanda were dry and aloof and a little scary, Uncle Jeb was fun.

I sat down in Grandma Catherine's easy chair and watched him flipping through a magazine, pointing out objects of interest to Jonah. Emma sat a few feet away with her arms around Gypsy, feigning disinterest, but I saw she was studying the magazine out of the corner of her eye.

"Climb up there, too, Emma," I wanted to tell her. *"Don't be afraid to let someone love you."*

Not that I had a lot of room to talk.

I thought of the last time I talked to Nicole. It was a few days after Christmas. She had called to thank me for the gifts I sent the kids.

"I don't know what we'd do without you, Michelle."

She seemed appreciative, though experience made me doubtful. Any time Nicole called I was suspicious. No matter what she said or how she said it, I braced myself, knowing she was buttering me up for something.

I was not a naturally suspicious person.

"I feel so bad," she went on. "The kids wouldn't have had a Christmas at all if it weren't for you."

"I'm sure things aren't that bad," I said, hoping she would leave me blissfully in the dark.

"Yes, they are. I got fired from my last job because I overslept a few times."

I cringed at the whine in her voice. I'd heard that excuse before.

"People without kids don't understand how it is," she continued. "It's hard to sit up all night with a sick kid and then get to work on time."

I didn't believe for a minute she overslept because she sat up all night with Emma or Jonah, and I wasn't feeling particularly generous. "Is the woman beater still with you?" I asked.

"How can you be so cold?" she snapped, the sugar gone from her voice. "If you mean Dean, yes, he's still here. He isn't going anywhere. I love him."

"Even after the last time," I said, referring to the beating he'd given her that resulted in the lost job at Denny's.

"You don't understand anything, Michelle. Sometimes people lose their tempers and do things without thinking."

"I understand all too well. I work in a hospital, remember? I see women like you every other night with their noses broken or their jaws wired because someone who *loved* them lost his temper."

"I wish for once you'd talk about something you know a little bit about. Dean's changed. He's not like he used to be. He isn't drinking as much, and when he's sober, he's as gentle as a lamb."

"That's good to hear. Has the lamb got a job?"

She snorted her disgust into the phone. "I don't know why I bother to call you. You are so hateful. Just because you don't need anyone in your life doesn't mean the rest of us can live like that. I want a man, Michelle. I want someone to tell me I'm beautiful, that I'm needed. I'm sorry I'm not as cold and self-sufficient as you are. No, wait a minute. I don't mean that. I'm not sorry. I'm thrilled I have feelings, to know I'm not made of ice. I couldn't bear to live like you."

"You mean in a house that's paid for, with a real job and a car that's not falling apart?"

"Thanks for the gifts," she spat. "The kids loved the toys, and the coat fits Emma perfectly. She really needed it."

I regretted losing my patience. I don't know why I needed to voice every thought that flitted across my mind. Even when I knew I was right.

"I'm sorry, Nicole. I don't mean to be so hard on you. I just want to see you—"

She cut me off. "I know what you want. You want me to be like you. Well, I can't. I'm a living, breathing human being with needs, whether you understand them or not. Merry Christmas!"

That was the last time I heard from her.

"*A living, breathing human being with needs....*"

I was a living, breathing human being. I had needs. I just didn't need a Neanderthal with a mean right hook to fulfill them.

I looked again at Emma, sitting close enough to Uncle Jeb and Jonah to see the pictures in the magazine but far enough away to protect herself from possible harm or worse, rejection. Is that how it started with me? Had similar fears turned me into the woman I was today? A workaholic who hadn't had a real relationship since high school?

My stomach tightened at the thought of that relationship. I thought I had been in love. Maybe I was as much in love as a person can be at seventeen. When Kyle Swann joined the Air Force I thought I'd never recover. But I did. And everything turned out fine. There was nothing wrong with me. I wasn't lonely. I didn't need a man to prove my worth. My worth came from a meaningful career and a loving heart.

Well, at least I had a meaningful career.

I pushed aside my thoughts of my sister and Kyle Swann. I didn't need to apologize for paying my bills on time and being a responsible member of society. And I certainly didn't need to apologize if I didn't want a man in my life.

Jonah yawned widely. I looked at the clock over the fireplace. It was nearly nine o'clock. It had been a long day for all of us. Jonah begged Uncle Jeb to go upstairs with us as I put them to bed. Uncle Jeb watched with arched eyebrows as Gypsy settled among the covers between them in Nicole's old bed. I knew what he was thinking.

"If Catherine Boyle was alive to see a dog living in her house, let alone sleeping in a bed like a person..."

I agreed with the part about dogs sleeping on furniture. Gypsy had never slept in a people bed in her life, but I couldn't separate her from Emma now. I wanted to get a little sleep myself.

"So, what are you planning to do, Peanut?" Uncle Jeb asked when we were back downstairs.

I shrugged. He hadn't called me by my childhood nickname in years. He had called me Peanut from the moment I arrived on the farm. Nicole had been Ladybug. Violet had several nicknames depending on Uncle Jeb's mood or what popped out of his mouth at the time, but typically he called her Daffodil, Sunshine or Tadpole.

"I don't know," I said. "It doesn't look like there's much I can do."

"Wanda says you're going to Children's Services."

I nodded. "I guess I won't have a choice. I mean if Nicole doesn't come back. I just hate to stir up trouble since this will probably end up amounting to nothing."

"I sure hope you're right."

He rubbed a rough hand across his chin. "With Nicole, it's hard to say. I don't want to think she up and abandoned her kids anymore than you do. But you gotta admit that's how it looks. If she was drunk or something and some man decided to bring the kids here without her permission, well, first off, he wouldn't know where to find you. And second, no man would think about birth certificates and shot records. Nicole knows what she's doing. She just didn't bother to let the rest of us in on it."

My heart sank. All day I'd held out hope Nicole was hung over somewhere, and as soon as she slept it off, she'd come and collect her kids. The last thing I wanted was to do her parenting for her.

Uncle Jeb leveled a hard stare at me. "I can't help but wonder what'll happen to Jonah and Emma if you send them back to Nicole. That is, if she can be found. If you took them back to her tomorrow, or let's say next week, what do you suppose would happen the next time she decided to take off?"

He didn't give me time to think up an answer. "She'd find somebody else to dump them off on. Somebody not as reliable as you. Or she'd keep them herself. Either way, those kids deserve better."

I opened my mouth to remind him Nicole needed to face her own responsibilities. It wasn't fair that she keep messing up and expecting someone else to fix the situation for her.

My arguments were valid. I had every right to live my life the way I chose without getting saddled with someone else's responsibilities. But my independence didn't matter to Uncle Jeb, and it apparently didn't matter to the two children upstairs in Nicole's old room.

"It'd be hard on Wanda." Uncle Jeb looked toward the window over my head and stared out as if thinking out loud. "Neither of us is as young as we used to be. But I suppose we could take those two young 'uns in before we sent them back to Nicole."

"Uncle Jeb," I cried. "You couldn't do that. At your age, you've got to consider your health."

It crossed my mind he could be trying to manipulate me into doing what he wanted, but Uncle Jeb didn't usually say things he didn't mean.

"My health don't matter if I think there's a possibility they're not being taken care of." He stood up. "You do what you need to, Peanut. I know you're busy with the hospital and all. I'm not playing games or trying to guilt you into anything. We all have choices to make. I've made mine."

He leaned over and kissed the top of my head like I was still a kid. "We'd love to see you in church tomorrow. It's the best place for kids. For you, too."

I nodded absently without accepting the invitation.

"Bring the kids over tomorrow afternoon," he said on his way to the door. "I'll take them up to the pond."

"We need to take a trip to Walmart first. They don't even have shoes."

"So I hear." He put his hand on his hip pocket. "You need money? Wanda and me can help out."

I shook my head. "No, no. I've got it covered."

I sat in the gathering darkness after he left, thinking about what he said. Yes, he was right. I hadn't thought about what it would be like for the kids when Nicole came back. They were better off away from her if she was unstable enough to leave them in my front yard without shoes and proper clothes. I certainly didn't want them raised by strangers. I wanted what was best for them. But couldn't the best be for their mother to get her act together and grow up?

Was that too much to ask?

As the room grew darker and my heart grew heavier, Grandma's words rang in my head. "You do for family, Michelle. Whether you want to or not, it's your Christian duty."

I didn't claim to be a Christian so I guess that left me in the clear.

Chapter Five

If I never learned another thing about children, I soon discovered a trip to Walmart with a benevolent aunt in possession of a debit card could bring even the most reticent child out of her shell.

I stopped at the Quick-Mart in Winona and bought two pairs of flip-flops before heading on to the county seat of Genoa another six miles down the highway. Even at an eastern Arkansas Walmart, it was no shoes, no shirt, no service. Inside the store we headed straight for the shoe department. Shopping with children didn't need to take my entire day. I wasn't like those weak-willed parents I often saw coaxing little Junior into the cart so they could head for the checkout. I would be in and out of here in thirty minutes.

I was so naïve!

Since it was August sandals were on clearance. Score one for Walmart. Judging from Emma's reaction, every Hurley woman was born with an extra gene that sent a rush of endorphins to her brain at the sight of a shoe sale. The white ones with a little daisy on top and hard soles that clicked smartly against the floor when she walked were marked down to three dollars. An iridescent-striped pair, also on sale, caught both Emma's and my eyes. How could I go wrong? They joined the others in the cart. Emma actually squealed with delight when she spotted a pair of black slip-ons with a chunky heel. They weren't on sale, but they were adorable. Into the cart they went. The whole point of the trip was tennis shoes, so we found a pair of simple canvas ones with a zipper closure for a paltry five dollars. I would have bought a pair for myself had they come in my size.

Fortunately for my pocketbook, whatever gene that made Emma and me ga-ga over shoes was missing in Jonah. He lost interest after picking out a pair of black and red, horribly ugly gym shoes. I found another suitable pair in his size in case I needed to dress him up a little and added them to the cart while he crawled up and down the aisle making faces at himself in the foot mirrors.

I had never spent more than twenty minutes in Walmart before, the checkout lanes notwithstanding, but now I was shopping with children. It was lunchtime by the time we exited the store. My shopping cart was so overloaded I almost lost control of it going across the parking lot. I even had to pull up to the front of the store where a disinterested young man in a blue vest waited with two new booster car seats that would surely gouge the leather backseats of my beautiful car. But the kids were set. I couldn't think of one thing they didn't now own.

I watched their smiling faces as I unloaded the cart. Emma swung her feet to admire her new sandals. Through their new 'shades', they watched the balloons we found placed strategically in the checkout lane. They cracked bubble gum, another checkout lane purchase, while making a horrible racket with toys I already regretted buying. I felt buoyant myself despite the breathlessness of my debit card, which had gotten quite a workout. The kids were happy—really smiling for the first time since I found them under the lilac bushes.

So this was how it felt to make a child happy. It didn't really take much. A little attention, a little cash and lunch at McDonald's.

I tried not to judge my sister. No one could afford to do this on a consistent basis. Still, if Nicole only made better choices in men, or realized she didn't need one at all and put a little thought into her future, her life might not be in such a sad state.

I couldn't get over how she had let her kids get used to such deprivation. For the moment I wasn't going to think about Nicole. I wasn't going to wonder where she was or what she was thinking. I was simply going to enjoy the good mood brought on by the rapture on my niece and nephew's faces.

After lunch and a half hour watching the kids play in the restaurant's indoor playground in their bare feet on a floor that had probably never seen bleach, I drove home and sent the kids outside with their new toys. I thought of Grandma Catherine's little TV with the grainy picture. I was overdue for a new one. Not to mention cable. Maybe not cable. I didn't want to bring that garbage into my house—a house that now contained preschool eyes and ears?

I took a deep breath and reminded myself not to get carried away. This visit was costing me a fortune, and Jonah and Emma had only been here one full day. I wasn't buying a new TV. Or cable. They needed shoes and car seats. The toys and sunglasses were no big deal. But I would not allow them to take over my life more than they already had. They would be out of my house and out of my life any day.

Things would settle down once I went back to work. Away from the farm, I could put the situation into perspective. I would make as few changes as possible and wait for Nicole to call and apologize and tell me she was coming to get her kids.

I called the hospital to take Monday off as a personal day. Meg, who worked the switch board evenings and weekends, nearly fell out of her chair. I had never used a personal day in all my years working there. Instead I took the money at the end of the year and bought mutual funds. Not because I feared poverty or because I was a workaholic. It was much simpler than that—I had no personal life and no loved ones on whom to spend money.

Everyone at the hospital knew it. I was the one they came to when they wanted to switch holidays or maneuver a long weekend out of the schedule. They knew I didn't have anything better to do than collect the triple-time pay that came with working holidays in ICU. The rest of them had wives, husbands, visiting in-laws, kids with soccer games and dental appointments. I had Gypsy. She didn't complain when she spent Christmas Day alone or if I didn't take her out of town for the Labor Day weekend.

When I first graduated from nursing school—back when I fantasized about having a life—I resented how my coworkers made a beeline to my locker when the holidays approached. I knew ahead of time who to expect just by looking at the schedule. Julie had a husband in law school who worked a night job so her early mornings were better spent at home. Dennis would sell a kidney for a three-day weekend so he and his wife could work on the early twentieth century house they were renovating. Deb's four kids were born during her five years between high school and nursing school. How she managed I couldn't imagine. Because she got on my nerves the least, she usually got first dibs on my Christmas mornings.

Still I resented how they assumed I had nothing better to do with my long weekends and holidays than trade with those of a lesser schedule. I had a family, of sorts. Back then Aunt Wanda always came over early to get a jumpstart on the holiday dinner preparations with Grandma. What right did my coworkers have to assume I would rather pull a double shift in the pouring rain in my underwear with a migraine and premenstrual cramps than stay home in the bosom of my loving family?

The first Christmas after Grandma passed away, I drew the preferred schedule. Just to throw them for a loop, I held onto my hours.

"I have plans," I told my coworkers. No one pressed for details, and I didn't offer.

After pulling twelve hours on Christmas Eve, I loaded an overnight bag and a barely housebroken Gypsy into the car and headed south. We spent two days in a virtually abandoned family resort village, walking the trails and keeping the minimal staff company. I hated it. Even Gypsy seemed depressed. I missed the hospital. I missed smiling and talking with the lonely patients who would rather be anywhere but in a hospital over the holidays. I missed the lame Christmas party food we all brought from home to share in the break room during quiet hours. I missed everyone's stories of misery over being away from their families, and funny ones of Christmases past. Come payday, I missed the check that was considerably smaller because of the missing holiday pay.

Most surprisingly, I missed Grandma Catherine keeping a plate of turkey warm in the oven for me when I stumbled home from work at seven-thirty. I missed Aunt Wanda's bellyaching over doing all the cooking. I missed watching the parades with Uncle Jeb.

After that year, I stopped resenting my coworkers' assumptions that I had nothing better to do on holidays and weekends than work. I didn't. Why pretend my life was something more than it was?

Poor Meg at the switchboard would think I had totally cracked when I called my supervisor Monday morning and took Tuesday and Wednesday as vacation days if Nicole hadn't appeared by then. That was another thing I seldom did. In the spring I took a week off to put out my garden. It was something Grandma insisted I do after I got my first regular job with vacation days and a habit I hadn't tried to break.

At the end of every summer, I took another week to harvest what we'd grown. That week coincided with the county fair where Grandma entered a quilt, some pies, jams, tomatoes, late flowers and any other category she qualified for. She'd been gone six years, and I still took those two weeks off. I loved getting my hands dirty with mindless work that left my back aching and hands blistered. I even enjoyed the week at the fair. I was the one who entered produce from the garden I no longer needed to raise and volunteered my time in the Band Boosters booth. It gave curious townspeople a chance to see me when they weren't under the influence of anesthesia. It also quelled the rumors for another year among the town's youth that I hid a forked tail under my scrubs.

I made no improvements to the house or farm except what was vital for human habitation. It was only Gypsy and me, and our tastes and expectations were simple. I had no future generations breathing down my neck, demanding I keep the place up for their sakes. So what if the front fence had no gate, the driveway needed paving or one or two upstairs windows were missing shutters and screens?

My savings account grew steadily, and I made maximum contributions to my 401K. What I was saving for, I didn't worry about. Retirement, I reasoned. A retirement everyone in town, including myself, knew would never come.

When an unexpected ringing jerked me awake at two-sixteen a.m. I reached automatically for the alarm. Then I remembered I wasn't going to work today.

I grabbed my phone off the bedside table. "Hullo?"

"Michelle, it's me."

I was instantly awake. "Nicole? Where are you? Are you all right?"

"I'm fine, I guess. As good as can be expected." Her voice contained the appropriate amount of self-pity and despair.

Now that I knew she wasn't dead, I got mad. "Where are you?" I repeated.

She let out a long, belabored sigh. "I'm all right, Michelle. Don't worry. I know you're probably really mad at me and I'm sorry—"

"Nicole," I interjected, "where are you? What's going on?"

"I told you, everything's fine. I'm sorry, but it couldn't be helped."

"What couldn't be helped? What are you talking about?"

"If you give me a chance to say two words without interrupting I'll tell you." She was not too irritated to maintain the whine in her voice. "It's a long story so I won't bore you with details."

I wanted details more than anything, but I wouldn't interrupt again.

"I can't keep the kids right now. I don't know how long it'll be, but I need you to keep them for me. I have some things to sort out in my life, and I can't do that and be Mommy at the same time."

I was never good at keeping my mouth shut when I thought something needed saying. There was so much I wanted to yell at Nicole right now. So much I could say. With great resolve, I clamped my teeth over the anger bubbling inside of me and waited.

"I don't know when I'll be back, Michelle, but please don't worry. No one is forcing me to do anything I don't want to do. As soon as I get my head straightened out I'll come back."

I wanted to tell her not to bother. She was the most selfish creature God ever put on the earth. She had no business with two great kids like Emma and Jonah. Of course I didn't say that. I wanted her to come back. Desperately. Her kids weren't my problem. Why should she get to shirk her responsibilities long enough to straighten her head out when every other mother on the planet had to stay home and play 'Mommy' whether they felt like it or not? I didn't say that either.

"Michelle? Are you still there?"

"I'm here. I'm trying not to interrupt."

"Well, I wanted to tell you thanks. I really appreciate everything you're doing. You don't know how much. I knew I could count on you."

Nicole paused for a moment. I heard a voice in the background. A man's. That figured. It was always a man. Nicole couldn't live one day without some loser in her life. I wondered if it was the same one Jonah said had dropped them off in my front yard.

Nicole put her hand over the receiver and said something I couldn't make out. Then she came back to me. "Well, I gotta go. I'll talk to you soon."

With a click, the connection was broken.

I sat in the dark with the dead phone in my hand and tried to figure out what had happened. Not only did my darling kid sister thank me for something I never agreed to do, she didn't ask one word about how Emma and Jonah were doing without her.

Chapter Six

I called Children's Services first thing Monday morning. The young woman on the other end of the line promised to have someone at the house by the end of the day. She sounded harried, overworked and genuinely distressed two children had been left in someone's front yard, even if said someone was a family member.

At one-thirty that afternoon, a small car pulled into the driveway and a young woman with her hair pulled back in what she must've thought was a businesslike, practical style, climbed out. From inside the front door, I watched her gaze around the property, sizing up my life with a critical eye. I thought of the missing gate, the drafty windows, the lack of air conditioning, the barn that leaned dangerously due south, and the electrical outlets that didn't have covers. I immediately resented the invasion of privacy. I had to impress this woman just so my worthless sister's kids could live here while Nicole was pretending she didn't have a care in the world.

Once we got to talking, I could tell the young woman hadn't been on the job long. She found my story duly pathetic.

At first I don't think she believed me. Her eyes suggested I found the kids in a parked car at Winn Dixie. Fortunately I had their birth certificates and shot records to back up my story. That made things go smoother. How thoughtful of Nicole to leave them in the backpack.

I expressed my concerns that I wasn't exactly a mothering type; I had a demanding job, a small car, and basically no room in my life for kids, although I didn't say it in so many words.

She nodded patiently before telling me as far as the law was concerned, I was under no obligation to provide for another woman's children. All I had to do was sign a few papers verifying my sister's children had been abandoned with me. The county would take the children into custody, then foster care, thus relieving me of the burden.

Even though it was exactly what I wanted to hear, watching the words form on her lips made me feel like an utter heel for bringing it up.

"Ideally in cases like this the best place for the children is with family members," she added. "Foster homes in this county, as in every county in the United States, are extremely overcrowded. We screen our foster parents, of course, and they are amazing, selfless people, but it's always better for children to remain in the home of a loved one where they feel at least a modicum of security. I'm sure you're not comfortable turning your niece and nephew over to strangers when they don't know where their mother is."

I sank lower in my chair.

"I'm not suggesting you've done anything wrong. I just want you to be aware that whatever you do could cause irrevocable damage to your family. Your sister brought her children to you for a reason. She could've turned them over to the agency in her county, but she didn't. She brought them to you. She trusts you. She feels confident your home is the best place for her children at this time. You need to carefully consider your next steps before you alienate your sister and her children. A rift like this among family members may never be repaired."

She smiled warmly and slid a stack of papers across the kitchen table at me.

"Fill out this paperwork. It's an order for temporary custody. Like you said, your sister could walk through the door by bedtime and all this will have been for nothing. But if she doesn't, don't you feel better knowing for the present the children are in good hands? When you're finished we'll go over a few things and you'll be all set. You can enroll them in daycare so you won't have to miss more work than necessary. In a few weeks if the kids are still here, I'll come back for a more thorough visit."

She opened the fridge to make sure it worked and contained some sort of food. I showed her the bathrooms, which were thankfully relatively clean, and where the kids slept. She smiled like I'd just won the lottery and announced I was awarded custody of my niece and nephew. She made her exit, promising she'd see me again in about a week.

I watched her walk back to her older model car with Gypsy sniffing her shoes the whole way. I couldn't believe my simple no nonsense life had been reduced to convincing a government agency I was fit to provide a home for my own niece and nephew. How had things come to this? All I wanted was to go to work tomorrow, leave the world to its own devices and keep it out of mine. Was I a terrible person because I didn't want to solve the world's problems?

The longer I thought about it, the less I cared what the Children's Services woman thought about me. I didn't want to raise Nicole's kids, even if they were my flesh and blood. I couldn't send them into foster care, but I didn't have to like how they had intruded into my life.

Even though I had basically sworn off religion and church for myself, it seemed like a good idea to enroll Emma and Jonah in a church affiliated daycare facility. If nothing else, they would learn respect and manners. I supposed memorizing a few Bible verses and singing a few Bible songs wouldn't force any twisted ideology upon them or make me a hypocrite.

There were two such places in Genoa. I didn't bother calling the one run by my old church. Just reading their ad in the telephone book brought back all the hurtful memories of Grandma and her Christian charity. I hadn't darkened the door of that church since Grandma's funeral. My adult rationale told me I shouldn't blame the church for Grandma's warped sense of Christian love and compassion, but I couldn't help doing exactly that. I wasn't about to let them get their hands on Emma and Jonah.

I listened to the slightly deranged sounding administrator of the second preschool explain their program. Could anyone really be that happy? I agreed to meet her Tuesday morning to fill out the appropriate enrollment paperwork. She had the answers to all my questions, not that I knew what to ask. It didn't really matter. She had me as soon as I realized the daycare center was located in the heart of Genoa on my way to work. If all went well on Tuesday, I would leave the kids for a half day. That would be enough time for them to get used to the place before I resumed my usual weekend schedule at the county hospital. Janet had already called to see if I could work. Without going into details, I told her I hoped so.

An impressive brick and wood building stood before me when I pulled into the parking lot of the Abundant Life Fellowship Church on Tuesday morning. The church had apparently begun as one building with a new addition added a few years later. The construction appeared recent, but you couldn't prove it by me.

Everyone says they are creatures of habit, but I truly am. The farm was located a few miles from Winona, a town of about eighteen hundred residents. To get to work at the University Hospital in the neighboring county, I had to drive through Genoa. I traveled the same roads whether going to work, the bank, the grocery or the county library every time I left the farm. My route never deviated. If they built a nuclear power plant one street over from the one I drove every day, I'd never know unless they rerouted traffic.

I parked my Mazda between a minivan and an SUV—both outfitted with multiple car seats—near a pair of double doors on one of the main building's many outcroppings. I thought of the little clapboard churches with spires shooting heavenward parked at a country crossroads like the ones depicted on postcards and calendars. Now churches looked more like businesses with pastors who resembled CEO's and deacons who looked like board members.

Before getting out of the car, I glanced into the back seat through the rearview mirror. Two terrified faces stared back at me. I pasted a smile on my face and climbed out.

My Mazda came with freestyle doors that looked great but which I never needed until now. With both driver side doors wide open, there was barely room for me to lean my hips in far enough to unbuckle Jonah's car seat. I stretched farther inside the cramped interior to unhook Emma. A shooting pain went up my back. She would have to get out herself. No wonder people with kids bought minivans by the fleet.

"You're going to have so much fun today," I said in a singsong voice. I immediately recognized the tone. It was same as the woman I spoke to on the phone. An occupational hazard from spending one's days in the company of children. "You'll make all kinds of new friends."

Neither looked interested in making friends.

"Will we be together?" Jonah's brown eyes, so unlike his sister's blue ones, were wide with terror.

I swallowed hard. I hadn't thought to ask the administrator how that would work. "I don't know, sweetheart. I'll ask the lady." I couldn't remember her name. I imagined real parents would never leave their children with someone whose name they hadn't bothered to remember.

The parking lot with its bustling parents and assorted, squealing children was intimidating enough but did nothing to prepare me for inside. We marched up the walk and into a vestibule. The walls were lined with hip level coat hooks and cubby boxes stenciled in colorful block letters.

EMERSON. KENTON. KENDALL. MONTGOMERY.

Didn't they allow children to use their first names at this school? How confusing for ones with siblings. Maybe they had to share personal space. That didn't seem fair.

An attractive brunette bustled forward. She gave me a brief smile before ignoring me completely and squatting down to eye level with the kids.

"You must be Jonah and Emma," she sang out with the enthusiasm of a TV infomercial hawker. I immediately recognized her as the woman I talked to on the phone yesterday. Her long curly hair was held away from her face by a wide, functional barrette. She wore minimal make-up and wash and wear clothes. I imagined our jobs weren't that different.

"I'm Miss Billie," she was saying. "I'm so pleased you could be with us today. We are going to have so much fun." She squeezed their hands and straightened. Her smile remained fixed in place. I doubted she could relax her cheek muscles if she tried. "You must be Ms. Hurley. I'm Billie Kirk, the school administrator. We spoke on the phone. Please, come into my office."

She took a step back, and nearly fell over a little boy who appeared out of nowhere. "Jordan!" With one quick hand on his chest and the other on his back, she artfully brought his full-tilt sprint to a standstill. "It's so good to see you this morning. Please don't run to the play area. We would hate for you to get hurt. Then you couldn't play with your friends."

"Okay, Miss Billie." The little boy grinned adoringly up at her and then walked sedately through the vestibule into a large, corralled area to our left teeming with children of all shapes and sizes.

Some wise individual had the foresight to fence the little angels in. I was impressed that a few soft-spoken words from the administrator could curtail the little boy's breakneck enthusiasm. Maybe there was more skill involved in doing this job well than a bubbly personality and low IQ.

I followed her into a tiny office opposite the play area. Emma and Jonah dogged my every step.

The administrator motioned us to the chairs across from her desk. I lowered myself into one. Instead of taking the other chair, Emma and Jonah leaned against my legs. It was the first physical contact we'd shared since I carried Jonah into the house Saturday morning.

"We are so pleased you chose Noah's Ark Preschool," the administrator said. "After you fill out the paperwork, I'll give you a tour of the facilities. We didn't discuss it yesterday, but I'm sure you want to see everything."

Not really. It hadn't occurred to me to doubt a word she said on the phone.

I was so not cut out for parenting!

I took my copies of the paperwork the woman from Children's Services had given me along with the kids' medical records out of my purse and handed them across the desk. Miss Billie got up to make copies on the machine behind her. "Have you been to preschool before?" she asked Emma and Jonah.

Emma shrank against my leg and stuck her finger in her mouth. Jonah stared at the administrator and said nothing.

"I don't think so," I answered for them. "Like I said yesterday, I haven't had much contact with them since they were born. They were pretty anxious about the whole idea of coming, so I don't think they have any daycare experience."

Miss Billie pulled the copies out of the tray and handed the originals back to me. She took her seat at the desk. "Okay." Her smile shone brightly under the florescent lighting. "I think we have everything we need to get started."

She ran through the preschool's program. Everything sounded simple enough. Payment was due every Friday for the following week. The amount gave me a bit of a shock, but this was just a temporary arrangement. Thank goodness. I could afford it for a month or two. Miss Billie said something about a monthly Sunday morning program in which they encouraged participation from children and parents. The kids took the stage in front of the congregation and sang songs and recited memory verses they'd learned that month in preschool. The idea of getting roped into attending church just for bringing your kids for daycare seemed a bit presumptuous. Leave it to a church to cook up such a scheme.

It wouldn't affect me anyway. Nicole would be back any day, and I'd be off the hook. Even if she didn't come back by the next Sunday morning program, this was still America. You couldn't force people to attend church.

I smiled and nodded at the appropriate pauses until she finally wound down and clasped her hands in front of her. "Do you have any questions?"

I only had one. "The kids are concerned about being separated. Because of the circumstances, I wonder if it's possible to keep them together, at least in the beginning. I'm not even sure it's a good idea to leave them today."

"Oh, that won't be a problem at all," the administrator said through her big smile.

She turned to Jonah and Emma. "A new place can be scary when you don't know anyone. But I have a feeling you're going to love it here at Noah's Ark. You'll make friends in no time at all." She stood up and looked back at me. "They're close enough in age to go into the same class, just to see how everything goes. Hopefully it won't be long before they want to separate into their own classes. If you like, I can show Jonah and Emma the play area and introduce them to the teachers while you fill out your paperwork. Afterwards I'll give you a tour of the facilities while the children have breakfast. By then they'll probably be more than ready to spend the rest of the morning here."

She held her hands out to them.

"Oh, um…" I looked from Emma to Jonah. They were staring at Miss Billie's outstretched hands. "I suppose that would be…if they want to…"

I couldn't explain the tiny nugget of betrayal when they reached out and took her hands. She led them from the room, talking a mile a minute about the fun stuff that went on at preschool, with not a backwards glance at me from any of them.

I bent my head over the stapled forms in front of me and went to work.

Food allergies, medical history, sleeping patterns. Typical stuff about which I knew nothing.

I filled in as many blanks as I could while trying to block the din coming from over my shoulder through the open door.

Someone plowed into the office and nearly fell over my chair. "Billie, have you seen—" came a masculine voice. "Oh, sorry."

I looked up to see a rugged-looking man with close cropped black hair in the doorway, dressed in khakis and a blue Henley shirt, his large hand on the doorjamb. "I was looking for Billie," he explained.

In an instant, his expression changed from rushed to recognition. "Michelle? Michelle Hurley? I don't believe it."

I gasped and jumped to my feet. Of all the people I expected to run into again, especially here in a church on a

Tuesday morning with a hundred screaming kids providing background noise, Kyle Swann wasn't among them.

In high school, he had been my one and only serious boyfriend. Until this moment, I thought I was over him.

For a split second I was torn between a handshake and the hug I wanted. Before I could decide, Kyle pulled me into his arms for a regrettably chaste embrace.

I ran my tongue over my teeth and prayed I didn't have bad breath. "Kyle. Hi. It's good to see you."

I hoped my voice didn't belie the condition of my insides. If possible, Kyle was more handsome than he'd been in school. His hair was as black as ever without the first gray one to spoil the effect. His shoulders had broadened in the last fifteen years, and his forearms rippled with definition. He'd gained weight, but it was all athletic muscle from the looks of things. Laugh lines had appeared at the corners of his deep brown eyes. Of course he would have laugh lines. I bet he kept his wife in stitches. Even while I resisted, my eyes shot to his left hand. No ring.

That didn't mean anything. Did it?

Even if there was no current Mrs. Swann, there were still children, possibly from several mothers, or he wouldn't be at a preschool in the middle of the week looking for the administrator.

I swallowed my illogical disappointment and tried to focus. It was tough with his LED smile directed straight at me. The smile that would make him recognizable in a crowd if I hadn't seen him in a hundred years. It was still easy and infectious and turned my insides to pudding.

Too bad I looked exactly the same except for an additional fifteen pounds and two vertical frown lines between my eyes that reminded me of Grandma Catherine every time I looked in the mirror.

"Wow, Michelle, you look great."

I see he had learned to lie in the past fifteen years.

"I didn't know you had kids." He turned to face the doorway. "Which ones are yours?"

"Oh, uh, they're not mine. I mean I don't…"

He turned back and studied me with that penetrating gaze that always seemed to see right through me. I struggled to maintain my focus as I looked past his broad frame. I spotted Jonah and Emma in the middle of the play area, apparently invisible to every other kid there. Emma's finger was still in the corner of her mouth. Jonah was studying his shoes.

I pointed them out. "They're my sister's kids. They are…um, staying with me for awhile."

The masculine scent emanating from him made it difficult to concentrate—spicy, woodsy, with a hint of musk. It smelled familiar. I was instantly fifteen old again. Flat-chested, knock-kneed and unsure of what to say in front of a boy. Kyle was sure of himself, even then. I remembered standing in front of my locker the first day of my freshman year, trying to get the lock open when he came up behind me.

"Here. Sometimes they want to do their own thing." He grabbed the dial on the lock and gave it a quick twist. "Try it now."

It worked. Heat rose in my cheeks. I knew all the freckles on my face were standing out against my pale skin. "Thanks," I mumbled as I peered inside the locker and wondered if I could squeeze inside.

"Sure," he said as he spun on his heel and disappeared down the hallway without introducing himself.

My first encounter with Kyle Swann—burned indelibly on my brain.

"You mean little Nicole? Those two are Nicole's kids?"

I nodded.

"It doesn't seem possible Nicole's old enough to have kids."

"She's not," I blurted before I could stop myself. "I mean she is old enough, obviously." Why couldn't I stop talking? "She's twenty-three. She's just acts immature sometimes."

"I didn't mean to imply she was too young. I just meant it's amazing how time flies. The last time I saw Nicole she was like…" He held out a hand to a height a little higher than his waist. "…what, eight-years-old? I think it was at our high school graduation. Do you remember that?"

Of course I remembered. It was the last time Kyle had seen me too—the day after our big break-up. He had announced he enlisted in the Air Force and was leaving for San Antonio in two weeks. Until that moment I hadn't considered how things would change after graduation. I wasn't an idiot. I had already enrolled in nursing school, and I certainly didn't expect Kyle to keep working at his uncle's gas station. In hindsight I realized I didn't want to think about how our lives would change. How *we* would change.

I hadn't exactly handled the situation with grace and dignity. More like screaming and name-calling.

But Kyle wasn't talking about us. He was thinking of eight-year-old Nicole and how much she looked like Emma.

I returned his smile. "Yes, I remember. Nicole was a handful in those days. I'm afraid she hasn't changed a bit."

He nodded and laughed. I laughed too, trying not to think about the Nicole who couldn't stay sober or keep a man or a job for more than six months.

"So what have you been doing with yourself, Michelle? Do you still live in Winona?"

I couldn't believe he didn't know. Everybody knew what became of me. Absolutely nothing. I attended the local college, lived much like I had during high school, except with double the responsibilities, and went to work as soon as I had enough training. I was the girl most likely to turn into a radish.

"Yes, I still live on Grandma Catherine's farm."

It wasn't Grandma's farm anymore. I'd held the deed since she died. I paid the insurance and property taxes every year, but still I felt like a squatter. As long as I lived, the farm would always seem like 'Grandma's farm' to me.

"I'm a cardio care nurse at University Hospital in Jonesboro," I continued. "I also work on contingency at the county hospital here in Genoa on weekends."

"Sounds like you're keeping busy, but you always did. You always talked about becoming a nurse when we were in school. You were the one to have around when someone needed something."

When someone needed something.

My ears burned with shame at the way I resented Emma and Jonah's intrusion into my world.

I motioned through the open office door. "Which ones are yours?" I asked to change the subject. For some reason I didn't like the idea of Kyle having children, though I didn't have any right to care. I'd feel a lot better if he'd gotten fat or lost his hair. Sometimes there was no justice in the world.

"I didn't think you'd be living around here. I thought after joining the Air Force and seeing what the world had to offer, you'd settle down in some exotic location."

The corners of his mouth turned upwards in that mischievous manner I remembered. "I don't have children. I never married."

I managed to control the urge to pump the air with my fist.

"Then what are you doing here?"

His grin broadened. "I work here. Not at the preschool, though this is where I start most of my days. My office is in the main part of the building. I come up here whenever I'm in the building to hear the children recite their pledges before classes start. The pledges to the American flag, the Christian flag and the Bible. Then I lead them in prayer. I transferred here in March."

"Transferred?"

"Yeah. I'm the church pastor."

He could've knocked me over with a feather. Kyle, a pastor? Playing in the NFL, maybe. A construction worker or even a schoolteacher. He always cared about people, and he got along with everyone. Even a therapist was within reason. But a pastor?

I hoped my shock wasn't obvious enough to insult him. "You don't say," I managed.

"I received my calling while living in Japan. I planned to make a career of the Air Force, but God had other plans."

I nodded like everyone I knew let God choose their career paths. "Where did you transfer from?" I asked conversationally.

"Tahlequah, Oklahoma. That was my first church. I pastored there for seven years. But Harrison County will always be home to me."

I nodded again like I chose Harrison County instead of just ending up here. I turned my eyes back to the play area. It was strange talking to Kyle as if there had never been anything between us. Stranger by far was the fact he was the pastor of the church I chose out of the phone book to bring Nicole's kids for preschool. If there was a God in Heaven, he was having a grand old time at my expense right now.

We watched as Miss Billie cheerfully settled a dispute over a baby doll between two little girls. She found Jonah and Emma in the crowd, said something to them and headed back to the office alone. "Morning, Pastor. How are you coming with the paperwork, Ms. Hurley?"

I glanced guiltily at the pile of unfinished papers on her desk as I tried to reconcile someone addressing Kyle as *Pastor*.

"She was interrupted," Kyle volunteered. "We're old friends. We were catching up."

"How nice." She smiled at both of us and then focused her attention on me. "It's almost time for breakfast. I can give you the tour of the preschool while the kids eat. Kyle, did you need something first?"

"I just came in for last month's attendance roster."

"Oh, I'm sorry. I haven't had time to get it to your office."

While she went around her desk and shuffled through her outbox, Kyle looked at me. "It was good seeing you, Michelle. We'll have to get together and talk over old times one of these days." He took the paper Billie held out to him and raised his free hand in a half wave. "Have a nice day, ladies."

I turned back to the administrator and tried to get the image of Kyle Swann out of my head.

The administrator was looking over what I had written on my forms. I saw by her arched eyebrows she couldn't understand why I didn't know more about the personal habits of my niece and nephew. How to explain? Rather than commenting, Miss Billie handed me a list of items each child would need—pencil box with crayons, kiddy scissors, glue, Kleenex, and on and on and on. My debit card groaned inside my wallet. Another trip to Walmart. I would also need a recent photo to put on Jonah and Emma's cubby boxes. Apparently, each kid got his or her own.

"It helps teach name recognition," Miss Billie explained. She continued to flip pages and study the lines I'd left blank.

I cleared my throat and scratched an itch on the back of my neck. "I'm sorry I couldn't fill in more of the forms. Like I told you yesterday, my sister sort of left the kids with me unexpectedly. I haven't seen them in over a year. Actually, it's been longer than that. Jonah was practically a baby."

I didn't understand my anxiety. The administrator was smiling benignly. I imagined she came across more hard luck stories perpetrated on children than I did in my work.

"My sister could waltz in here tomorrow and take them back," I explained. "I almost feel guilty asking you to do all this paperwork when it may be for nothing."

Her smile stiffened for the first time since I'd walked through the door. "Do you think that's wise?"

I blinked. "Don't I have to do the paperwork regardless of how long they stay?"

The patient, long suffering smile returned to her face. "I don't mean the paperwork." She studied her hands before answering. "I mean about the children." She gestured with her head at Jonah and Emma, who were sluggishly getting in line with the rest of the kids. "Is it in their best interest for their mother to waltz in tomorrow and take them away as if none of this happened?"

"Um, I, uh, don't have any right to keep her from doing whatever she wants. I mean, she is their mother. Like I said, I haven't had any real contact with her since last Christmas. I don't know her situation except that she needs me to keep them a while."

I realized I was defending Nicole and myself much too vehemently. I stopped talking.

Miss Billie leaned forward and rested her elbows on the desk blotter. "I understand. It's difficult to decide what's best for children when family ties are involved. You don't want to hurt anyone's feelings."

"It isn't that."

"Personally, I don't believe it would be fair to you or the children for your sister to feel like she can breeze in and out of your lives whenever the mood strikes her. You won't know, and certainly the children will have no idea, when this behavior will repeat itself. Children need security, structure. They need to know who is in charge and when or if a situation may change. I imagine they are better off with you for the time being. You obviously care a great deal for them. You've gone to all this trouble; bringing them here, paying, taking care of everything before you go back to work. I know you don't have children of your own and this is a huge adjustment. It might be a good idea for you to seriously consider what you'll do when and if your sister comes back."

I sat across the desk from this sweet diminutive woman, stunned. The chance of Nicole not coming back had been a nagging fear in the back of my mind since I picked Jonah up off the dew covered grass and took him and Emma inside. Sure, Uncle Jeb had said much the same thing the other night, but I knew he couldn't stand up to Nicole any better than I could.

I kept telling myself Nicole would come back any minute, and my life would go right back to the way it had been since Grandma Catherine died. Back to when I was in charge. No more at the mercy of the choices made by my absent parents. No more hearing what a strain my existence had been on Grandma. I was finally free.

I hadn't thought about what would happen when Nicole came back. I didn't think about Emma and Jonah worrying and wondering the whole trip back to Memphis—if that's where she chose to take them—when it would happen again.

How could I hand them over to her irresponsible care even if she was their mother? How could I sleep at night knowing the next time they might end up in the front yard of someone other than me?

I watched the news. I worked in a hospital. Even in my secluded little world, I was aware of the evils that befell children every single day. But Emma and Jonah weren't better off with me. Couldn't anyone besides me see that? They would've been better off born to a family who actually wanted and appreciated them. Preferably a family with two parents, a minivan, a dog and a mortgage they couldn't afford.

Not Nicole, and certainly not me.

No matter what Miss Billie thought, I wasn't the person for this job. I kept odd hours. Sometimes I didn't eat vegetables for a week. I didn't drive a minivan. I didn't know the words to a single nursery rhyme. I had no business taking care of kids. I didn't have a problem stepping in to help out long enough for Nicole to get her life straightened out, but the sooner she came back and relieved me of this burden, the happier I'd be.

Chapter Seven

“Aunt Shell."

The tiny voice behind me startled me as I prepared another supper, courtesy of Betty Crocker and Kraft. Since this morning my thoughts had flitted from what Miss Billie said about the kids staying with me to Kyle Swann's appearance in the administrator's cramped office. I couldn't get over seeing him after all these years. Nor could I get over how much I *cared* about seeing him.

I set the box of dry macaroni on the counter and turned around. Jonah stood directly behind me with his neck tilted back as far as it would go to look up at me.

After my tour of the preschool, I'd left the kids there for three hours while I ran errands and tried to gather my thoughts. When I picked them up before lunch, they seemed none the worse for wear. Jonah shrugged when I asked how his morning went, but later he mentioned playing with someone named Ben. Emma said even less. Her answers were a simple yes, no or a noncommittal nod.

I considered it a victory they hadn't cried and screamed and shrank away from the teachers in teachers. We would stick with the half-day plan for the rest of the week. Hopefully I could go back to my regular work schedule next Monday. I hadn't figured out what I'd do about the preschool closing at five-thirty and me working a twelve-hour shift on Mondays and Wednesdays. I hoped Aunt Wanda and Uncle Jeb could pick the kids up for me and keep them till I got home though I hadn't asked yet.

"What is it, Jonah?" I asked, sounding more compassionate than I felt.

"Emma's crying."

A rush of annoyance washed over me. Again? What was it this time? That girl was a bigger crier than any reality TV star. Crying kids was not my area of expertise. I'd know exactly what to do if she was a fifty-eight-year-old chain smoker who'd had her chest cracked open the day before. I was good in those situations. Here, I didn't know what I was doing. What Emma needed I couldn't give her. I couldn't turn Nicole into a better mother no matter how much I wanted it to happen. As much for my sake as Emma's.

I took a deep breath and tried to muster up some patience. Emma had every right to cry. She went to bed one night in her own bed—or so I assumed—and woke up under a stranger's lilac bushes. What a nightmare for anyone at any age.

"Why is she crying?" A dumb question, but it bore asking.

"She wants Carrie."

My jaw dropped. I forced it shut again. I turned the heat off under the pan of water heating for the macaroni noodles and squatted down in the narrow space between Jonah and the stove. I gazed into his concerned face. "Who's Carrie?"

"Our neighbor. She takes care of us when Mommy's sick or with Dean."

Dean again—boy, what I wouldn't give to meet this character. I would worry about wringing his neck later. Right now I needed to focus on getting as much information out of Jonah as possible. This was the first insight into their lives either of them had revealed since they got here.

"Where does Carrie live?" I asked carefully.

"Across the hall. She's real nice. She reads to us and makes us peanut butter and jelly sandwiches and lets us sit on the couch with her and watch TV."

My jaw clenched at the thought of the simple pleasures my niece and nephew obviously lacked.

I took a deep breath to ease the fresh wave of anger at Nicole. "That sounds wonderful," I said to Jonah. "How long have you lived across the hall from Carrie?"

He shrugged. "Long time."

"As long as you can remember?" I asked hopefully.

He shrugged his thin shoulders again.

"Is she old like me or old like Aunt Wanda?"

He pursed his lips thoughtfully and cocked his head to study my face. I braced myself for the insult about my age that was surely on its way.

He touched his finger to my forehead. "She's got lines on her face like you, but they're bigger." He put both hands on either side of my mouth and drew more lines. "She's got lots of lines here." He touched the corners of my eyes. "And here. Lots more than you. Her hair's brown and white."

So she was closer to Aunt Wanda's age.

Jonah giggled. "And she's got a big belly. It's real soft and squishy. I put my head there sometimes when I'm watching TV and I can hear it thump-thump." His smile faded and his brown eyes misted. "I miss Carrie too. Do you think you could take us to her apartment?"

I straightened. My knees were beginning to lock in their squatted position, and I needed to get away from those puppy-dog eyes. I tousled his hair the way I saw Uncle Jeb do and hoped he found it comforting. "Sweetheart, I don't even know where Carrie lives."

"I told you." His voice rose an octave. "She lives across the hall."

How could I make him understand I didn't know where Nicole lived? I assumed Memphis but had nothing solid on which to base my assumption. "Does Carrie have a phone?"

His reply was a blank stare.

"Do you know her other name, her last name?"

This time I got a definite shake of the head. What was I going to do? I didn't know where Nicole lived. The last number she'd given me had long since been disconnected. Why didn't I pay closer attention to her when I had the chance? Why was I so satisfied with keeping her totally out of my life? Even if I knew Memphis was the right city, it wouldn't get me any closer to finding Carrie with no last name or to finding my sister.

I was going to have to figure this out on my own with no help from anyone, and no one with whom the kids were close to, to comfort them when I couldn't.

I took Jonah's hand. "Let's go see if we can make Emma feel better." He looked as doubtful as I felt.

Oh, Nicole, I groaned inwardly. *How does it make you feel that your children are crying for another woman, and have yet to ask about you?*

I had never sat idle in my entire life. That wouldn't change because I had two small children in the house. I wasn't due back to work till Monday, five whole days away. I planned a trip to the local Sherwin Williams to pick up some paint for Nicole's old bedroom while the kids got used to the preschool. The room hadn't been painted since before Nicole moved in when she was three. If the drab, faded eggshell walls depressed me, I could only imagine what they did to Emma and Jonah.

Dressed in a stretched out tee shirt and gardening pants with ripped knees and a bleach stain on the right leg, I made the drive to Genoa to drop the kids off. My fine honey blond hair that frizzed mercilessly in the Arkansas humidity was pulled back in a non-flattering ponytail. My face was void of make-up. No one ever accused me of being a fashion plate, especially when there was work in my immediate future.

I had painting on my mind and nothing else. It never occurred to me until I pulled into the church parking lot that I may run into someone other than Miss Billie at the preschool or the old guy who mixed paint at Sherwin Williams.

I was still struggling with the release on Emma's booster car seat and not thinking of my appearance when a shiny, late model black pickup pulled into the parking lot at the edge of my peripheral vision. Just another parent I didn't need to impress and had no intention of making friends with.

After causing irreparable damage to my thumbnail, the lock on the car seat released. Emma shrugged out of the restraints. I shoved a tendril of hair that had escaped my ponytail out of my face and backed out of the car.

"Good morning, Michelle."

Kyle!

I spun around, one hand fiddling with the ponytail that wasn't even centered on the back of my head, and the other assisting Emma out of the car. "Kyle, hey. Fancy meeting you here. Just when I got all prettied up."

He didn't even raise an eyebrow as he surveyed the mess that was me. "How did the kids like their first day of preschool?"

"Fine, just fine." I blew ineffectively at the strand of hair that refused to stay behind my ear.

"That's good." He looked at Emma and then Jonah who was waiting at the curb. "Do you like coming to preschool?"

Emma stuck her finger in her mouth and ran over to Jonah.

"I'm sorry," I told Kyle. "They're shy around new people."

"I imagine so after everything they've been through."

Miss Billie sure didn't waste a second before airing my family's dirty laundry all over the county. Every teacher in the preschool probably knew, too, what a terrible injustice had been done to sweet little Emma and Jonah by their irresponsible mother. Did they also know my role in turning Nicole into a narcissist?

"Praise God for watching over them and sending them to you," Kyle said.

I wanted to tell him if God had been watching over them, he would've given Nicole a righteous kick in her thinking place the first time she thought about deserting her children under my lilac bushes. Instead an indignant "humph" escaped my lips.

"They're blessed to have you, Michelle," he reiterated.

"I'd rather not discuss this in front of the kids," I said in a voice only he could hear. "They've been through enough without hearing my opinion of my sister or a God who would give her two beautiful children to neglect in the first place."

Kyle's eyebrows practically met in the middle of his forehead. "I see."

I glanced pointedly at my watch. "I've got tons of things to do this morning before I pick the kids up at eleven-thirty."

"Of course. I didn't mean to hold you up." He reached around me and shut the car door and then followed me onto the sidewalk. I walked slowly, giving him plenty of opportunity to go his own direction. He didn't. Instead, he picked up his pace and reached the door two strides ahead of me. He held it open for us to walk through.

"Any time you need to talk, Michelle, my door's always open," he offered graciously. "I know this is quite an adjustment for you, and you might need a neutral ear."

I nodded in response and bent my head over the sign-in sheet. Kyle finally took the hint and walked away. I ushered the kids to the play area and then beat my retreat in case Kyle or any other do-gooders were waiting in ambush with more meaningless platitudes about a merciful God watching over my niece and nephew. It was the last thing I needed to hear. Nicole was lazy, irresponsible, immature, and self-serving—period. She had answered no divine call when she dumped her kids in my front yard. As usual she was thinking only of herself and not about how her actions would affect anyone else.

God, if he even existed, had not blessed Emma and Jonah by sending them to me. My life had been turned upside down. Emma and Jonah were devastated. And Nicole, well, who knew about her? She was probably passed out drunk this very minute. How could God be in any of it?

It wasn't until I buckled my seatbelt, put the car in gear and caught a glimpse of my reflection in the rearview mirror that I remembered what a mess I was. I no longer cared. Hopefully Kyle didn't have the fortitude to approach me again. I had enough complications in my life without worrying what an old boyfriend thought of me.

Aunt Wanda was waiting on the front porch when I got home. I groaned inwardly but pasted a smile on my face for her benefit. I already had barely enough time to move furniture, take down pictures and wash the walls before I had to go back to the preschool to pick up the kids. I didn't have time for company.

"Morning," I called out as I went around to the trunk to retrieve the paint and supplies I'd bought at Sherwin Williams.

"Good morning," she called back as she started down the path toward me. "I see you have a project this morning." She reached into the trunk and took out a gallon of paint. "Ooh, what a pretty shade of blue."

I smiled my thanks at the compliment. "I'm painting Nicole's old room." I lifted two more cans out of the trunk. "I got a soft yellow for the walls. I thought I'd tack up some trim a foot or so from the ceiling and paint the top area blue."

"Sounds pretty. You always had an eye for colors."

I wondered what merited all the compliments. I'd never designed anything in my life. I could barely coordinate my socks with my slacks. The only time I painted was out of sheer necessity. My one attempt at hanging wallpaper had ended in upside down roses so I never tried again.

"I stole the idea from HGTV."

Aunt Wanda followed me through the back door and set the gallon of paint next to mine in the mudroom. "Does this mean you've decided to keep Emma and Jonah?" she asked gently.

Aha. Her true purpose for being here. Uncle Jeb had obviously told her about our conversation the other night. She was afraid she was going to get stuck with Nicole's kids.

I went into the kitchen and headed for the coffeepot. "It doesn't look like I have much choice at this point. I've been meaning to spruce up around the place anyway. Now is as good a time as any since I've got this unexpected vacation. You want some coffee?"

"I always have time for coffee." Never one to settle into the role of guest, Aunt Wanda headed straight for the sink and the dishes I'd left from breakfast.

"I'll get those later," I said half-heartedly. I already knew how this game would play out.

The sink was already filling with lemon-scented bubbles. "I don't mind," she said cheerily. "There's only a few."

I flipped the switch on the coffeemaker and started straightening the kitchen table. Now that I no longer lived alone, my table was actually used for eating. I stacked the magazines and bills into orderly piles and slid them to the far end of the large table. I straightened the place mats and refolded the napkins to slide into napkin rings.

At some point long ago, I went out and bought beautiful place settings for display to fit the motif of a country kitchen. I kept up the façade for close to a week before my typical disorganization crept back over the table. Soon the placemats were stained and wrinkled and hidden under a mountain of whatnots that never seemed to make it to where they belonged. Someday I'd put away the magazines, maybe cancel a few subscriptions, file the bills and take back my kitchen table—someday.

Aunt Wanda wrung out the dishrag and carried it to the cleared off end of the table where she attacked a collage of child sized fingerprints. "Jeb and I have been talking, and we think it's best this way. This is probably the first chance those two little ones have had at a normal life."

She was right. She was absolutely right. Miss Billie was right. Even Kyle was right. But why was I the one doing all the work?

I sank into one of the chairs and curled a leg under me. "It was kind of pitiful. Their reaction, I mean, when I took them to Walmart Sunday. They are totally unaccustomed to getting anything new. Emma was crying again yesterday, but it wasn't for Nicole. She wanted someone named Carrie."

Aunt Wanda shook her head and went back to the sink. "Those poor little darlings."

"This Carrie, whoever she is, is probably worried sick about the kids too. I wish I had some way of getting in touch with her and letting her know they're all right."

"Neither Jonah or Emma know her last name?"

I shook my head, but realized Aunt Wanda had her back to me and couldn't see. "No. Jonah said she lived in the apartment across the hall. I don't know if he meant Memphis or somewhere else altogether."

Aunt Wanda's head wagged back and forth. "Those poor darlings," she repeated, though I figured she didn't even realize she had spoken out loud. "It's such a blessing they have you."

Not that again.

She pulled the stopper from the sink and tore a paper towel from the roll on the holder to dry her hands. "Nicole was about Emma's age when your mom took off outta here. It's beyond me how someone can do something to someone else when they know firsthand how horrible it is." She tossed the paper towel in the wastebasket at the end of the counter and turned to face me. She crossed her arms over her chest and wagged her head again. "No one thinks about anyone else anymore."

I went to the pile of magazines at the far end of the table and picked up the first one. It was a November issue. If I hadn't read the magazine in nine months, it was a pretty safe bet I never would. I either had to find room for my clutter or expect my family to turn me in to one of those life improvement shows on TV. I sat down and started putting the magazines in chronological order. I didn't want to think about Mom or when she left.

Aunt Wanda, on the other hand, was ready to reminisce. "How Nicole carried on when your mom left. Do you remember that, Michelle? Of course, you do. You were what, fourteen? I thought Nicole'd never stop crying and hollering for Ruth." She clicked her tongue. "Mom never had patience for tears. She used to threaten to whip Nicole if she didn't stop crying, but she wouldn't stop. I don't suppose she could."

"Of course, she couldn't," I snapped, enraged at the memory of Grandma Catherine standing over Nicole, scolding and threatening her. "She was four. She wanted her mother. She didn't understand what was going on. Screaming at her wasn't the way to explain it."

"I know, Michelle. I'm the one who calmed Mom down every time Nicole started in. You think that bawling didn't grate on my nerves too? It was all I could do to keep Mom from beating her half to death when she took to carrying on like that."

"I'll be sure to have Nicole thank you the next time she sees you."

"There's no need to get all up in arms at me," Aunt Wanda cried. "None of it was my fault. I'm not the one who convinced your momma to take off the way she did. Her place was with you girls. We all wanted her here, but she quit listening to us years before. If we'd'a had our druthers, she never would'a married that worthless Hurley in the first place. It was all his doing. She was a practical, responsible young woman just like you, until he got his claws into her, that is."

I'd heard all this before more times than I cared to count. Grandma used to have this conversation with anyone who'd sit still long enough to listen. Aunt Wanda was usually willing to lend an ear when Grandma got into one of her griping moods. Back then, the two women were interchangeable in my book. If Grandma wasn't reminding me what a yoke my parents had tied around her neck by taking off with no thought of her age or failing health, Aunt Wanda was telling Uncle Jeb in a voice loud enough for me to hear how unfair it was of Ruthie and that worthless Hurley to impose on Grandma the way they did.

That worthless Hurley. I don't think I ever heard Grandma or Aunt Wanda use Dad's real name.

"He wasn't worthless." I put all the indignation I bore as a child into my voice. "For eleven years he was a wonderful father. He and Mom had their differences. It happens to a lot of couples."

Aunt Wanda snorted derisively. "Eleven years does not get a kid raised. It takes a lifetime. If a person doesn't have a lifetime to give, then they have no business bringing children into the world."

I took a deep, cleansing breath. There was nothing to be gained by debating my father's parenting skills with her. Besides, on this point she was right.

"In a perfect world, adults would never consider bringing children into the world unless they were able to handle the job," I conceded. "Dad made mistakes. He still is making them obviously, since we haven't heard from him since he left twenty-two years ago. Mom made mistakes too. But she and Dad weren't the only ones. Grandma never should've made Nicole and me feel like we were a burden to her. It wasn't our fault our parents dumped us on her, but she made us feel like it was every single day. Maybe that had something to do with the way Nicole turned out."

"Mom did the best she could," Aunt Wanda defended her, though meekly. "She was an old woman. Your parents had no business forcing you girls on her."

"I know. I know. She told me all the time. I heard it so many times I could quote her word for word. If she wasn't such a fine Christian lady, I'd be in an orphanage somewhere, while Nicole would be adopted by a nice family who wanted a pretty little girl to love. According to her, people didn't adopt girls like me. I'd be stuck in that orphanage working in the kitchen like a galley slave. I should've been grateful for having it as good as I did."

Aunt Wanda's face softened. She dropped her arms to her sides. "Mom shouldn't have told you that."

I let out my breath. It was unfair for me to take out my pent up anger at Grandma Catherine on Wanda. I was too old to hold onto anger at an old woman who said insensitive things. Aunt Wanda was only defending her mother's memory. Grandma had been part of a different generation where people had different attitudes concerning children. At least the kids in my family.

I was no better than her. I'd been having the same thoughts about Emma and Jonah since the moment they showed up under the lilac bushes. Like Grandma Catherine, all I thought about was how their presence affected me. They forced me to use precious personal and vacation days, costing me money and wrecking my routine.

Nicole and I had been a burden to Grandma and were reminded of it everyday. Now the shoe was on the other foot. I was the beleaguered one while Emma and Jonah were the crosses to bear. Maybe I hadn't said anything out loud to make them feel unwelcome, but my actions and attitude spoke volumes. Like Aunt Wanda pointed out about Nicole, I knew firsthand how it felt to be abandoned by those who were supposed to love me more than anything and left with someone who saw me as nothing more than a yoke around the neck.

My attitude needed to change. Like it or not, Emma and Jonah were here for the foreseeable future. What if, like Mom and Dad before her, Nicole never came back? If she did, how could I go back to my comfortable life as if nothing had happened?

Chapter Eight

Thursday morning I awoke determined to get an early start on painting the remainder of Nicole's old room. Yesterday after the kids got home from preschool, I took them upstairs with me. I poured a small amount of yellow paint into two old bowls and let them paint along the bottom of the wall. With the drop cloths and newspapers I spread over the floors, messes were minimal. I opened the windows for ventilation, and by the time we finished we were dripping with sweat. But it had been fun. The kids giggled and talked while they painted. I mostly listened. They soon forgot I was in the room and talked more candidly and openly than they would if I had joined the conversation.

This morning I planned to finish the job. All I had left to do was the trim around the doors and windows and the crown molding. Two hours max if I got right on it. I'd be finished before time to go back to the preschool or the sun got around to that side of the house. I hoped to convince Uncle Jeb to come by this weekend and help hang the chair rail I bought at Home Depot.

I woke the kids a half hour earlier than usual.

Jonah sat up in bed and rubbed the sleep from his eyes. "Are we going back to that school today?"

I reached inside a drawer for a clean shirt and shorts. "You're going every morning this week, remember? Starting next week you'll go every day for the whole day while I'm at work except for Friday. I don't work on Fridays?"

Emma swung her legs over the side of the bed. Jonah scooted over next to her. They stared up at me, their faces forlorn. They looked more like brother and sister than I had noticed before.

My stomach tightened. What was up? "You like the preschool, don't you?"

Jonah shrugged. Tears formed in Emma's eyes. Impatience welled up inside me. I didn't have time for this. The minutes ticked away on the clock beside the bed as the sun climbed higher in the sky.

"What's the matter?" I asked a little too brusquely. With great effort, I softened my voice and began again. "I thought you had fun yesterday. Don't you like all the toys they have and playing with the other kids?"

An almost imperceptible nod moved Emma's head. I went on, encouraged. "Well, see there. You'll have friends in no time. You'll learn all kinds of things too."

"We want to stay here with you and paint," Jonah said.

I tossed an outfit on the bed for each of them. "Not today. I'm painting on the ladder and neither of you can reach that high. If there's any paint left when I'm finished, you can help me paint the backside of the barn after you get home."

What damage could they do to the backside of the barn?

They brightened immediately.

"After that we'll go into town for ice cream."

This had them bouncing on the bed. They squealed with delight.

I smiled to myself. I was brilliant. This parenting stuff didn't have to be complicated. Keep them busy. Feed them ice cream. Never let them smell fear or indecision.

"Can we get some Play Doh when we go to town?" Jonah asked.

I grimaced inwardly. Wasn't that stuff messy? "Play Doh?"

"They have it at school, but we haven't got to play with it yet."

I looked from one expectant face to the other. Play Doh in my house and on my rugs. Ice cream I could do. I could even stand in the blazing sun this afternoon and supervise while the kids splashed leftover paint on the barn. But Play Doh? That meant I'd have to put an old sheet on the floor. I'd probably have to pull the table apart afterwards and clean Play Doh out from between the cracks. I'd have to keep an eye on Gypsy and make sure she didn't eat any of it. For that matter, Jonah and Emma might eat it. Could the human body digest Play Doh? This was becoming a hassle I'd rather avoid.

Emma turned to Jonah. "Mommy says Play Doh's too messy. Remember? That's why we can't have it."

Her words didn't register for a moment. I was too surprised she had spoken at all. Three whole sentences out of her mouth, one right after the other. Was this some kind of breakthrough, or was she simply preparing her little brother for the inevitable disappointment she saw coming? They couldn't have Play Doh because it was too messy, too much of a bother for Mommy.

I was about to give them the same excuse.

"It is messy." I gave them a solemn look. "But I have an idea. We'll buy some Play Doh after school and save it for rainy days when we can't play outside."

The light in their eyes was worth whatever inconvenience this would cost me. "You have to promise to be careful and not get any on the floor where Gypsy might get it and make herself sick," I said in stern reminder.

They squealed again and pumped the air with their fists.

"And we gotta put the lids back on so it won't dry out," Jonah said.

"Right. We mustn't let it dry out," I admonished.

They leaped off the bed and started slinging arms through sleeves. I stole a surreptitious glance at them on my way downstairs to let Gypsy outside for her morning routine. I wondered briefly if I'd been duped into buying the Play Doh by the mention of Mommy saying no. I didn't think so. Neither of them seemed to have a manipulative bone in their bodies.

I hadn't given in so easily because I was a totally selfless person. I was beginning to like the way their eyes lit up and the infectious giggles that escaped their mouths when something made them happy. My heart swelled when I saw the simple delight in their eyes at the prospect of painting the barn or getting new shoes at Walmart. I was making them happy, but in return they brought joy into my life. A joy I had forgotten.

I left the windows in Nicole's room open a crack for ventilation but drew the blinds to keep out the brunt of the afternoon sun. Mid-August. Relentless heat. Little rain. It was the same story every year, yet people still gathered in general stores throughout the state and tried to remember a summer that had been as miserable.

"Let me think. Oh, yeah, I remember—last summer!" I wanted to scream every time the conversation occurred within my hearing.

I drove to the school with the AC on high. It was Emma and Jonah's last half day. Uncle Jeb agreed to pick them up for me next week on Mondays and Wednesdays, which were my long days, until I found a sitter. I hoped it wouldn't be long.

It was too hot to play outside. Inside the fellowship hall the preschool staff was trying to keep eighty-five preschoolers from raising the roof off the church with their pent up energy. They had been divided into playgroups. I assumed that helped keep them under control. Nonetheless the fillings in my teeth vibrated from the noise.

Miss Mary, Emma and Jonah's teacher, approached. A smile lit up her round, warm face. She seemed unaffected by the chaos pulsating around her. I wondered if the State issued ear protection for preschool teachers.

"Did you finish your painting?" she asked me.

I smiled and scratched at a smear on my forearm I had missed during clean up. "All finished until I get another creative urge."

She chuckled, and then her face sobered.

I braced myself. Which one? Emma or Jonah? I had my suspicions.

She clasped her hands in front of her and announced, "This was our first tear-free day."

I exhaled. "Thank goodness."

She took my arm and steered me a few feet away. "Emma talked a little today. She's not done that before. If she speaks at all, it's through Jonah. We try to discourage it."

"I know. I'm sorry."

"Don't be. It's fine. She's a delight. She even started playing with one of the other little girls."

"Wow! That's encouraging."

"Yes, it is. Jonah spent his first morning stuck to Emma like glue. Then he started moving around the room, feeling out the other boys and finding a place for himself."

I wasn't surprised. Jonah had already proven he was the type who'd get along anywhere. It was Emma who concerned me. My heart ached for her. She made a friend. Tears pushed at the back of my throat.

"Most of this morning Emma stayed close to me the way she always does," Mary explained. "Not talking or anything. Just sitting next to me and watching what I was doing. Every chance I get, I talk to her about anything I can think of. She never says anything back. She just watches my hands if I'm cutting or preparing the next day's lesson. Sometimes she nods, but that's about it. Then today out of the blue, she told me she and Jonah painted yesterday."

The lump in my throat tripled in size. "I'm painting the room they're sleeping in. I let them help. They seemed to enjoy it."

"You don't know how much. While she talked about it, she positively glowed. You're doing a good job with them. I know it's hard on you, but you're doing fine. It shows."

I wasn't sure how to react to her praise. I wanted the kids to be happy and adjust to the situation. I wanted them to be comfortable in my house and feel secure. I wanted Emma to make friends and start speaking for herself. I just wasn't sure I wanted to get good at this mothering thing. It wasn't my job. Nicole *would* come back. Just when the kids got used to me and I got used to them, she'd stroll in like nothing was out of the ordinary and resume her place as authority figure in their lives. No matter how I questioned her parenting skills, she was their mother.

Wasn't it best for me to hold the kids at arm's length until then?

I already knew the older woman's answer to the question ,so I didn't ask. "Thank you," I said instead. "It's a learning process for all of us."

"After telling me about the painting," Mary continued, "I saw her studying another little girl in the room who tends to play on the edge of the crowd as well. I had a brainstorm and called Caitlyn over to us. I asked her to hand me something.

Then she looked at Emma, Emma looked at her, and the rest is history." Miss Mary's eyes scanned the playgroups. "There they are. They've been together ever since."

I followed her pointing finger and saw two heads—one fair, the other carrot-topped—bent over a wooden puzzle.

"Now I won't feel so bad about the kids staying all day next week."

Miss Mary patted my arm. "You shouldn't feel bad for one minute. They'll get along fine."

I smiled appreciatively before starting toward the two little girls working on the puzzle. Mary put her hand back on my arm. "Don't forget. This Sunday is our Sunday morning program. All the children gather in Miss Jennifer's classroom fifteen minutes before morning worship."

My reply was a blank stare.

"It's been posted all week."

I didn't need to tell her I didn't read the notices posted next to the sign-in sheet. It was written all over my face.

"I'm sure Miss Billie mentioned it when you enrolled Emma and Jonah," she reminded gently.

I still had no idea what she was talking about. I had a ton of things to do today and needed to get going.

"Once a month the children from the preschool sing a few songs for the congregation and recite their memory verses. Many of our preschoolers don't have a home church, and it gives the church members a chance to see what goes on in the preschool all month."

Oh, yes. Now I remembered.

"Sounds wonderful," I lied, "but I'm working this weekend." I set my expression into a study of regret. I hadn't planned to work at the county hospital, but that could be changed with a simple phone call. They always needed the manpower on weekends.

"That's too bad. Maybe you can make it next month. Emma and Jonah have been practicing the songs with the other children. Jonah loves to sing, don't you know?"

No, I didn't.

"Maybe there's someone else in the family who could bring them Sunday morning," she added hopefully. "Even a sitter would be fine. That way they could meet more people from the church and the preschool. It may help them get used to things quicker. I guarantee everyone who attends will be blessed."

I was sure they were, but I wasn't about to suggest Aunt Wanda and Uncle Jeb skip their own church service just so they could see Emma and Jonah performing on stage here.

I gathered the kids and the papers they'd made that day and exited the preschool as quickly as I could. Almost as if they had a will of their own, my eyes sought out Kyle's usual parking spot in front of the doors that led to the main building. His truck wasn't there. A worm of disappointment worked its way into my belly. I didn't know why. I wasn't even sure why I bothered to look for him. Maybe so I could tell him how disgusted I was with his scheme to lure people to church. Was he such a poor preacher he had to trick unsuspecting parishioners to get them through the door?

I considered my appearance and was glad I wouldn't run into him today. My clothes were paint spattered. I probably didn't smell very good either. My hair was falling from the confines of its sweaty ponytail. I was naturally fair-haired and fair-skinned like Emma, so my complexion was red and splotchy on the best of days, especially when I got overheated. Most women with my coloring disguised it with makeup. I seldom bothered. It was bad enough I came out in public at all in my current state, but I'd promised to let the kids paint with the leftover paint. I hadn't seen a point in showering before I left the house.

Kyle was nothing more than an old boyfriend from high school. Hardly a boyfriend really. We dated some, spent a lot of time together and even talked about the future. Who didn't do that in high school with at least one person?

I wondered again about his alleged 'call to preach' as he put it. He hadn't been particularly religious in high school. His parents had dragged him to church every Sunday like Grandma Catherine did me.

"In this family we go to church," she chanted every time I complained.

"Why?" I would demand. "What good does it do?"

"Don't sass, young lady," came the inevitable reply. I never got a more sufficient answer to my question.

The kids had already eaten lunch at the preschool, so we headed straight to Walmart. "No toys," I warned as I pulled into the parking lot. "We're only here for Play Doh."

They didn't look like they would complain, even if I broke my promise. They seemed pretty used to disappointment.

Inside the store they didn't ask for a thing. Besides helping me choose the right colors of Play Doh, they didn't make a peep. I almost caved and offered to buy a DVD because they were so respectful and obedient but stopped myself in time. I wouldn't spoil them. There was no need to fill my house with insipid kids' movies when they wouldn't be living here that long.

I didn't point out the Play Doh castle or ice cream parlor I noticed nearby on the shelf. One or both would be a nice surprise some other time. I picked up a few other things we were running low on around the house and headed toward the registers. It was amazing how two tiny people could change the entire simplistic way a house ran in a matter of days.

Emma and Jonah sat cross-legged in the cart, holding onto the Play Doh. They studied the writing on the packages as if they could read the words and occasionally smiled at each other. A wordless communication passed between them. They had been privy to each other's sufferings for as long as they lived. Now they were almost like one. When one hurt, they both hurt. When one rejoiced, the other experienced the same joy. Sharing the Play Doh, like the paint, ice cream and new shoes, delighted one because it delighted the other. I almost envied their bond until I remembered why it was so strong. If not faced with so much neglect and loneliness on a regular basis, they would never have developed such a close relationship.

The weight of their bodies at the front of the cart made it difficult to maneuver. I seldom required a cart when I shopped. This time seventy pounds of preschoolers threw off my rhythm. I rounded a corner and had to hold back hard on the handle to keep from careening into a man suddenly in my path. My gaze slid upward. With a sinking heart, I realized the man was Kyle.

Kyle stuck his hands out defensively and caught hold of the front of the cart. I couldn't help noticing the strength in his hands and wondering what in his job description left his arms so tanned and defined.

"Whoa, there," he said, his face open and friendly. He looked up and recognized me. He grinned and managed to scowl playfully at the children at the same time. "Are you trying to run me over?"

Emma giggled and gazed up at him through lowered lashes.

Jonah got onto his knees and proudly thrust his four pack of primary colored Play Doh toward Kyle. Emma had chosen the pastels. "Look what we got, Pastor Kyle."

Pastor Kyle. I would never get used to that. It was too holy, too reverent for the Kyle I remembered. Nor did it describe the man in front of us, sporting jeans and a plaid button-down shirt and carrying a pack of strawberry licorice in one calloused hand.

Kyle's eyes widened. "Play Doh! I love that stuff. Looks like you're going to have some fun."

"Not today?" Jonah's serious tone matched his expression. "We've got to paint. The Play Doh's for rainy days."

Kyle nodded like the explanation made perfect sense. He smiled at me. My insides puddled. What was wrong with me? Fortunately Kyle turned his attention back to the kids before he noticed how my sweaty palms could barely maintain their grip on the shopping cart.

"I hope it rains soon." He tousled Jonah's hair and smiled gently at Emma. She beamed discreetly under his perusal. How did he know she wasn't ready for the easy familiarity with which he treated her brother?

"What are you painting?" Kyle directed the question at me.

"The kids' room." With a start I realized it was the first time I didn't called it Nicole's old room.

Kyle noticed something in my eyes. Acceptance? "I guess you know how well they're doing."

I nodded. "I talked with Mary today about that very thing."

"We're glad to have them."

I nodded. Did he expect me to say I was too?

When the silence lengthened, he looked down at the kids. "I'll see you two at school Monday." He glanced back at me. "Unless you're coming to the preschool program Sunday morning."

Emma and Jonah turned to me, expectant and hopeful.

I resented being put on the spot like that. I looked past the kids straight at Kyle. "I don't think so."

I thought about telling him I had to work like I'd told Miss Mary, but there was no need to lie. I was a grown woman. I didn't need to make excuses to anyone. My life had changed enough without adding church attendance to the list of things I was required to do now that I was in charge of two small children.

I ignored the disappointment on Emma and Jonah's faces. I wasn't a fairy godmother who could make them happy by waving my wand. I had changed enough in the past week to accommodate them. I had to stand up for myself somewhere.

Kyle didn't ask for an explanation. "The invitation is open any Sunday. Have fun with that Play Doh," he said to the kids. "Don't get it all over the floor."

"We won't," Jonah assured him cheerily as Kyle moved past our cart in the narrow aisle.

With one more wave to encompass all of us, Kyle moved out of sight. I pushed the cart toward the registers. Emma and Jonah watched warily as I put my things on the belt to be rung up. They could tell something was bothering Aunt Shell. They just weren't sure what. To tell the truth, neither was I. I'd been invited to church countless times since Grandma passed away.

For a while after she died a group of ladies from her church visited to make sure I was all right and to see if there was anything they could do. They were certain my despondency over losing Grandma was what kept me from taking my place in our usual pew every time the church doors were open. I finally admitted to the pastor and his henchmen I only went to church as a courtesy to my grandmother since I lived rent-free in her house. Now that she was gone I was no longer under that obligation. While shocked and dismayed by my candor, my confession did the trick. They never came back.

Even though I presently lacked the nerve to say the same thing to Kyle, I wasn't going to let him use Emma and Jonah to guilt me into anything.

Chapter Nine

Gypsy, the traitor.

For the past six years, barring the occasional night on the porch, she slept on a discarded quilt I left crumpled on the floor next to my bed. After Grandma died I made it known I was in the market for a dog. The neighbor of a woman at work owned an Australian Shepard who had engaged in a tryst with a handsome stranger of questionable lineage. The dog's pedigree didn't concern me in the least since all I wanted was a companion, an alarm system and another warm body in the house. Owning a dog had been an off limits topic with Grandma, who viewed most living creatures as a thorn in her flesh.

I drove an hour north almost into Missouri to meet the man with the wayward Australian Shepard. I fell in love with Gypsy at first sight. I trained her rigorously and shaped her into what I wanted in a pet. It wasn't hard. She was smart as a whip.

She lived up to my expectations and beyond. She was my best friend and I was hers. She hung on my every word and thought I was the most fascinating being in creation. In return, I chased her around the yard, pretending to want the soggy tennis ball clamped in her jaws. She was the last thing I saw every night when I laid down to sleep and the first thing I tripped over in the morning when I stumbled out of bed—until the morning the kids came.

Now she spent every night sprawled across the foot of the double bed in Nicole's old room. I wasn't thrilled about a dog on the furniture, but I didn't have Grandma's mettle. After everything the kids had been through, there was no way I could tell them dogs belonged on the floor, or in Grandma's opinion, tethered to a doghouse in the back yard.

Gypsy wouldn't understand either. She knew where she was needed. I loved her. I kept her clean and groomed and healthy. I filled her dog dish, but it was Emma and Jonah who needed her more than I ever would. Gypsy knew it. I knew it. The kids knew it.

Grandma Catherine's garden had completely gone to rot and ruin in the two weeks since the kids showed up under the lilac bushes. The weeds had overtaken the tomato plants, and the cucumber vines had wrapped around the green peppers. I called the administrator at the county hospital and told her I couldn't work weekends for the foreseeable future. Uncle Jeb and Aunt Wanda were already helping out by picking the kids up from preschool on the evenings I worked until seven. Until I found a reliable babysitter, I couldn't ask them to give up their weekends too. Besides, I had things to do around the house.

Before the dew had a chance to burn off the plants, I dressed in my old work clothes and stopped outside Nicole's old bedroom door to motion for Gypsy before I made my way to the garden.

I was a little surprised to hear her padding along behind me. It was the first time she'd been out of the kids' sight in two weeks. I knew it was only because they were still asleep, but I appreciated the company, nonetheless. I grabbed a hoe from the shed and started to work on the east end of the garden, the end where the sun was already beating down. By the time it got unbearably hot and I was good and tired, I'd be in the shade, and the work wouldn't seem so arduous.

After a circuit of the yard, Gypsy plopped down in the dew-covered grass in the shade of the hydrangea hedge to watch, one ear cocked toward the house in case a tiny pair of feet hit the hardwood floor upstairs.

I smiled at the dog and attacked the weeds with vigor. For all its tedium, I enjoyed working the garden. Things had certainly changed from when I was young. I hated working out here when Grandma was the one giving orders. Not only was she unreasonably particular about her garden—no dirt clods bigger than a nickel, rows perfectly straight, cucumbers to the east, carrots and radishes to the west and the weeds went without saying—she had the ability to suck the pleasure out of any project.

I became adept at blocking out Grandma's presence, whether physical or implied, from my mind. While she seemed to rejoice in searching for the bad in any situation, I decided I would do the opposite. I would make a game out of everything, whether canning beans, snapping peas or scrubbing the living room floor. I closed myself into my own little world where everything was fun, mysterious or an adventure.

It wasn't just for my benefit. Regardless of the amount of chores, I still had to keep an eye on Nicole. When working in the garden, I'd sit her at the end of the row close to where Gypsy currently lay and tell her a story about a fairy princess held captive in a tower or a beautiful girl waiting for her brave knight to return from battle. There were always countless obstacles that kept the knight from returning or the princess locked in the tower depending on how much work I had to do in the garden.

The favorite story for both of us was the one in which Nicole was a princess left in my care, her Royal Guardian. Her parents, the king and queen, had lost their kingdom to an evil knight, and had gone home to try and regain it. Princess Nicole had to wait at the end of each garden row and never take her eyes off me. If she did, the evil knight, who could be hiding anywhere, might jump out of the bushes and get me. Then she would have no one to protect her until the handsome prince, who was slaying dragons at the time, could come to rescue both of us. Every now and then to keep things interesting, I'd drop my hoe in the dirt and growl and yell and run at her, pretending the evil knight had tricked her by pretending to be the Royal Guardian. She always squealed and leaped to her feet and ran a few times around the garden until I caught her or she dropped into the grass in gales of laughter and pretended to be scared.

Every summer we added more details and characters to our stories until they often overlapped, which only added to the fantasy. I always thought I'd write them down someday after my chores were done and Nicole and I were relaxing on the couch or the front porch. Like so many other things, I never got around to it.

I couldn't remember exactly when we stopped playing games and making up stories. Probably around the time I started college. I was still responsible for whatever might go wrong around the farm whether present or not.

And things started to go wrong fast.

Grandma hadn't liked me from the first time she laid eyes on me. Anyone could see it. Mom tried to make light of it, though she wouldn't insult me by flat out denying Grandma's disdain. "That's just how she is, Michelle," she'd say. "She's set in her ways. Don't take it personally."

I didn't. I didn't take anything personally. If I had been the delicate sort like my cousin Violet, I wouldn't have made it past eleven.

Still, living with Grandma Catherine's Christian charity waxed sore on even the strongest of constitutions. She wouldn't let me forget what a burden I was.

"It's not your fault, girl," she'd say after a good scolding over some infraction I'd committed. "It's that worthless daddy of yours."

Like that's what I wanted to hear.

"He's the one that took off and left your mama with no choices."

Grandma would click her tongue and stare out the window, her gnarled fingers flexing and relaxing around the ends of her rocker arms. I knew she was imagining wrapping her hands around my missing daddy's neck and squeezing as tight as she could. "I told Ruthie he was no good the first time she brought him home."

I always stopped listening whenever Grandma got tuned up like that, knowing full well how the story turned out—at least Grandma's version.

She would push her rocking chair back and forth, faster and faster with her spindly legs. The madder she was, the faster that rocking chair would rock.

"I remember telling your grandpa, 'Gib, that boy'll amount to nothing but trouble. He's worthless. Too pretty for his own good.' A man shouldn't be that handsome. It always leads to trouble, sure as I'm sitting here. Yes, indeedy."

I never understood how good looks automatically overrode any good quality a person might possess.

"Thing were okay as long as your daddy was working steady," Grandma always went on, relishing the taste of the story on her tongue. "I have to admit he took pretty good care of you and your momma. I knew it was a matter of time, though, before he'd mess up and leave my poor Ruthie high and dry. After the plant shut down, that's when it happened. It takes a strong man to stare adversity in the face and bounce back. Your daddy, oh no, he wasn't the bouncing back kind."

For years after Dad left, I wondered if he knew what his leaving did to us. Had he known how Grandma would treat us, he would come back. I was sure of it. He wouldn't knowingly do this to his family. But how could he not know? Surely he realized his wife would end up back home with her family in Winona. Mom, Nicole and I would be forced to put up with a hateful old woman he couldn't bring himself to visit since I was little.

Why had he done it? Hating us was one thing. Leaving a wife he no longer loved was another. But forcing us onto Grandma when he knew she wouldn't turn us out, which would have been the kindest thing she ever did to a person, was beyond cruel on his part.

I put my hand on the small of my back and stretched. I hadn't dwelt on this baggage in years. After Grandma died I decided it took too much effort to harbor bad feelings toward her, Dad, Mom or anyone else. I would move on with my life, get serious about saving for retirement, take some courses, move ahead in my field and leave my family problems buried in the past where they belonged.

I made an effort to get my mind off its dark path and plan breakfast instead.

Waffles were always a popular choice. The kids loved them. Emma wouldn't eat until she'd filled each little divot with syrup. Jonah tried, but he wasn't as coordinated. He always dumped half a bottle on his plate before I'd get impatient and do it for him. The syrup never went to waste though. He licked up every drop no matter how big the puddle. I would remind myself life was too short to worry about going through a bottle of Golden Griddle each week.

I'd gained three pounds in the two weeks since Emma and Jonah arrived. I didn't have a figure that could afford three pounds here and three pounds there. If Nicole didn't come back soon I wouldn't fit into my scrubs. The frequent stops at McDonald's, the fish sticks and macaroni and cheese, were all catching up with my hips. More gardening, less waffles, I told myself as I worked my way into the shade.

Uncle Jeb showed up at the backdoor as we were restoring order to the kitchen after a late breakfast of waffles and cantaloupe. "What's all the ruckus in here?" he demanded in his fake gruff voice. He glowered down at the kids from his six-foot height, but the gleam in his eye was evident to all, even Emma. "I could hear you all the way across the field."

"Uncle Jeb!" Jonah squealed. "Are we going fishing today?"

Emma stayed near the safety of the table but studied Uncle Jeb's face, equally anticipating his response.

I jumped to his rescue. "Come on, you two. Uncle Jeb has taken you fishing three times already. Maybe he has other things to do."

Uncle Jeb winked at me and looked back at Emma and Jonah. His bushy gray eyebrows pulled into a frown. "As a matter of fact, I've got a million things that need taken care of today and don't have time for no pestering kids. I've got to bush hog around the pond. Then I gotta put the horses into the north field. After that, Wanda wants me to clean out the barn and the field next to the house so maybe we can have a barbecue tonight."

Jonah and Emma exchanged glances. "A barbecue?" Jonah asked. "Do we get to come?"

Uncle Jeb rubbed his chin and chewed his bottom lip. "Well, I expect Wanda'll be calling here in a little bit to see if you wanna come. But I told her, no, there's too much work needs done to be planning some silly barbeque."

"We can help, Uncle Jeb," Jonah offered.

Emma took a brave step forward and nodded emphatically.

Uncle Jeb dismissed them with a wave of his hand. "Nah. You wouldn't wanna ride around on that old hot tractor all day. And I know you don't like them horses."

"Yes, we do! Yes, we do!" Jonah assured him, jumping from one foot to the other.

"How about it, Emmy?" Uncle Jeb said. "Is that so?"

She nodded again and said in a small voice, "We like the horses."

Uncle Jeb pulled his mouth into a bow as if considering the validity of their words. "Well, I guess if you're sure."

"We are. We are."

"Okay, then. Michelle, how about I put these two whippersnappers to work today? If they work really hard, they can go into town with me to get some steaks and hotdogs and whatever else we'll need for a barbecue."

Emma and Jonah turned pleading eyes to me.

"Well, I don't know," I said, playing along. "Neither one of them look big enough to be much good on the tractor."

Jonah puffed out his chest. "Yes, we are. I'm strong. So's Emma."

I paused thoughtfully and grinned at Uncle Jeb over their heads. "Oh, all right. Go upstairs and put on long pants. I don't want you bringing ticks home to Gypsy while you're bush hogging."

They tore out of the kitchen, squealing and waving their hands in the air.

"Don't forget you're coming to work," Uncle Jeb called after them. "Like the Good Book says; ya don't work, ya don't eat."

"'Kay, Uncle Jeb," they called back as they thumped their way up the stairs, though I was sure his Bible reference was lost on them.

I turned to my uncle. His face was lit up with a thousand stars. "You know you don't have to do this," I told him. "You and Aunt Wanda fool with the kids enough during the week. I'm sure you'd appreciate some time to yourselves."

"That's all we've got, Peanut. Time to ourselves. It don't look like me and Wanda's going to have grandkids anytime soon. If we do, they'll be all the way over in Fayetteville with Violet. I love having the kids around. Doc's always telling me I need a little recreation. Those two kids are better than any blood pressure medicine."

"Are you sure about them on the tractor?"

"Don't you remember you and Violet ridin' all over the farm on that thing? While you were at school, Nicole sat right there beside me while I got my work done. I bet I babysat that girl a thousand hours on top of that tractor."

"But we were used to it. Emma's awfully bashful. What if she forgets to hold on and you have to scold her? She'll start crying and that will ruin everyone's day."

"You get used to something by doing it." Uncle Jeb brushed his knuckles across my cheek. "If I didn't know better, I'd think you sound like a worrying momma."

"No, no, I'm not worried…" My voice trailed off as a flush warmed my cheeks. "If you're sure…"

"I'm sure." He put his hand on the screen door. "Send 'em over to the house with Gypsy when they get downstairs. I'll be puttering around somewhere. I'll light the fire for supper sometime around six."

"Sounds good. I'll be there. Thanks, Uncle Jeb. You made those kids' day."

"No problem." He was halfway out the door when he turned back. "Michelle, you could return the favor and make my day tomorrow by bringing the kids to church with your Aunt Wanda and me."

So his good deed came with a price.

"Now, Uncle Jeb, you know I don't do church."

He waved his arm dismissively. "Yeah, I know. But you may want to reconsider for the kids' sake. It ain't just you anymore."

I checked the irritation welling up inside me. Uncle Jeb didn't mean to use the kids as a way to get me to do what he wanted. He cared about me and the condition of my soul. I wished there was a way to convince him his concerns were unnecessary.

"I'm fine and so are Jonah and Emma. I don't need to dress them up and drag them to church every week to prove I'm a good person."

He swallowed hard to check his own irritation. "Goin' to church don't have nothing to do with being a good person. Be that as it may, I hate to see you let a bad experience sour you on the Lord. You're right that the church ain't perfect. That's because it has people in it. Regardless of the way his children sometimes behave, there's still only one way to the throne. Through his son Jesus Christ who shed his blood on the cross for saints and sinners alike."

"I don't know if I believe in a merciful God who sent his only son as a way to redeem sinners. If there is a God and there is a Heaven, it has to be a very empty place. I haven't met one single person who lives according to what I remember reading in the Bible. The people going to church every Sunday are just like me. We work and pay our bills and don't break any laws. The only difference is I'm not fooling myself into thinking I'm better than everybody else."

Uncle Jeb let out a long sigh. "I'm sorry you feel that way, Michelle. I'm even sorrier you can't see God's light shinin' through me. I serve him the best way I can, and I'm doin' him a disservice if my own niece can't see my witness."

"I didn't mean you," I backpedaled. "You're not a bad person. I just meant most people—"

"I know what you meant. My Christianity is who I am. If it ain't apparent to the people I come across in my daily walk, well then, I need to reexamine myself. 'Study to show thyself approved, rightly dividing the word of truth.' Don't forget, dinner'll be ready around six."

He backed out the door and stepped off the porch. I watched him head across the field that separated our properties. I wanted to yell and tell him I was sorry. I didn't mean to insult him. He was a good man. If anyone was going to heaven, he would surely be among the elect few. But it was too late. He would know I was apologizing because I hurt his feelings, not because I hadn't meant what I said.

I thought of Kyle. Would my thoughts insult him, too, if I voiced them to him as I had Uncle Jeb? Were all Christians so sensitive about their calling, or did Uncle Jeb take the whole witnessing business more seriously than most? Grandma never worried about what anyone thought about her or her witness. It would never occur to her to step back and examine her behavior if anyone ever had the nerve to accuse her of not living like a Christian.

I wasn't an atheist. I knew too much about science to believe every living organism was the result of a huge cosmic accident. It took more faith to believe that theory than Creationism in my book. It was like suggesting the Empire State Building was the result of an explosion at a steel mill.

My logical mind knew there had to be some truth to the whole Creator God idea. My problem came with the thought of a benevolent Father figure looking down from heaven, listening to our prayers and solving our problems. A merciful, benevolent God wouldn't allow some children to be born into loving homes with loving parents while others were born in bathroom stalls and thrown into dumpsters. If God was up there, why wasn't he watching over kids like Emma and Jonah? Why did he allow the Nicole's of the world to treat their children like puppies they'd grown tired of?

Emma and Jonah scampered back into the kitchen. Their faces fell when they saw only me. "Where's Uncle Jeb?"

"He headed home. He's waiting for you to catch up."

They darted for the back door without another word. Gypsy plowed out from under the kitchen table, her toenails scraping across the linoleum to gain traction.

"Take Gypsy with you," I called unnecessarily.

"We will," Jonah said over his shoulder as he and Emma disappeared out the door with Gypsy on their heels.

I watched as they hurried in the same direction Uncle Jeb had gone. I could see the top of his John Deere hat disappearing over the rise. I needed to do something to fix the hurt my careless words had caused. A more thoughtful niece would have said no thanks to his church invitation and left it at that. I turned toward the cabinets. If I had the ingredients, I'd make the German chocolate pie he loved so much, the one he wasn't supposed to eat. Wouldn't he be surprised when it showed up on the table other than at Thanksgiving dinner?

Chapter Ten

"Ms. Hurley."

I was instantly suspicious of the look on the preschool administrator's face when she approached me Monday morning. I pasted a smile on my own face, albeit a pale imitation of hers, and waited. Were the children being asked to leave? Was Emma crying all the time or not participating? Was it Jonah? Had he bitten someone? Children under stress did that sometimes. Last month a five-year-old showed up in the emergency room during one of my weekend stints with a bite-size hunk missing from his cheek where his little sister decided she'd had enough of his bullying.

"Yes?" I said calmly when she was within speaking range though my heart was racing.

"I wanted to make sure you saw our signup sheet." She nodded benignly toward the table just inside the vestibule with the sign-in roster, a lost and found box full of small toys, sunglasses, miscellaneous children's wear, and the sign up sheets for field trips or calls for volunteers.

I noticed the paper taped on the table next to the clipboard where I had just signed Emma and Jonah's names. Miss Billie probably knew by now I was one of those clients who rushed in and out every day in too much of a hurry to notice anything other than what demanded my immediate attention. I wondered what else I'd missed in the past two weeks.

"We're taking the children to the park on Friday," she said.

I feigned interest by looking down at the paper and nodding.

"Each child needs to bring a sack lunch. I know you're usually off on Fridays and don't bring the kids in, but I know they'll enjoy it. If you decide to bring them, you need to sign here and here." She pointed to two blank lines. "That lets us know you're aware of the trip. There will be permission slips for you to sign the day of the trip too."

I nodded again. "Sounds like fun," I said noncommittally.

"And since you're off that day…" She clasped her hands in front of her and beamed. "We're always looking for volunteers. Any time we leave the facility, we try to have as many adult volunteers as possible. It's always a lot of fun," she added in response to the look of panic that swept across my face. "It gives you a chance to meet the other parents and get to know your child's friends."

I wasn't interested in meeting parents, and I doubted any of Emma or Jonah's friends were felons or deviants or otherwise needed my attention.

"I'm sure Emma and Jonah would love to go," I mumbled.

"Does that mean you're volunteering?"

"I—I don't know. What exactly would I have to do?"

"Oh, nothing really. We just need plenty of warm bodies to give the illusion the adults are in charge." She laughed merrily. "And you're a nurse. You'll be the stabilizer for all the other parents. I'm sure nothing upsets you."

"I used to think so."

She laughed again, obviously delighted by my wit. She put her hand on my arm. "Don't forget to pack a lunch for yourself. We're leaving the school at 9:30."

I walked out of the church, feeling like I'd been tricked into doing something I would regret.

I had not seen Kyle since I almost ran into him with my cart at Walmart the day the kids and I painted Nicole's old room. I felt bad for insulting Uncle Jeb over his invitation to church. I didn't want to put myself in the same situation with Kyle. I successfully put him out of my mind until I saw him climbing behind the wheel of one of the eighteen-passenger vans at church Friday morning. It never occurred to me he would go on the field trip with the preschoolers.

In all the confusion of assigning seats, holding hands, making sure everybody went to the restroom and was in the right group, I barely had time to look up, let alone notice what was happening around me. Besides the teachers and staff whose names I couldn't keep straight, there were three mothers, one dad and somebody's teenage sister helping get the kids wrangled into some mass of organization. Over all of us reigned Miss Billie whom I had yet to see flustered.

Each child chose a partner with whom to hold hands while crossing the parking lot. From there the partners would ride to the park together in either the church vans or one of the teachers' or parents' minivans to whom they'd been assigned. Mine was the only sports car in the parking lot. I felt like a fish out of water. At least it got me out of driving duty. I don't think my nerves could've handled it.

Jonah joined hands with the little boy he'd been sitting next to all morning. I'd learned earlier the little boy was his friend Ben. I worried how Emma would react when Jonah paired up with someone else. I scanned the crowd and saw her standing against the wall, whispering and holding hands with the lovely red-haired girl she'd been playing with the day we painted. I exhaled gratefully.

Miss Mary witnessed my reaction. "Emma has certainly blossomed in the past week. She's still quiet, but that's just her nature. She doesn't give me a moment's trouble. She and Caitlyn do everything together. They're like peas in a pod."

"I'm so glad. She's opening up more at home too. She had me worried for awhile."

"No need for that. She's a bright little girl and very resilient. She'll be fine."

We watched a few moments as Emma and her friend leaned on the wall, whispering and smiling at each other while they waited for the call to line up. A sense of pride surged through me.

I wondered if Nicole was enjoying herself enough to make up for everything she was missing here.

Miss Billie came into the large room where we waited and announced it was time to leave. The only dad in the group looked at me and smiled. "Is this your first field trip?"

"Is it that obvious?"

He grinned, revealing a quirky smile and nearly perfect teeth. "You've got that deer in the headlights look. Don't worry. You'll be an old hand at this in no time."

I didn't bother to tell him I didn't plan to be in this position long enough to get good at it.

I didn't see a wedding band on his left hand, not that I was looking. Was he divorced or a deadbeat? I was relatively certain deadbeat dads didn't go on field trips with preschoolers. He had the type of looks that could grow on a person with a straight nose, nice square jaw, dark hair and intense dark eyes nearly the shade of his hair.

He extended his hand. "I'm Barry Schilling." He glanced across the tops of the children's heads milling around us and motioned to the only redhead in the crowd. "That one's mine. Caitlyn."

She obviously got her red hair from her mother, though I could see Barry in her face and effervescent smile. "You're kidding," I said with a laugh. "The blonde with her is mine. I mean, she's my niece Emma. My nephew Jonah is around here somewhere."

I thought I should explain why I was about to embark on my first field trip with a niece and nephew instead of their mother. I figured it would take too long, and Barry probably didn't care anyway. Families came in all sorts of combinations. I just didn't want him to think I was misrepresenting myself, that I volunteered while their mother was deployed overseas or something when really she was God only knew where, doing God only knew what.

The line started to move forward, and my chance to explain vanished.

I tensed. *Stranger danger*, my insides screamed. What if one of them was snatched while I was looking at some other kid? Where was Emma? I couldn't see Jonah in the milling sea of boys who all looked alike from this angle with similar clothes and nearly the same haircut. What group was he in? I couldn't remember. He had been moved out of Miss Mary's class last week and put into…whose? I couldn't remember his teacher's name. What kind of guardian couldn't remember the name of her child's teacher?

The children pushed forward as anticipation reached a fever pitch. I rested my hands on the shoulders of two children close to me and tried to look like I wasn't freaking out. What if someone ran under the wheels of a minivan? What if they didn't stay in line? What if one of them ran away or was kidnapped?

Barry must've read the terror in my face. "Things will settle down once we get everybody buckled into the van. It's getting them ready to go that's hectic."

I took a deep breath. "I'm ordinarily very calm. Believe it or not, I'm a nurse. I'm trained to handle emergencies. It's just with kids…it's different."

"Especially when they're your own." He chuckled and moved forward to hold the door open.

I opened my mouth to tell him Emma and Jonah weren't mine. I was just the aunt. That's all he needed to know. The kids surged forward through the double doors like water spilling over a ruptured dam. Now wasn't the time to tell anyone anything.

Our orderly lines fanned out as children crowded toward the vans or went off with the parents assigned to drive. Kyle stood at the open side door of the first van, lifting children inside.

"Stay with your partners," the teachers called out over and over.

"Fasten your seat belts."

"Austin, stop kicking the back of the seat."

"Kali, sit on your bottom."

The parents finished loading their charges into minivans and waited with their engines running in a caravan behind the church vans.

What an undertaking just to drive three miles to a park. I was exhausted already.

After the children were loaded there were still two empty spaces in the recesses of the van Kyle was driving.

"Michelle?" Kyle said when I stepped forward to climb inside. "So that was your name on the sign up sheet. I thought it was a typo."

"Ha ha, very funny." I put my foot on the step and held my hand out. "Are you going to help me up or not? They must make these vans taller than they used to."

"I'm sure that's it." He took my outstretched hand to steady me as I heaved myself up and inside the cramped space between the seats.

With my body nearly bent in two, I lurched to the rear of the van. A rookie mistake I would soon regret. I finally managed to buckle myself between the boy who had been kicking the back of the seat and his equally ornery looking counterpart.

Barry climbed in after me and took a seat two rows ahead. He turned around in the seat and smiled. "You all right back there?"

"I'm fine now. They're strapped down. What could possibly go wrong?"

He arched his eyebrows, and the lines around his mouth crinkled into a mischievous grin. "You'll find out," he said as he turned to face forward.

I glanced up and saw Kyle watching the exchange in the rearview mirror. When he caught my eye, he looked forward and started the ignition.

I stared at the back of his head as he put the van into gear and pulled out of the parking lot. He didn't look up again. I wondered why he had in the first place. Did he have a problem with me talking to Barry? Did he know something about the guy I didn't? Was he jealous? I smiled at the thought and immediately banished it from my head. Kyle had no reason to be jealous of me and a man I just met. I had no reason to want him to be. He was only watching because he found it amusing that I chose the back seat. I already wished I hadn't. The van swayed, the noise level was deafening, exhaust fumes were making me nauseous and dear little Austin was kicking the back of the seat again.

I concentrated on breathing through my mouth and tried to ignore the swaying and kicking. It was only three miles.

I spent the morning running from swing to swing pushing little ones who soon learned I couldn't say no, and helping others to the bathroom where it turned out they preferred playing in the sink over actually doing what they'd come in to do. Through no intention on my part, I ended up sitting across the picnic table from Caitlyn's dad during lunch. For a moment I allowed myself to believe he planned the whole thing. I wasn't exactly a bad catch. In the right clothes, with a little make-up and a decent haircut, I could hold my own. I'd had a date or two in my time and had turned down more than one opportunity. But I was too busy for men and relationships. Eventually they stopped asking. Or maybe I stopped putting myself into a position to be asked. I wasn't sure which. I think I sent off a vibe, if anyone said vibe anymore. Somehow men knew. Maybe they discussed it at the meetings. Don't approach. Waste of time.

All work and no play had made Michelle a dull girl.

After opening what felt like a hundred juice boxes, unwrapping sandwiches and peeling back the stubborn plastic over ready-to-eat lunches, I lowered my posterior onto the seat board of our picnic table. Even after eleven hours on surgery prep duty, it never felt this good to sit down.

"I never caught your name," Barry said the first time I glanced up from my sack lunch.

"Oh, I'm sorry. I'm Michelle Hurley. You met Emma and Jonah." I nodded at Emma, who sat four children down on my side. Jonah was at a different table, surrounded by a group of rowdy boys who couldn't be bothered with boring aunts.

"I hear about Emma all the time. They're pretty new at the preschool, right?"

I nodded as I swallowed a bite of peanut butter on wheat. "They've been here for three weeks. Since my sister…" I hadn't meant to get into this right now. "They're staying with me awhile. They're warming up to the whole preschool thing. I hear a lot about your Caitlyn, too."

He chuckled. "I'm glad. She doesn't make friends easily. She's been at the preschool for a few months, but Emma is her first real friend. She's always been shy—like her daddy."

"Oh, please," I said, smiling.

"Well, a long time ago. I guess I got over it."

We nibbled at our sack lunches. Between rising up and down from our seats to assist little hands, Barry managed to tell me he worked nights. It worked out well with Caitlyn. He was free to attend many of the morning field trips and help out on special days. He shared custody with his ex-wife who kept the little girl at night while he worked.

I wondered why he was telling me so much personal stuff when we'd just met. Did he want me to know there would be no jealous ex knocking my door down if something developed beyond today? Was he killing time until we headed back to the school? Was he an easy talker who didn't know a stranger?

I didn't offer much about myself. There wasn't much to tell besides why Emma and Jonah were living with me in the first place. I sure didn't want to go into that.

I looked around in a subtle attempt to spot Kyle. I found him sitting at the table directly behind me with Miss Billie and a few of the teachers. I couldn't see him without turning completely around in my seat or giving myself a neck ache. But I could hear him. The table behind me erupted into laughter. His was the only adult male voice, deep and resonating. Just like I remembered. He could even make Grandma Catherine laugh, which was no easy feat. I wished I knew what they were talking about. It sounded like they were having so much fun. I should've paid closer attention when I chose my seat.

What was I thinking? I didn't want to sit next to Kyle—the pastor. What would we talk about? My past sins? My many shortcomings as a human being? No thanks. I already knew most of them.

After a lunch that ended all too quickly, the adults cleared the picnic tables while the kids charged back to the playground. Kyle moved through the crowd, playing games with the kids, pushing swings, being one end of the teeter-totter with two boys perched on the other squealing with delight. Everyone loved him. I couldn't help noticing how much.

"How are you holding up?" he asked pleasantly the one time we got close enough to speak.

I smiled broadly. "I'm hanging in there." I stopped pushing a swing long enough to tuck a strand of hair behind my ears. Next time I'd wear a ponytail.

"I hope we haven't scared you out of volunteering again."

"Oh, no, I'm having fun. I can almost tell some of the kids apart. I played a game where I was a shark and fifteen screaming kids were the bait. I've pushed this swing for twenty solid minutes. My only question is, when's naptime?"

"Not soon enough."

"I can see how they roped me into volunteering, but what about you? Couldn't you come up with some kind of excuse?"

He chuckled and gave his swing another push. "To tell you the truth, I don't mind at all. I seldom have a free day, and when I do, I enjoy spending it with the kids and getting to know some of the parents better."

I nodded like it made perfect sense. In truth, I wondered if his personal life could possibly be as pathetic as mine. A whistle shrilled through the heady August heat. Kyle brought his swing and rider to a halt.

"Okay," he shouted. "Time to load up."

The little boy on the swing I was pushing leaped off before I could bring it to a safe stop and took off running toward the van. "Not a moment too soon," I said. But Kyle had already moved away and was herding kids into groups.

As soon as we got back to the preschool, I climbed into my steaming Mazda long enough to start the engine, crank the AC and jump out again. The interior of the car was at least 115 degrees. I could just imagine what those seats would feel like against bare preschool skin.

I headed into the building to collect Emma and Jonah. They could nap at home. I met Barry coming out with Caitlyn in tow. "Nice meeting you, Michelle," he said as he held the door open for me.

"You too, Barry. And you, Caitlyn."

She shrank against her father's leg and smiled up at me.

"Maybe we could get together sometime," he said. "Plan a play day for the kids… or something."

His dark eyes twinkled at the 'or something'.

This was not what I needed. Not now. Barry was friendly and not bad looking and obviously a caring father. But the Big D was a major consideration. I ran into plenty of divorced dads at the hospital, but I never dated one. They knew before they even met you what they were looking for. It all depended at what point they were in their lives. They either wanted a mother for their children, a mother for themselves or something warm for a night. They weren't looking for a wife until after they realized it was easier to fill all three roles in one fell swoop.

They were always in a hurry—a hurry to strike up a conversation. A hurry to get you to dinner. A hurry to let you know how miserably they'd been treated by their ex's. A hurry to get you out of the restaurant to see if the rest of the evening would go as they hoped. Divorced men were about as high maintenance as you could get in my book.

My life was complicated enough.

"We'll see, Barry," I said as gently as I could. "I've got a lot going on right now with the kids and work…and everything."

Understanding registered in his eyes, followed by disappointment. "Sure. Me too. Well, I'll see you around. Maybe at the next field trip."

I went inside, hating myself for being so cold, and hating society for putting me in this situation. Barry didn't seem like the typical divorced guy. If he had been out for one thing, he would have tried to cajole me out of my rejection.

All the way home and for the rest of the evening, I agonized over giving him the brush off. I wasn't dead. Maybe I should've taken a chance with him. It would be nice to dress up and go out with someone who could cut his own meat. I liked to think I wasn't interested in becoming part of a couple. I liked the way my life was. I wasn't sure it was the whole truth. Right now I was too busy to be lonely. The day might come, however, when I wanted something more. When I was no longer satisfied with sharing my home with only Gypsy.

There had to be a few guys out there with redeemable qualities. Even divorced ones. Maybe Barry was the one, and I had missed out on the perfect opportunity to get to know a really great guy.

Just before tucking the kids into bed, I realized what was bothering me so much about the whole thing. If Kyle had been the one who asked to get together, I would've jumped at the chance.

Chapter Eleven

Miss Billie gave me the number of a stay-at-home-mom from her church who did daycare in her home. The woman sounded stable and responsible over the phone, accepted second and third shifts and had two openings. She agreed to pick Emma and Jonah up from the preschool at four o'clock on the days I worked twelve hours. She would also watch them on weekends when the county hospital couldn't do without me. I told her I wouldn't work more than two weekends a month although I dreaded losing out on the money.

Barring any criminal record, she was hired as far as I was concerned. While we talked I did the math in my head and was staggered by the amount it was going to cost to hire this woman and continue paying full-time rates at the preschool. I could plainly see my 401K contributions going bye-bye. So were the frequent trips to Wal-Mart for shoes and toys and meals at McDonald's.

Angie Burkheimer, the stay-at-home-mom, had two girls of her own, one in first grade and the other in kindergarten.

When Jonah, Emma and I arrived for our interview, I saw two babies in playpens and two little boys, about the size of Jonah, playing in her daycare room. Jonah was immediately satisfied with the arrangement. I figured Emma would enjoy playing with the babies. I was right.

I recognized Angie from high school. She was a year or two behind me, but I remembered her. Winona High School only had about five hundred students between ninth and twelfth grades so nearly everyone shared at least one elective or study hall.

Angie had converted the large family room off her kitchen into a daycare area. We left the kids there to play and settled at the kitchen table where we were still within sight and earshot to go over details.

"How is Nicole these days?" she asked discreetly.

I was getting used to explaining to people why I was keeping my sister's kids while skipping over most of the embarrassing details. I hated for every person in the county to know what a terrible mother my sister turned out to be. Angie, though, would need to know the whole story if she was going to spend much time with the kids.

After I finished explaining the last three weeks of my life, she took a sip of her coffee and sighed. "I didn't know Nicole that well. She was a lot younger than me. But I know of her. I'm sorry to hear things haven't worked out better for her."

I nodded in agreement. There was no need to deny it or be embarrassed. Most people around here knew *of* Nicole, even if they'd never met her. She hadn't lived in Winona for over three years, but her legacy was fresh in everyone's minds. I guess I was partly to blame for the mistakes she made, but there was no use apologizing for that either. If I had done a better job teaching her the difference in right and wrong, if I hadn't given into her so easily, if I hadn't sheltered her so much from Grandma Catherine and let her face more of the consequences for her decisions, maybe she would be a different person today. Better equipped to handle life's trials and disappointments.

"I saw in the church bulletin the fourth is the next preschool Sunday," Angie told me. "Are you bringing Emma and Jonah?"

Another preschool Sunday already. Where did the time go?

"I haven't thought about it," I answered truthfully.

"We'd love to have you. The preschoolers are always such a blessing."

Another blessing. It seemed everyone in that church found blessings in the simplest things the rest of the world ignored.

"I haven't gone to church since Grandma Catherine passed away."

Angie took another sip of her coffee. I studied her face for condemnation. There wasn't any.

"That's a shame," she said. "It's hard enough for a person to get through life with no anchor in the Lord, let alone when there are children involved. I don't know how I would navigate the waters of motherhood without my Heavenly Father for guidance."

"Fortunately for me, I don't have children. I'm just filling in while Nicole's doing whatever it is she's doing."

Angie's eyes widened for a brief instant. She set her cup into the delicate matching saucer and smoothed the edges of the tablecloth. "Oh. I thought…" She motioned with her head at Jonah and Emma playing on her family room floor. "I thought since you had custody... I mean I know they're Nicole's kids, but since they're living with you I thought it was a permanent arrangement."

I remembered the first day I took the kids to the preschool. Miss Billie had tried to make me feel guilty for not taking some sort of permanent action to get custody of Emma and Jonah. Neither she nor Angie could possibly understand how difficult this was for me.

"This is definitely a temporary arrangement," I said, leaving no room for misunderstanding. "I care for Emma and Jonah, but I'm not ready to be somebody's mother. Nicole will come back, and my life can go back to the way it was."

She gazed at me over the rim of her cup. "Are you sure that's what you want? For life to go back to the way it was?"

I gritted my teeth. I was getting tired of people asking me the same questions every time it came up. "Sure I'm sure. I'm helping my sister out of a jam. But the sooner things go back to the way they were, the better."

For the next twenty minutes, we chatted about the passage of years. I even got up the nerve to ask Angie what she thought of Kyle as a pastor. Angie didn't say anything more about making my arrangement with Emma and Jonah permanent or a Heavenly Father who would be willing to help me through this trying time if I only asked him.

I don't know what woke me in the middle of the night. The bottom half of the window that faced the security light next to the barn was blocked by a window air conditioner seven months out of the year. The light that filtered through the shades didn't do much to illuminate the room.

I strained my ears for whatever woke me out of a sound sleep. Probably Gypsy moving about. Had it been anything more than the usual night sounds of an old house, she would be barking and carrying on. Then I remembered the kids. Though three weeks had passed since their arrival, their presence still eluded me in the early waking hours.

I swung my legs over the side of the bed and headed across the hall. I stopped outside their bedroom door and peered inside. A Gypsy-shaped lump at the foot of the bed shifted, sighed and repositioned itself. I continued down the hall, stumbled into the bathroom and groped in the top drawer on the left of the vanity for my eye drops. I tilted back my head and blinked away trails of overflow that slid down my cheeks.

The noise that had presumably woke me in the first place sounded again—a muffled thump and shuffling from Nicole's old bedroom. I listened for a pronouncement of danger from Gypsy. As long as she wasn't alarmed, there was no need that I be.

Fully trusting her judgment, I used the bathroom and washed my hands before heading back down the hall. Closer to Nicole's door, I heard more shuffling and whispering. I rapped the doorframe with my knuckles and stuck my head inside.

"Is everybody okay in here?" I asked into the darkness.

The shuffling and whispering stopped.

"Emma? Jonah? Are you awake?"

The blankets shifted and Jonah's head appeared against the white pillow. I stepped into the room and closer to the bed until I could distinguish his tiny face. The blanket shifted again and Emma appeared beside him. Her long hair stood up from static electricity and clung to her soft face. She pushed her hair out of her eyes and stared solemnly up at me.

I sat down on Jonah's side of the bed. My weight displaced them, and they shifted toward me. Gypsy gave me a dirty look before going back to sleep. I rested one hand on the other side of Emma, a sort of embrace encompassing both of the kids. "Is everything okay? Can't you sleep?"

Emma stuck two fingers in her mouth. Jonah glanced at her before turning to me, the spokesman for the two of them. "When's Mommy coming to get us?"

Three weeks and this was the first time either kid had used the dreaded M word. I knew it would happen eventually.

I reached out and smoothed the hair away from his face. "I don't know. Soon, I'm sure."

Why did I go and say that? I had no idea when Nicole would show her face. Maybe never. Wasn't that exactly what

Dad and Mom did? I watched for them for years, expecting them any day at the end of the driveway. They never came, either of them. I always wondered if they met up somewhere far away from Winona, Grandma Catherine and their responsibilities. I imagined them smiling, joining hands and going back to whatever it was they were doing before they got burdened down with kids and bills and the redundant things that make a person wake up one morning and wonder why they were ever put on the earth.

I imagined Dad turning to Mom and saying, "Ruthie, what took you so long?"

She'd clasp his hand and smile and say, "Oh, you know how it is, Bobby. First one thing and then another. I'm here now. That's all that matters."

Apparently, it didn't happen that way since we heard from Mom from time to time. She even showed up on the farm on a few occasions. She didn't come to Grandma's funeral though. No one knew where she was living at the time to notify her. By the time she called again, Grandma had been dead for over a year. Mom already knew about it. I never asked how she knew or where she'd been all that time. I was too mad by that point to care what she did.

"Are we going to live with her again?" Jonah's brown eyes were round as saucers in the pale moonlight squeezing between the curtains.

"Well, I don't know."

Which would be better? Kinder? An outright lie that Mommy would come back, and they'd live like all the other kids at the preschool with a Mommy, a Daddy, a maw-maw and paw-paw who loved them and took care of them and didn't disappear without notice? Or should I give them the facts now?

"Listen, kids, since you brought it up, there's something you need to know. The thing is, your mommy's a nutcase. Nobody knows who your daddies are or where they are. Your

mommy might come back, but there's a good chance she won't. See, long before you were born, her mommy and daddy did the same thing to her, so she grew up all messed up. She doesn't know how to be a mommy because the only person she had to teach her was Aunt Michelle. And we all know Aunt Michelle is no better equipped to be a mommy than...well, than Gypsy here. I don't know when your mommy's coming back, so if I were you, I wouldn't hold my breath or anything."

They probably weren't ready for that much truth.

"I know Mommy loves you and wants to be with you. But for now, me and Aunt Wanda and Uncle Jeb think it's best if you just stay here."

They looked at each other. I couldn't see their expressions well enough in the darkness to tell what they were thinking. I prayed Emma wouldn't start crying. A headache was developing behind my eyes. I wanted to go back to bed and put this whole conversation behind me.

"If she does come back," Jonah said, catching me off guard by using *if* instead of *when*, "can you tell her we want to stay here?"

My jaw dropped. I clamped it shut as quickly as I gained control of myself. I couldn't believe my ears. They preferred living here on this dreadful farm with me rather than with their own mother.

"If that's what you want."

"Do you think she'll be sad?" Emma asked in a quavering voice.

That was their concern. They didn't want to go back to Nicole, but they didn't want to hurt her feelings or make her mad by telling her so.

"Naw," I said confidently. "She'll be glad you're here where Uncle Jeb can take you fishing and you can go to preschool with your friends."

They exchanged another meaningful glance. The tension visibly eased. "You sure?" Jonah asked.

"Sure, I'm sure. I'll tell her myself. Don't worry about it. Now, why don't you go to sleep." I leaned forward and kissed their foreheads. We still hadn't progressed to much of a physical relationship. They hugged Uncle Jeb and climbed all over him. I'd even seen them kissing Aunt Wanda. But the three of us limited our contact to hair tousles or awkward shoulder pats. Sometimes I wondered if they saw me the way I used to see Grandma Catherine.

I stood up and moved to the foot of the bed. "You go to sleep, too, Gypsy." I took her head in my hands and kissed her loudly on the furry spot between her eyes. Jonah and Emma giggled. "Night, everybody. See you in the morning."

"G'night, Aunt Shell,"

I walked back to my room in disbelief. They didn't want to go home. They would rather live with a crotchety old aunt they barely knew than with their own mother. Was it because they got what they wanted most of the time and had Gypsy to play with and sleep with? Or was it because they knew when they woke up in the morning, they would be in the same bed they went to sleep in the night before?

Poor Nicole. Couldn't she see what she was doing to her kids? Did she even care? I laid in the dark and stared at the ceiling for a long time before I finally drifted off to sleep. In no time the alarm was ringing in my ear and it was time to face another day, another day with children. I had told Angie I didn't want to be anybody's mother. I could walk away any time. I knew now that wasn't entirely true. I still wasn't crazy about having my life overtaken with the responsibilities of parenthood, but I knew there was no walking away from it now.

Chapter Twelve

With Emma and Jonah singing Bible songs and reciting memory verses all over the house, I didn't have a chance of forgetting Preschool Sunday or coming up with a valid excuse not to attend. We arrived at the church fifteen minutes before the regular morning service was to start. A greeter at the door ushered us through the relatively quiet fellowship hall and down the hallway to the classrooms. Most of the doors were closed since the Sunday School classes were still in progress.

Halfway there, we could hear animated voices of preschoolers coming from one of the classrooms. Emma and Jonah quickened their pace. Jonah grabbed my hand. "In here, Aunt Shell."

He led me inside the room where nearly every teacher from the preschool, dressed in their Sunday finery, presided over about twenty children. What a relief! Apparently, I wasn't the only parent/guardian who didn't participate in Preschool Sunday.

Jonah dropped my hand and was immediately absorbed into the crowd of boys dressed in an assortment of apparel sold for little guys. Everything from suspenders, clip-on ties and smart miniature vests to shorts and tee shirts. The girls' clothing was more consistent with traditional church wear. All of them were in dresses, complete with ruffles, frills and ribbons. Hair was teased, curled, braided and/or tied back with an elaborate bow that complimented the outfit. Even the patent leather shoes and ruffled socks in every color of the rainbow matched the rest of the outfit.

I felt like an old maid in a potato sack. At least Emma wasn't overdressed as I first feared. When Aunt Wanda heard about Preschool Sunday, she insisted on taking the kids shopping and returned with a wardrobe befitting any little princess or prince attending church.

Billie greeted Emma and Jonah and then turned to me. "Michelle…" We had since graduated to first names. "…I'm so glad you could make it this morning. Jonah has talked of nothing else all week. I'm afraid you've got quite the little performer on your hands. You'll see what I mean when he gets onstage."

I smiled, though I wanted to remind her Jonah wasn't on *my* hands. I was just filling in. Why was that so hard for people to remember?

She put her hand on my elbow and steered me toward the door. "Go into the sanctuary and find a seat. It goes smoother if there are no nervous parents around to watch us getting ready."

I hesitated. "Um, I won't interrupt class if I go in before church starts?"

"It's nearly over anyway, and they're used to late arrivals. Make yourself at home." She pushed me into the hallway and shut the door behind me.

I dragged my feet down the hall toward the double doors leading to the sanctuary. I wasn't sure what was holding me back. I wasn't normally a shy person. A career in the medical profession had taught me the hazards of hanging back. Better to rush in and take charge than let things happen of their own accord. Many of these people I would recognize from the community or work. There was nothing to be nervous about. They would welcome me with open arms in the love of Christ. Right?

That was precisely what I dreaded most.

I took a right turn at the end of the hallway and entered the ladies' room instead. I managed to kill four or five minutes there and another thirty seconds at the drinking fountain. For lack of further detours or delays, I moved to the heavy, double glass doors of the sanctuary and reached out.

A beaming deacon or usher or whatever title this church used, saw me coming and pushed the door open for me before I could pull from my side. "Praise the Lord, sister," he exalted in a hushed tone. "Come on in."

I smiled back and squeezed past him. A balding man in an off-the-rack gray sports coat and black Dockers stood at the front of the room, an Ipad in one hand, the other gesturing toward the crowd to drive home a point. His lips turned upward in a welcoming smile when he saw me but didn't miss a beat in his oratory. I smiled back even though his eyes were already scanning the congregation.

I spotted Aunt Wanda and Uncle Jeb seated a few rows up from the back. I made my way toward them, trying not to call attention to myself. They had missed the service at their own church to be here for Emma and Jonah's stage debut. Aunt Wanda had to see for herself how Emma was received in all her dressed up glory. I knew she'd disapprove when she saw the simple fashion in which I'd secured Emma's mountain of hair. I wasn't a hairdresser, especially to a little girl who couldn't hold still for more than a minute at a time. At least I'd used the hunter green hair bow with the trailing streamers that reached halfway down Emma's back and looked gorgeous against her pale blonde curls. That would make up for my lack of hair fashion.

Aunt Wanda saw me coming and wiggled her fingers in greeting. I smiled and slid into the pew.

"Are the kids excited?" she whispered, her face aglow.

"Jonah is," I whispered back. "Emma isn't saying much."

It took another twenty minutes for the typical opening hymn, announcements, an over-long prayer by Brother So-and-So and collection of tithes and offerings. I dropped a tightly folded five into the collection plate so I wouldn't look like a complete cheapskate.

Finally a line of nearly thirty preschoolers filed up the center aisle and took their place on a set of risers on the stage. They burst into a hearty rendition of "This Little Light of Mine" followed by two songs I'd never heard, and then a recital of a memory verse from the book of Joshua. Aunt Wanda dabbed her eyes with a tissue from her purse. Even Uncle Jeb's eyes were shining. I couldn't believe the lump in my own throat. Anyone with eyes in their head could see Jonah was the most talented one up there. I reminded myself neither he nor Emma belonged to me so I needn't get puffed up, but I couldn't help doing so just a little.

After the ten-minute performance, the children left the stage and joined their parents—or guardian in my case. They sat quietly at my side while the choir led the rest of us in a few choruses, and then Kyle took his place behind the pulpit.

I had spent the days following the field trip putting Kyle Swann completely out of my mind. The last thing I needed was for my heart to get used to the idea of renewing an old flame. That wasn't going to happen. Kyle wasn't interested in me. I didn't know if I was interested in him. He was a pastor—one of 'those people'. But when he took his place behind the pulpit, I had a hard time separating the man in the dark suit expounding the necessity of living a godly life from the boy I dated in high school. Could this be the same Kyle? Popular, funny and handsome. At ease in any situation.

His sense of humor was still evident after all these years. He elicited chuckles from the congregation several times as he drove home a point, but always respectful of his position and message. While I lacked his conviction, I enjoyed the sermon for its forceful delivery and unapologetic message of the need for holiness.

The shallow, fleshly side of me enjoyed watching the trim, athletic pastor as he moved from one end of the stage to the other, occasionally descending the stairs and moving across the front of the sanctuary as he spoke. I wondered how many other women in the church were distracted from the message by the messenger.

Once or twice I entertained myself with questions about why Kyle wasn't married. Then I forced my mind back to the sermon. Kyle's personal decisions were none of my business. People wondered the same thing about me. Some of them were so bold as to come right out and ask.

Maybe Kyle was set in his ways and liked his independence. Couldn't fault him there. Maybe the right person had never come along. Maybe he was stingy with a dollar and abhorred the thought of supporting a wife. Pastors didn't make much money, at least that's what they liked the rest of us to believe.

After the service we shook a few hands and joined the throng making its way toward the exit. A familiar voice sounded behind me.

"Morning, Michelle."

I turned and saw Barry Schilling looking pretty good in a burgundy mock turtleneck with a sports coat and slacks. He glanced at his watch and laughingly corrected himself. "I guess I should say 'good afternoon'. Sometimes the message goes a little long and it's after twelve before we get out of here."

I ignored the lightly concealed insult directed at Kyle. "I didn't know you attended church here."

I looked down at the copper-haired Caitlyn. She was studying Emma, who was studying her in return. Emma's first two fingers were planted firmly in her mouth. Caitlyn worried the fabric of Barry's trousers. Though best friends at preschool, the two girls were struck dumb in the strange and crowded surroundings of the church sanctuary.

"We usually come when Caitlyn is spending the weekend with me, especially on Preschool Sundays," Barry replied. "She loves Sunday School, especially since Miss Gail is her teacher."

"Oh, yeah? I didn't realize some of the preschool teachers teach Sunday School here. Next time I'll try to get here early enough."

Why did I say that? I was not coming back.

Barry smiled. "I saw you sneaking in at the end of class. Nice trick."

"I wasn't sneaking in," I assured him, though that's exactly what I'd been doing. I changed the subject. "The preschool program was great. Too bad more parents don't give it a chance."

Barry shrugged. "Everybody's busy."

I had used the same excuse, but I believed people found time for what they thought was important. I caught hold of Aunt Wanda's sleeve and turned her toward us. I made the necessary introductions, which included Uncle Jeb even though he had left the line to chat with a farmer he knew.

"Nice to meet you, Barry," Aunt Wanda said. "What a little doll you have there. I've heard so much about Caitlyn from our Emma."

Barry beamed at the praise. "And I hear plenty about Emma. I'm so glad Caitlyn made such a good friend."

Someone from the crowd spoke to Barry and he offered his regrets for leaving our company. After he moved away, Aunt Wanda leaned toward me. "What a nice young man."

"Yes, he is," I agreed. "I've never seen a more dedicated father."

Barry appeared to be a gentleman, and I wasn't exaggerating about the dedicated father part, but I still wasn't sure how I felt about him. I couldn't tell if it was my aversion to divorced men, his comment about the length of the service, or the fact he wasn't Kyle Swann that kept me from getting pulled in.

When we finally reached the front door where Kyle was shaking hands, he groped his chest in mock disbelief.

"Very funny," I said at his reaction.

He reverted to the sober man of God image and clasped my hand. "I couldn't believe it when I saw you walk through the door. I nearly fell out of the pulpit."

So much for the sober man of God.

"You are hysterical," I said with a mischievous smile. "Too bad you can't bring some of that wit to your sermons. You wouldn't have so many parishioners falling asleep on you."

"Michelle!" Aunt Wanda hissed behind me, scandalized.

Kyle dropped my hand and grabbed hers. "Don't worry. Michelle and I go way back. There's nothing she can say to shock me. Believe me, she's tried." He kept hold of Aunt Wanda's hand but turned his gaze on me. "She always liked to get under my skin."

"Well, as long as you know how to take her," Aunt Wanda said uncertainly.

Kyle released Aunt Wanda's hand and gave me his full attention. "What did you think of the sermon?"

"Not bad, though I was kind of disappointed at the lack of fire and brimstone. I always enjoy a good roof-raiser."

Kyle slapped me on the shoulder and nearly knocked me out of my flats. "You keep coming back, sister. I guarantee you'll hear one the next time the Lord lays it on my spirit."

I wasn't sure if he was serious or not. With Kyle, it was hard to tell. The way he talked left me a little unsettled. He talked almost…spiritual, as if he and God had some sort of easy rapport going on. At the same time his dry wit bordered on irreverence according to my memories of 'church men'. He sure didn't remind me of the ministers from Grandma Catherine's church. His youth probably explained it. He would undoubtedly grow stodgy and boring like them someday.

Of that I was certain.

Chapter Thirteen

That evening I sat on the front porch swing with my nose in a romance novel that had been lying around the house forever. It was hard to concentrate. I couldn't stop peeking over the top of the book every few minutes to watch Emma and Jonah at play with a hodge-podge village of Army men, Barbie dolls and Lego characters they'd constructed on the porch floor. Gypsy lay nearby, her nose on her paws, seemingly asleep but on the alert in case plans changed and the kids took off to do something else.

She didn't stir when the phone rang inside. I jumped off the porch swing to run inside to answer it. I wasn't one of those people who always carried her phone with her at home. Why bother when it hardly ever rang? I didn't have friends, per se, so the only people who called were Aunt Wanda, Uncle Jeb or someone from work. Now that the kids were here, my phone rang or alerted me to a text much more often.

"Hello, Michelle?" said a masculine voice. "It's me, Barry Schilling."

I ignored the flutter of disappointment in my stomach. Who had I been hoping for?

I recovered instantly. "Hi, Barry, how are you?"

"Great. Hey, I've been sitting here and I couldn't stop thinking about seeing you this morning."

I'm sure he meant to flatter me. Instead, my disappointment changed to apprehension. "Oh, yeah?"

"Yeah. I know I mentioned it before and it wasn't a good time, but I was thinking it might be fun to get the kids together for a picnic or something. Anytime would be fine with me. I know your schedule changes a lot, but I have Caitlyn every other weekend. I thought maybe some weekend while it's still nice out we could take the kids to the lake or something."

He paused. I could almost hear the gears turning in his head, going over his invitation and wondering if he'd adequately pled his case or if he needed to add something to sweeten the deal. Aunt Wanda was right. He was a gentleman. The kids would have fun. I might, too, if I relaxed a little. I did sort of miss male company, not that I'd had much in more years than I cared to count. So what if he was divorced—who wasn't these days? It was only an invitation to a picnic. It wasn't like he proposed or anything. It would do the kids and me good to get out of the house and spend time with someone who wasn't related through work or family. The thoughts rushed through my head in less than the blink of an eye.

"Sure, that would be fun," I said and meant it. "I work next Saturday, but I'm off Sunday."

"Caitlyn will be with her mom next weekend. What about the following one?"

I wasn't scheduled to work at all that weekend. I wasn't sure I wanted to make it too easy on him, but I wasn't good at playing hard-to-get. I wasn't good at playing at all.

"That will work perfectly for us," I said simply.

"Great. How about I pick you up around one? Unless you'd rather we go to church together and drive out to the lake afterwards."

"No, that's all right. I'm not much of a church-goer."

Besides, I didn't want Kyle to see me at church with Barry and get the wrong idea.

"No problem."

I could tell by his voice it really wasn't. Since everyone I came in contact with lately was preaching to me about how I needed to get the kids in church, it was almost unsettling to find someone who wasn't concerned with the condition of my soul. I'd tell anyone who asked I was a non-believer. Barry didn't seem anymore interested in living a Christian life than I was. Still it seemed odd he wasn't trying to save me.

"Caitlyn and I will see you around one," he continued. "I'm an all right cook, but I'm not so great with sweets. How about I bring everything but dessert?"

"You don't have to do all that. I can bring my share."

"No, I want to. This was my idea. See you Sunday after next."

I nearly said, "It's a date."

I caught myself just in time and just gave a simple 'bye' instead. I clicked off the phone and dropped it into the pocket of my baggy, hanging-around-the-house shorts. I wouldn't tell the kids about the invitation until later in case something came up and we couldn't go. For some reason, I couldn't work up much enthusiasm about my first date since Gypsy was a puppy.

Between work and racing to the preschool or Angie's house to pick up the kids, it started getting hard to keep track of what day it was. Almost before I realized it, it was time for my 'date' with Barry. It rained nearly the entire following week and I started to think our picnic would be canceled after all. But on Saturday afternoon the rain tapered off and by Sunday, the sun sat high in the sky, promising the perfect day for sitting on the water's edge.

Emma, Jonah and Caitlyn were relatively quiet, considering their ages and excitement level as we drove to the lake in Barry's car. While the girls whispered back and forth and covered their giggles with their hands, Jonah managed to make his presence known. Barry and I exchanged smiles and stole surreptitious glances to the backseat.

"Can we go feed the ducks?" Jonah asked before he was halfway finished with his chicken drumstick. It was the third or fourth time he'd asked, the first time being before Barry even turned off the engine.

"Finish your lunch first," I admonished. "All of it." Bossing people around came naturally for me so maybe this mothering thing wasn't outside my wheelhouse.

He took a huge bite of the drumstick.

"Don't choke yourself there," Barry said. "We've got all day. Those ducks aren't going anywhere."

Jonah chewed faster. He cast a dubious glance toward the water to see if Barry knew what he was talking about. I smiled at Barry over the top of Jonah's head. The man was definitely patient and understanding with children. He had gone out of his way to make the day fun for the kids. I didn't appear to be his top priority, which suited me fine.

Was he trying to woo me by winning over the kids first, or was this day for Caitlyn's benefit, and he couldn't invite Emma without Jonah and me tagging along? Either way, I was having more fun than I expected to.

I studied Barry out of the corner of my eye. While not traffic-stopping handsome, he was growing on me. I had always liked them tall, dark and handsome. Probably because it was such a contrast to my own petite, pale and ordinary. Or maybe because Kyle also happened to be tall—taller than

Barry by several inches—also dark-headed and incredibly handsome. But Kyle wasn't here. The only place he'd invited any of us was to Preschool Sunday.

Barry seemed like the whole package. He obviously loved his daughter and would do anything for her. In my years at the hospital I ran into plenty of fathers who did not share his commitment. I wondered if he'd be interested in me after Emma and Jonah went back to Nicole and there was nothing left in the equation for Caitlyn. Did I want him to be? Before the kids, I was perfectly happy with the idea of remaining single and independent the rest of my life. I didn't need a man for financial support. I could take care of my own lawn and car. A month ago I couldn't think of a single reason why an intelligent, capable woman would tether herself to a man. Now with the kids to think of, I couldn't help looking at things differently.

Nicole needed to come home and come home quickly, or I was going to find myself married, barefoot and pregnant. Perish the thought!

I tore a crust of bread off my sandwich and stuck it in my mouth. Marriage was not in the cards for me. Children hadn't been either until my irresponsible sister thrust hers upon me. Fortunately the situation was temporary.

Emma and Caitlyn were also finishing up their meal. They were as anxious as Jonah to get near the water to see the ducks. I stood up and started stuffing empty sandwich bags into the picnic basket Barry had carefully packed. He stood up on the other side of the picnic table to help. Within moments, all evidence of our picnic was gone and the children were scampering toward the water. Barry and I hurried to catch up.

"I knew this was a good idea," he said as we watched the kids tear apart pieces of bread to throw into the water for the gathering ducks.

I nodded and put my hands into the pockets of my Capri pants for something to do with them. "They are having fun."

The silence lengthened between us. It had been so long since I'd been in the company of a man who was neither a doctor barking orders, a technician accepting them or a patient doing both, I didn't know how to handle the situation. I knew I should fill the silence but couldn't think of a single intelligent thing to say.

"So am I."

I turned to look at him, wondering if he was talking about the kids. He wasn't. The corners of my mouth turned up in a self-conscious smile. I was flattered but also a little nervous. I thought back to my last date. It had ended disastrously with the man mumbling something about calling later as his car tires churned gravel on his way out of the driveway.

Barry took my smile as encouragement. "I don't usually meet women I feel so comfortable with. In fact, I haven't dated anyone since my divorce."

Fabulous. A rebound relationship.

"We aren't dating, are we?" I detected a hint of panic in my voice.

He grinned, obviously amused by my reaction. "Not yet."

I looked back at the kids playing by the water. Jonah's foot slipped out from under him and he stumbled. While miles from harm's way since he was several feet from the water's edge, and the water was only about a foot deep there anyway, I dove onto the distraction, nonetheless.

"Careful, Jonah. Not so close."

"'Kay," he called over his shoulder without taking his eyes off the ducks.

I wasn't ready for dating. I wasn't ready for Barry to think about dating. I was still getting used to the idea of having two little people dependent on me. I didn't know a thing about Barry, and he didn't know a thing about me. I couldn't remember what he did for a living. I shouldn't have come. I should've taken the kids fishing at Uncle Jeb's pond and ignored Barry from here to eternity. But he was a sweet guy.

How could I tell him what a mistake this was without hurting his feelings?

Why did I care? I was a trained professional. I was paid to administer pain. I could do this.

I took a deep breath and opened my mouth.

"Daddy, we're out of bread." Caitlyn held up the empty bread bag for us to see.

All three children looked imploringly at Barry. "We need more bread," Jonah said, stating the obvious.

Barry held out his hands. "Sorry. That's all we brought."

"Can we get some more?"

"The ducks are still hungry."

"We need more. Pleeeze."

Barry looked helplessly at me and shrugged. I was just thrilled the shortage of bread got me off the hook for a while.

"Why don't we walk one of the trails," I suggested.

"But what about the ducks?" Emma's blue eyes were wide with concern.

I put my hand on her shoulder. "They'll be fine. Now that they've had their bread, they can go fishing for bugs."

Emma and Caitlyn squealed in disgust.

"Cool," said Jonah.

Barry stuffed the empty bread bag in his hip pocket, and we set off in the direction of the closest walking trail. I stayed busy for the next thirty minutes explaining what kinds of bugs ducks preferred, what kinds of trees and grass we were passing, why snakes didn't have legs and how come the lake looked brown when everybody knew water didn't have a color.

Only Barry didn't ask questions. I was glad. His were much more difficult to answer.

Chapter Fourteen

Almost without my realizing it, the weeks passed with comfortable regularity. After one home visit, we didn't see anything more of my caseworker. She was busy and overworked, and I'm sure she was thrilled a relative had been close at hand to take Emma and Jonah in, thus relieving her office of the burden. She called me once at work to 'chat'. I later discovered she had also spoken with Billie and Angie about me. Everything was fine. The kids were blossoming. They were clean and well fed. She could spend her time on more pressing matters.

Our lives on the farm settled into a dull routine. Mornings were punctuated with mad scrambles for shoes, socks and misplaced personal objects that couldn't be left behind. I didn't bother to cook breakfast. I woke the kids thirty minutes before we had to run out the door. They dressed, brushed teeth and lolled on the floor with Gypsy until the last minute when I started stressing out. At work my thoughts turned to them more and more. A teacher would tell me some little bit of progress Emma had made or something funny Jonah said or did, and I would think about it the whole day. I wondered if the preschool was serving something they liked for lunch. I worried if one of them hadn't slept well. I started paying attention to interest rates on new cars even though I told myself I did not need a larger vehicle. My Mazda would work fine for the short time Emma and Jonah were staying with me. Soon enough it would be me and Gypsy again. No trade-ins, no minivan or even a sedan. I had worked too hard for that sporty, navy blue machine in my parking spot. It wasn't going anywhere.

I sometimes worried the kids were getting along too well without Nicole. Other than a time or two early on when Emma cried for Carrie, neither of them mentioned anything pertaining to their life before moving in with me. I wondered if they should see a therapist. I'd heard good things about a juvenile specialist who worked at the county hospital's clinic. I was confident he wasn't a crackpot. But would talking to him make their living arrangement more apparently dysfunctional to them?

The old adage "*If it ain't broke, don't fix it,*" kept me from asking him about the kids' plight. If they suffered inwardly, they were keeping their pain to themselves, and I was hesitant to bring it up.

Barry called one Tuesday evening in early October as we were sitting down to dinner—another feast of chicken nuggets and macaroni and cheese. I was a nurse. I should know better than feed the kids such things.

"Michelle, hey."

I glanced at the kitchen table where Emma and Jonah were dipping nuggets into great pools of ketchup. I turned to face the wall. "Hi, how are you?"

"Great, and you?"

"Fine." I nodded imperceptibly as if he could see me through the miles separating us. I couldn't think of much else to say.

"How was work?"

"Good. Busy."

"Yeah, me too."

I wondered if he was experiencing the same sense of drowning I was.

"I was thinking, maybe we could do something this weekend, just the two of us. You know, no kids this time."

"Oh, I'm…"

He jumped in to fill my lapse. "I thought we could see a movie or something. Or try that Italian restaurant in Genoa. I've never been there, but I hear good things."

I hadn't been there either. I never saw the point in getting dressed up to go to a restaurant by myself before the kids came, and these days it was Mickey D's or Burger King.

"I don't know, Barry. I've been working a lot and I feel guilty leaving the kids with the sitter so much."

"Oh. Okay. I get it." Did he really? "I just enjoyed our picnic last month and I've been thinking about you a lot. Maybe I should…I'll give you some time. It's just that, well, with Caitlyn and all…"

"Barry?"

He sounded relieved at the interruption. "Yeah?"

"I know it's been awhile since we got together, but everything in my life is moving so fast right now. These changes, well, there's quite a few of them, and I think I need to step back and take a breath."

"Sure, I understand. Well, hey, you have my number. Whenever you want to try that Italian place, just call. The invitation's open."

"Thanks, Barry. I appreciate it."

"Okay, then. See ya."

I hung up and took my place at the table. My chicken nuggets lay limp and greasy on my plate. I couldn't believe I actually planned to eat them. I was too old for such a diet. I pushed one absently around my plate. What was wrong with me? Barry was a great guy. He could… could what? What need did I suddenly have for a man in my life just because I had children to care for? And what was behind his comment about Caitlyn? Was that his motivation for pursuing me, if that's what he was doing? Did he want a mother for his daughter, knowing I would also benefit from having a man around the place? I sure didn't want to become another little girl's surrogate mother.

Good grief. When did things get so complicated? All I knew for sure was I wasn't ready to date Barry or anyone. Nicole would be home any day, and my life would return to normal. She could walk through the door right now.

I stole a glance at the back door half expecting to see her. Nothing. I sighed and got up to return the chicken nuggets to the metal baking dish. I wasn't hungry.

"We played with the parachutes at preschool today," Jonah said.

"You did?" I was glad for the change of subject. "Was it fun?"

He was off and running. Even Emma contributed a comment or two. I pushed every other thought aside and gave them my full attention, thankful I no longer had to worry about Barry and my nonexistent feelings toward him.

Uncle Jeb drove the tractor across the field Saturday to bush hog. Emma and Jonah heard him coming and ran outside to meet him. By the time I got to the porch, he was hoisting them up beside him to perch on the tractor fenders.

I went out into the yard and gave him a grave look. "Are you sure this is such a good idea?" I called over the roar of the motor.

He waved dismissively. "They know how to hold on. Get back inside and enjoy the time to yourself. We'll get this done as quick as we can. It's supposed to rain later."

I shrugged in defeat, waved at Emma and Jonah who waved back exuberantly, and turned back to the house. A free Saturday. I'd be a fool not to take advantage of it.

I breezed through the pantry and jotted down a grocery list on the back of a store receipt. I had learned a trip alone to the grocery store did less damage to my checking account than with two little angels tagging along. I got in and out a lot quicker, too, with exactly what I needed and not an item more.

I grabbed my purse, phone and car keys and headed out the back door. When Uncle Jeb made another pass on the tractor, I held up my keys and jingled them with a questioning look on my face. He nodded and waved. The kids waved too, their faces aglow. I headed for the car.

I dashed through Winn Dixie, not wanting to take advantage of Uncle Jeb's kindness even though he loved spending time with the kids. I could see in his eyes it made him feel young again. A crash of thunder announced the rain Uncle Jeb predicted had arrived. Within moments, a heavy torrent beat down on the roof above my head. The lights flickered, throwing the store into total darkness for a brief instant. An intake of breath and a chorus of dismay went up among the shoppers. Several of us joked that it would be a treat getting from the front of the store to our dry cars.

Back outside, a rushing torrent raged through the parking lot and overflowed storm drains. The backwash was as deep as the fenders of the cars that braved their way through. Several shoppers huddled under the store awning and waited for the rain to subside. I squeezed my cart in among them and waited. Usually storms that came this suddenly and ferociously passed just as quickly. I thought about Uncle Jeb and the kids on the tractor and hoped he got them inside before the storm hit.

If he knew I was worrying, he'd laugh and say, "This ain't my first time on top that old tractor. Ain't my first thunderstorm either. You're acting like an old mother hen."

Maybe I was.

"I don't think this is going to let up anytime soon," an elderly woman spoke up under the awning.

"We can always use the rain," someone else said.

A young man told his wife to wait and dashed into the squall to fetch their car. We watched him run as fast as he could onto the wet pavement. His cotton shirt was instantly plastered to his back.

"Here goes nothing," another man said. He hunched his shoulders, gripped the handle of his cart and took off. Several others did the same, while most of us chose to wait and watch the rain.

"I'm going for it," one woman finally said. "I've got to get home."

We laughed and wished her well. By the time she reached her car with her cart of soggy groceries, she was soaked to the skin. So were her groceries.

"I think I'll call my nephew," the elderly lady said. "He works over at the bank. He can be here in a few minutes." She set a gigantic purse on the handle bars of her cart.

I wished I had someone to call, though I would be too embarrassed to even if I did. It was just rain. I wasn't thrilled about braving the onslaught of rain, nor did I want to spend my afternoon in front of the Winn Dixie. But I had a fifteen-minute drive home and there was ice cream in my cart. I couldn't stand here thinking about it much longer. A bolt of lightning pierced the sky over the Burger King. Rain was one thing…but lightning. I'd wait another minute or two.

A man in a drenched tee shirt that outlined every rippling muscle in his shoulders and chest came running toward the store. His shoulders were hunched against the rain. He held the bill of a baseball cap low over his face.

"Hubba hubba," said the elderly woman as she returned the phone to her purse. The rest of us laughed.

He looked familiar. When he got close enough, I saw it was Kyle. My cheeks pinked at how we had appreciated watching him run across the parking lot in his soaked shirt. I wondered what the other women would think if they knew he was a pastor. What would Kyle think about our ogling him? I wondered if it would inspire a sermon.

"Do you think it'll rain?" I joked when he reached the awning.

He took off his cap and shook the rain out of his hair, showering my cart. "Michelle. What are you doing out in weather like this?"

"It wasn't raining when I left the house."

"Yeah, me either. Are you stuck?"

"Sort of. If it doesn't slack off in another minute or two, I'm going for it. Uncle Jeb's watching the kids and I really need to get home."

He turned and scanned the parking lot. "Where're you parked?"

I pointed toward my Mazda at the far end of a row of parked cars. I never parked near the store entrance even when the kids were along. I didn't want my car dinged by careless car doors or runaway carts. The extra exercise wouldn't kill me either. Today I longed for one of those handicapped placards so I could park up front in the extra wide slots.

Kyle heaved an exaggerated sigh. "That figures." He held out his hand. "Give me your keys. I'll get it."

I gasped as a jagged bolt of lightning sliced through the ashen sky. "I can't let you do that."

"Come on. I can't get any wetter."

"It's all right. I can wait."

More shoppers were exiting the Winn Dixie while cars pulled along the front to let others out. Before long I'd be crowded out from under the awning.

Kyle waved his hand impatiently. "Michelle…"

"Okay." A boom of thunder crashed over our heads and echoed against the stone walls of the building. I flinched. "But be careful."

Kyle arched his eyebrows at me like we were playing a game, ducked his head and headed back into the rain.

I held my breath as he dodged cars and ankle deep puddles on his way to my car. I flinched again at another flash of lightning. I exhaled with relief when he slid inside the car and started the engine. When he drove over a storm drain, the water came up to the car doors. I grimaced. I'd have to take it easy on the drive home. The car hydroplaned like nobody's business on wet roads.

Kyle waited for another car to load up and then pulled in front of me. I dashed out from under the awning and pushed my cart to the back of the car. Kyle and I threw in bags with abandon, not caring if bags overturned or the cookies ended up under the orange juice. We laughed as we reached for the same bag and our hands tangled in each other's.

Finally the job was finished, and I ran to the front of the car. "Thanks, Kyle," I said, before shutting the door behind me. "I don't know what I'd've done without you."

He smiled, exposing those toothpaste commercial teeth, and lifted his hand in acknowledgement. He took my empty cart and headed for the protection of the awning. He turned to watch me so I threw up my hand and waved. A grin split his face though he had to be uncomfortable with his dark hair sopping wet and his clothes plastered to his body.

I caught a glimpse of my reflection in the mirror and groaned in horror. After taking the brunt of the downpour on my behalf, Kyle managed to look rugged and desirable. I, on the other hand, was an absolute fright. My hastily applied mascara had left black puddles under my eyes. Tufts of hair stiffened from hairspray stuck out at odd angles all over my head. My old lady support bra was evident through the fabric of my wet blouse.

I pushed thoughts of my appearance out of my head. A smile tugged at the corners of my mouth as I thought of Kyle dashing through the rain to get my car. I hadn't been rescued by a knight in shining armor in a long time.

My thoughts immediately turned to Barry. Kyle was simply being polite when he retrieved my car. He probably would've done it for any helpless old woman in his congregation.

Barry had actually shown interest in me as a woman. He called to ask how I was. He sought out my company. If I allowed it, a relationship might develop. He would've gone after my car, too, had he pulled into the Winn Dixie ten minutes ago and saw me stranded under the awning. Still, it meant a lot more that Kyle was the one to do it.

Chapter Fifteen

I stopped in Emma's doorway, fumbling to fit my earring into the hole in my lobe. After all these years I still could barely manage it without a mirror. Emma sat on her bed dressed in the new outfit we'd bought the other day but still with no shoes or socks on her feet.

"Hurry up, sweet cheeks, or we're going to be late for the party."

This was the first birthday party Emma and Jonah had ever attended in their lives. They told me so when they proudly presented two invitations from preschool last week. Some courageous and questionably off in the head mother had decided to invite every single child from the preschool to a party in honor of her darling's "Number Five" at Chuck E. Cheese's. Billie assured me it wasn't that big of a deal since at least half of the invitees never showed up to these things. Regardless, the thought of forty-plus preschoolers at a birthday party—Saints, preserve us!

I displayed the proper amount of enthusiasm and decided Emma and Jonah would be among the half who wouldn't attend. They were easily distracted when I played my cards right. They could go fishing with Uncle Jeb that day. A walk in the woods would make them forget the party. And if they didn't, they'd get over any pang of disappointment the instant I waved an ice cream sandwich under their noses.

My plans didn't change when Jonah said they'd never been to Chuck E. Cheese's. They'd seen the commercials and drove past the one at the shopping center near their apartment but had never been inside. My resolve faltered a bit until I reminded myself children all over the world never went into a Chuck E. Cheese's to play in the contaminated ball pit or hit randomly appearing moles on the head with a mallet for sport yet managed to grow up and lead productive lives.

Then Emma asked if there would be a cake at the party.

When I told her every birthday party had a cake, she and Jonah exchanged wide-eyed glances. It was then they informed me they'd never been to a birthday party, and the closest they'd come to a real live birthday cake was looking through the glass at the ones in the display case at the grocery store.

Even a hard nose like me couldn't say no after hearing that. Never attending a birthday party—who could imagine such an injustice? Surely Nicole could have at least thrown a party at home for their birthdays and baked a simple cake. When had my baby sister become so selfish? She wasn't brought up that way. Well, maybe she had been. But to turn around and deny her own children the simple pleasure of a birthday party—and a cake—it was beyond me.

We would go to that party. I'd spend twenty bucks on a gift for a child who most certainly didn't need it. I'd join the other adults at the parents' table, whose sole purpose was to buy tokens for overpriced, lopsided games, eat bad food, smile a lot and engage in banal conversation about preschool policies, work and the potty-training habits of younger brothers and sisters.

I went the rest of the way into Emma's room and bent down to look at myself in the child-sized mirror over her dresser. Emma had moved into my old room two weeks ago. My things had been moved into Grandma's room shortly after I inherited the farm. As the new homeowner I had no sentimental qualms about claiming the biggest bedroom at the front of the house under the blessed shade of the old oak tree as my own. Jonah now had Nicole's room to himself. So far things were working out well—no tears or bad dreams. Everyone seemed to be adjusting to the living arrangements. Even me.

Emma cocked her head and gazed up at me through the mirror's reflection. "What'd you call me?"

I wiggled the earring post into place. It took a second to remember what she was talking about.

Oh, yes, 'Sweet Cheeks'.

Had the nickname hurt her feelings? Uncle Jeb was always calling her something silly like Cricket or Emmy Doodle, and she seemed to like it. Then I noticed the glint in her eyes. I secured the earring and turned to face her. I set my hands on my hips. "I called you sweet cheeks. Hasn't anyone ever told you what sweet cheeks you have?"

She shook her head from side to side as a pink blush crept up her cheeks. Her sapphire eyes glittered.

I leaned forward, twisted my fingers into claws and started toward her. She shrank into the pillows and giggled. Her blush deepened.

"You've got the sweetest cheeks I ever saw," I said in a cackling voice. I sank to my knees in front of her on the bed and put my hands on either side of her face. "I'm going to eat them right off of you."

I put my face against hers and nibbled at her cheeks and tickled her neck. "I'm going to eat you up," I said over and over, my voice growing louder and more maniacal with every word. It was almost embarrassing how easily the imitation came to me.

Emma squealed with delight. Her childish laughter pierced my eardrums. I kept tickling. She kept wiggling and giggling and pretending to hate it. This was the first time I'd really tousled with her. I had always felt awkward initiating contact, afraid she would feel threatened or uncomfortable. Or maybe I was the one who'd be threatened and uncomfortable.

Finally, I collapsed, breathless, on the bed beside her.

Emma shoved the pillows aside, propped up on one elbow and studied me for a moment. Then she leaned over and kissed my cheek. "Aunt Shell, you're pretty."

I was so shocked I couldn't respond. Emma wasn't a cuddly, demonstrative child. At least not with me. No matter how used to each other we'd become, she still only spoke to me when absolutely necessary. I had to watch for clues to determine if she was happy or distressed. She only truly opened up with Jonah or Uncle Jeb, and only when she thought I wasn't watching. If Aunt Wanda, another adult or I were in the room, she remained tense and on guard. Trying to get her to relax only made her more self-conscious so I stopped trying. I figured she'd come around in her own time.

I rolled off the bed, not sure what to say or do. I leaned over and smoothed out the wrinkles on the lavender and white candy-striped duvet Aunt Wanda had bought her at Kohl's. "You're pretty, too, sweet cheeks," I said, barely looking at her. I headed for the door. "I'm going to go light a fire under your brother. Get your shoes on so we can leave in a few minutes."

"Okay." She slid off the bed and dropped to her knees to retrieve her shoes from under the bed.

Her voice stopped me at the door. "Aunt Shell?"

I turned back to look at her.

"I love you."

I swallowed hard and sniffed away the tickle in my nose. "I love you, too, Jelly Belly."

The sound of the words out of my mouth were more unsettling than hearing them come out of Emma's. Even more unsettling was the realization that I meant it. I did love her. And Jonah too. Not the distant love for someone because they're kin and it's required. But the gut-deep, take-a-bullet-for-them sort of love I had never experienced for anyone. When had it happened? Nothing good could come from it, that was for sure. I was setting myself up for heartache. When Nicole came back—and she would come back someday to take them away—I'd never see them again. Then what would I do?

Unaware of my inner turmoil, Emma stuck her head and shoulders under the bed, her rump in the air, and dug underneath for the pink canvas sneakers that matched her outfit.

My heart continued to do all sorts of weird things inside my chest. I wanted my house back. I wanted to work weekends without paying an arm and a leg for childcare. I wanted to sleep late and work in the garden and eat cereal for dinner. I didn't want to be awakened in the middle of the night by a child with bad dreams or a wet mattress. Was that too much to ask?

If there was a God in heaven, why was he doing this to me? I was a good person. I respected my elders. I stuffed five-dollar bills into the Salvation Army buckets outside every store in town at Christmastime. Being a nurse had to count for something. I gave more of myself in one day than most people did in a month.

I shook my head to clear it and headed across the hall where I heard Jonah talking to his plastic action figures. I could almost guarantee he wasn't ready for the party either. Instead of my customary aggravation, all I could think was, the only thing greater in the world than a child's laughter in my ear was being loved by that same child.

The first face I recognized upon entering the loud, crowded, confused location for the party belonged to Barry. Before I could think about losing myself in the crowd, he spotted us and cut across the restaurant to greet us. Then I realized he was actually following Caitlyn, who was making a beeline for Emma.

So much for being irresistible to the opposite sex.

Still, he seemed pleased to see me. We hadn't seen each other since our picnic at the lake. I wasn't intentionally avoiding him. I liked him. He just made me feel self-conscious and clumsy. I never knew what to say. I couldn't tell what he was thinking.

The real problem was I didn't know how to be a woman in a relationship. I wasn't sure I had the fortitude to learn.

"You decided to brave the birthday party, too, I see," he said when we met in the middle of the floor.

I nodded and raised my voice to be heard above the din. "The kids have never been here before." He didn't need to know it was also their first birthday party—ever. I smiled and added, "Neither have I."

"Then you're in for a treat. Here, let me help." He took the oversized gift bag out of my hand and led us toward the rear of the restaurant, if this type of establishment qualified as a restaurant.

I looked around and down for Emma, Jonah and Caitlyn. Satisfied they were within sight and easy reach, I started walking. I was suddenly paranoid about losing them. Everybody knew these kinds of places were breeding grounds for kooks who preyed on small children.

Jonah's eyes were roaming everywhere at once. He veered left, and I grabbed his shoulder to bring him back on course.

Oh, no, buddy, you're not getting out of my sight.

The birthday girl's mother had gotten here early and moved tables and chairs and covered them with paper tablecloths. Barry set our gift bags on an overloaded table against the wall and motioned me toward two empty seats in the middle of a long table occupied by adults and a few little brothers and sisters who were too shy or too small to be turned loose in the melee.

I wasn't sure I wanted to spend the duration of the party next to Barry. What would we talk about? I still didn't know anything about him except that he loved Caitlyn. I couldn't imagine many other fathers giving up a Saturday afternoon to escort a four-year-old to a birthday party unless forced into it by a wife. He was intelligent and certainly not the least interesting person I'd ever talked to.

So why was I so reluctant to give this getting-to-know-you phase a try?

I sat down in the chair he pulled out for me. I'd never get to know him if I didn't put some effort into it. Not every relationship started with fireworks and racing pulses. I wasn't necessarily looking for a relationship with anybody, but maybe it's exactly what I needed.

Emma bounded after Caitlyn to a group of little girls surrounding the guest of honor. Someone called Jonah's name, and he headed in that direction. I forgot about getting to know Barry as I followed Jonah with my eyes. I smiled with relief when a little boy grabbed his hand and pulled him onto the floor where five or six other boys were playing. He was popular. All the boys liked him and even most of the girls from what I could tell. He had adjusted to this situation better than I could have hoped.

Barry leaned toward me to ask what I wanted to drink. I looked up to see a waitress at the ready.

I smiled my thanks to Barry, told the waitress what I wanted and turned my eyes back to the kids. Fortunately, I didn't need to get their attention to ask what they wanted. It was provided by the party girl's parents.

It was a good thing someone with a clear head had taken care of everything. The entire ordeal was almost more stress than I could take. My eyes flitted around in my head like a pinball machine, determined to keep Jonah and Emma in my sights at all times while scanning the crowd for lurking weirdoes, waiting for a change to grab one of them. When they got up to play games, I followed. When I finally relented to Jonah's begging and let him go play with a friend and the boy's father outside my line of vision, I warned them to stay together. The dad didn't bother to conceal an eye roll as he assured me he never let his child play unsupervised.

After they disappeared into the crowd, the mother put a placating hand on my arm. "I know how it is, honey, but don't worry. Ryan is really careful with the kids. Just let the boys have fun."

Easy for her to say. She didn't have to do this on her own. Dear responsible Ryan was here to help, not like the losers Nicole had chosen to father her kids.

During the eating of dry pizza and even drier cake, I relaxed enough to enjoy the sheer rapture in Jonah and Emma's eyes as the birthday girl unwrapped her gifts. I fantasized about the elaborate parties I'd throw when their birthdays rolled around. The guest list was formed in my head before I realized they'd surely be back with Nicole by Valentine's Day, which was Emma's fifth birthday.

I almost resented Nicole's disruption of my plans for our Emma's big day.

A voice came over the loudspeaker and wished a happy fifth birthday to Amelia. The little girl clasped her hands over her mouth. All the children clapped and squealed. "Amelia, that's you. They said your name."

My eyes sought out Emma. She was standing on a booth seat with three other little girls trying to see the gifts as they were unwrapped. She didn't look envious, just happy to be with her friends.

I was envious. She'd get her party, that is, if Nicole didn't come back and spoil everything.

At the end of the party, we gathered our things. The entire afternoon had been confusion, but now it was amplified. Tired, cranky kids whined about leaving. Parents exposed frayed nerves. I was nearly sick from too much pizza and soda.

Jonah pulled on my shirtsleeve. "Can I go home with Gregory?"

"No, you've been with Gregory all day. You'll see him Monday at school."

Jonah stomped his foot and pulled harder. I nearly dropped my purse. "I wanna go. I never get to do anything."

I had never seen this side of the child and wasn't in the mood for it now. He was too young for a sleepover. Not only that, he'd be well off learning throwing a hissy fit in public was not the way to talk me into something.

"We're going home. Where's your sister?"

"Too much soda," Barry explained at my side like a seasoned veteran. "Don't let it get to you."

"I don't know if I agree with that. Kids seldom need artificial stimuli to turn into brats."

I felt instant remorse at the surprise on his face. He always went out of his way to be polite. I had no right to snap at him.

"It isn't all Jonah's fault," I conceded, softening. "I am a little short tempered and headachy."

"Yeah, me too. But you'll get used to it."

"I don't know if I want to," I said without thinking.

His eyes widened in surprise. "Don't want to what?"

Barry still didn't know the complete circumstances of how I ended up with Nicole's kids. I hadn't decided if I wanted him to.

I gave him a half smile. "I just mean I don't know if I'm up for any more parties, at least not one on such a grand scale."

"I know what you mean. I'm glad you came to this one though. It gave me someone to talk to."

I smiled again. Now wasn't the time to point out I had barely spoken two words to him all afternoon.

"Maybe soon you can find the time to get together with me and no kids."

I looked into his sincere ebony eyes and wondered why not. He was a nice guy. He didn't seem to take offense when I ignored him to helicopter-parent the kids. He put his daughter's needs first in every situation. And he asked me. There weren't a whole lot of people doing that.

"I'll check my schedule, Barry, and see what we can work out."

His eyes bulged. "Really?"

I laughed. "I better get the kids rounded up for now. See you around, Barry. Come on, kids. Bye, Caitlyn."

I extracted a sullen Jonah from his shrinking group of friends and led him and Emma from the restaurant before Barry had a chance to try to nail down a date. I was already second-guessing my decision. Yes, he was a great guy. I just didn't want him getting the wrong idea. I had a feeling he was looking for something I wasn't ready to give.

Chapter Sixteen

I couldn't remember a more enjoyable holiday season. In the past the period from Halloween till New Year's was marked by an increased number of patients in the emergency room, overtime and coworkers bugging me to switch holiday hours. Not this year. After shopping for the kids, I took them to purchase small gifts for each member of the preschool staff with something extra for their own teachers and Angie their babysitter. They couldn't reach a compromise about what to get Uncle Jeb so he ended up with twice as much as everyone else.

Besides shopping, there was a tree to decorate. Not the puny four-foot artificial one I usually set up in front of the living room window. There were lights to string on the bushes outside, Christmas cards to be sent to relatives who had never met Jonah and Emma and parts to learn for the preschool Christmas program. The unending Christmas carols sung around the house the entire month of December in tiny, high-pitched timbre was enough to put even an old Scrooge like me in the Christmas spirit.

I denied Aunt Wanda the pleasure of buying a dress for Emma to wear to the Christmas program. One day after work I stopped by the mall in the city. I'd driven past the exit for the past five years but never felt the inclination to actually stop until now. The incredible selection in the Little Girls' Department made for an agonizing decision, but I eventually settled on a midnight blue velvet number to bring out the shine in Emma's eyes. In the Boys' Department, I found a blue velvet vest of almost the same shade and a matching bow tie. I bought new black trousers with the most darling cuffs and pleats I'd ever seen for Jonah to wear with the white button down shirt he already owned.

I left the store via the Women's Department. I never had a need for dress clothes, but I was tired of showing up for Preschool Sundays in the same black skirt and outdated blouse that did nothing for my figure. Not that I had much in the figure department. I chose two pretty but practical ensembles I didn't think would go out of style for at least a decade. I chastised myself for spending money on clothes I would probably never wear after Nicole came for the kids. In the back of my mind I secretly loved choosing the outfits. Besides, it was beginning to look like Nicole was in no hurry to come back.

I wasn't sure how I felt about that.

The Monday morning before the Christmas program, Jonah's teacher, Miss Jennifer, met us at the door as we marched in. After asking Jonah and Emma about their weekend she turned to me. "Michelle, hi. I've been meaning to talk to you." Her effervescent smile told me nothing was wrong with Jonah's performance at preschool, so I relaxed. "It's about the program Wednesday night," she said.

"I hope you're not going to ask me to make any shepherd or angel costumes."

She gave my arm a playful slap. "Of course not. It's much simpler than that. We teachers are looking for a few parent volunteers from each class to help line the kids up in the hallway before we enter the sanctuary. I promise you'll have plenty of time to get inside and to your seat so you won't miss anything. It's really no big deal. Not a lot of work. It's just helpful to have a few level heads present. It can get a little frantic."

She put her hand on my arm again and leaned toward me conspiratorially. "We only ask certain parents. We'd rather not have any stage mothers helping, or the ones who manage to get their own kids crying, if you know what I mean?"

I knew exactly what she meant. "Sure, I'd love to help out."

Aunt Wanda could hold my seat until I got back into the sanctuary. We'd already decided to arrive early and get seats as near the front as possible.

She squeezed my arm one last time. "Great. I really appreciate it. Jonah is so excited about his part. He does it flawlessly during rehearsal."

"He does it all the time at home, too." I smiled down at him and Emma who showed no interest in our conversation. They finished hanging their coats on the hooks and headed toward the play area.

"Hey, wait a minute," I called after them. "Didn't you forget something?"

Two little faces turned up to me, lips puckered. I put my hands on either side of Emma's face and planted a kiss, and then Jonah's. "Have a good day. Learn stuff." The same admonishment every day followed by the same reply.

"We will. Bye."

I smiled a farewell to Jennifer, signed the kids in and headed for the door. The air outside was cold and blustery. My hair immediately flew across my face blinding me. Absently I shoved it aside. A familiar Christmas carol pealed from the church bell tower, totally appropriate for the bite in the air and the song in my heart. It was going to be a perfect Christmas. I didn't realize until later that I couldn't remember the last one.

Emma, Jonah and I arrived much too early for the Christmas program. When we got to the designated classroom, half the teachers hadn't even arrived yet. There were only a handful of children present, but they were already keyed up. I didn't know how the teachers would get them calmed down in time. I wished I hadn't arrived so early. Now Emma and Jonah would have too much time to get bored and antsy. But I couldn't have stayed home any longer if I tried. I was totally caught up in the moment. Aunt Wanda had picked up the kids from preschool early while I was at work so she could set Emma's hair in hot rollers—something I didn't know still existed.

About the time I got home from work, the curlers came out and the hair ribbons went in. Thank heaven for Emma's patience. Her hair was a masterpiece. I couldn't remember Cousin Violet's hair ever looking so marvelous. When I said the same to Aunt Wanda, she shrugged. "Violet got her fine limp hair from your grandma's side of the family, same as you. I never could do anything with it. Emma's, on the other hand, you can stick a brush in it and it'll stay there." She proceeded to demonstrate.

After helping get the kids in semi-orderly lines outside the sanctuary doors, I sneaked inside and up a side aisle to where Aunt Wanda and Uncle Jeb were seated. Next to them sat Uncle DeWitt. I smiled in surprise and squeezed in next to them.

Uncle DeWitt seldom left the farm except for errands he couldn't avoid. I hadn't noticed any particular interest on his part in Nicole's kids, yet here he sat. On the outside at least, he was as crotchety and cantankerous as I was. Was it all a ruse to get people to leave him alone? It sure hadn't worked so far for me.

I barely settled into my seat when the double doors opened. A rustle went through the crowd as five hundred parents, grandparents, siblings and church members turned to face the back of the sanctuary. Uncle Jeb pressed the record button on the camcorder. I fumbled for the camera function on my phone like nearly everyone else in the sanctuary. My vision blurred with unexplained, unshed tears so I doubted I'd get a decent shot.

Music filled the auditorium and two lines of forty children deep filed into the church. Each child carried a small bell. Most of them were ringing the bells the way they'd been taught. Some, like Emma, clasped their bells in front of them like a shield, shoulders rigid and eyes wide with terror. The more rambunctious ones—Jonah included—were ringing the life out of those bells. I feared any minute the insides would go flying and put out someone's eye. People shifted in their seats and elbowed for a better view as their own youngster came into view. Two or three actually stood up, blocking the view of the parents behind them.

As the children marched past us, they sang.

"Little children, rise and sing. Ring the bells of Christmas. 'Tis the birthday of our King. Blessed child of Christmas."

While my heart practically ached at the sweetness of the moment, I couldn't help feeling sorry for Nicole. Where was she? Did she have any idea what she was missing? How could she be so self-absorbed, so hardened, that this moment wasn't worth experiencing? Even gruff Uncle DeWitt, who had worn bib overalls to his mother's funeral, had known what was important.

Over and over the chorus was sung until all the children had filed through the sanctuary and formed four long rows across the stage. Eighty little voices rang out above the music proclaiming their excitement and love for their Savior's birthday. Jonah and Emma were positioned on opposite ends of the stage. I had hoped for a picture of them together, but I was sure it would happen later. Uncle Jeb panned the camcorder back and forth from one to the other. Aunt Wanda didn't try to quell the tears streaming down her cheeks. Uncle Jeb's eyes were glistening too. I couldn't see Uncle DeWitt seated on the other side of Uncle Jeb, but I liked to think he was as touched by the procession as the rest of us.

Forty-five minutes later the curtain rose for the last time. Once again, the children held the bells in their hands. The music started, an upbeat tune that had all of us tapping our feet. The children began to sing.

"Come on and ring those bells, light the Christmas tree. Jesus is the King, born for you and me. Come on and ring those bells, everybody sing. Jesus, we remember it's your birthday."

Jonah was in the front row near center stage, singing his heart out. I blinked away tears when I overheard two women behind us discussing the sweetheart in the blue vest. After a little searching I spotted Emma in the back row with the older children. Her hips swayed to the music as she rang her bell and sang. A smile brightened her features.

The children sang the song through twice before leaving the stage in the same way they'd come in, still ringing their bells as they headed toward the fellowship hall. This time every bell rang enthusiastically; all signs of timidity having disappeared.

There was an invitation on the back of the programs for the audience to partake in refreshments after the program in the fellowship hall. We all stood and waited our turn until we could leave our seats and claim our children. The bad part about having a good seat close to the front for the program also meant we would be among the last to leave the sanctuary.

"I hope they have some cake left by the time we get there," Uncle Jeb grumbled jokingly.

Refreshments were the farthest thing from my mind. "I hope the kids don't start worrying that we forgot them."

"Don't worry about that, Peanut. Didn't ya see the looks on their faces? They're having a blast."

Aunt Wanda turned in the aisle and squeezed my hand. "Wasn't it beautiful, Michelle? They did so good. All the kids were adorable."

I nodded. "I'm so proud of Emma. She's been just short of terrified all week."

"Don't forget Jonah," Uncle Jeb said. "Did you see him up there belting out those songs? That boy's got real talent."

"Uncle Jeb, he's only three."

"Don't argue with me, Peanut. I know talent when I see it. That boy's got it. Must take after my side of the family."

"He doesn't have a drop of Rowe blood in him," Aunt Wanda reminded him.

"Then he must have got it by proxy."

"What did you think, Uncle DeWitt?" I asked the tall, somber man at the end of the aisle, waiting patiently for our row to be dismissed. "The kids will be so happy you made it."

Uncle DeWitt kept his gnarled hands clasped in front of him. He gave me a slow nod and pursed his lips. He never spoke or reacted quickly to anything. We had learned over the years to let him speak his piece in his own time without rushing him. If you rushed him, he'd clam up and not speak at all. He was truly a man of few words.

"Yup. Fine job," he said finally.

We waited politely to see if he had more to add. He didn't.

A hand fell on my shoulder. I turned to see Kyle in the pew behind me. My heart did a little stutter step. I hadn't seen him close enough to talk to since the day he risked drowning and electrocution to fetch my car at the Winn Dixie. He sure looked different in dry clothes with his Christmas-red dress shirt accentuating what remained of his tan and that jet black hair. I couldn't decide which look I preferred better. He wore them both so well.

"Emma and Jonah did great tonight," he said. "They're like two different kids."

"Aren't they, Pastor?" interjected Aunt Wanda. "We're so proud of them—and of Michelle here too. She's just what they needed."

All eyes shifted to me. "I don't know about that," I said, uncomfortable with the attention. "I'm not the only one with input in their lives."

Aunt Wanda put her hand on my arm. "But you're doing the brunt of it, sweetheart." She looked back at Kyle. "You should see her with them. You've never seen such devotion. She's practically refurnished her entire house. It isn't cheap raising two kids, but you never hear her complain. Those two don't want for nothing. Do they, Jeb?"

"Well, I—"

"She's given up all her free time too. Hasn't she, Jeb? They couldn't've asked for a better aunt. Nicole's lucky to have a sister who is willing to do what Michelle's done."

I was beginning to feel like a lame racehorse Aunt Wanda was trying to pawn off. Kyle was listening with a bemused expression on his face. I wanted to crawl under a pew.

"The teachers did a great job with the kids tonight," I said as soon as Aunt Wanda paused to inhale. "I can't imagine the hours that went into putting something like this together."

Kyle nodded. "Billie outdoes herself every year. I'm glad all I have to do is get up there and make whatever announcements she tells me to."

It was finally our turn to leave our pew. Kyle circled around the pew he was in and fell into step behind me. "Are you staying for refreshments?"

I couldn't explain how his question thrilled me even though he probably asked the same question of everyone who came to the program.

"The kids'll be too wound up to leave right away," I said.

"I know it thrilled you to see them onstage."

If he only knew how much. "It's a shame their mother wasn't here to see it."

He put his hand on my elbow and slowed down, forcing me to slow down along with him. Aunt Wanda, Uncle Jeb and Uncle DeWitt moved on with the crowd, unaware we were no longer right behind them.

"Have you heard anything from Nicole?"

I tried to focus on his words and not the warmth of his breath on my cheek.

I shook my head and whispered back. "Not a word."

He shook his head in time with mine. "Are you getting along all right? Is there anything we at the church can do to help?"

I was touched by his offer. "Thanks so much. I never thought I was cut out for this mothering business, but now I almost can't imagine life without the kids in it."

Heat rose in my face. Where had that thought come from? Life without Emma and Jonah had been—and would be again soon—much simpler. It was just the spirit of the season and the emotion of the evening making me think such silly thoughts.

Why in the world had I admitted them to Kyle?

He squeezed my elbow before letting go of my arm. "I hoped that would happen. You're really good for those kids. Just what they needed like your aunt said. I only see them now and then at preschool, but I see the change in them, especially Emma. You've been such a blessing to them."

There was that word again. Blessing. I wasn't blessing anybody. I was just doing what needed done. It was in my nature. It's what I'd been trained to do.

Still I couldn't help feeling a little prideful when he spoke so highly of the kids.

I would've loved to talk with him more, but everyone in the church wanted a piece of him. He gave me one last smile as we reached the fellowship hall before leaving to mingle with the crowd. I spoke with several of the parents I had gotten to know over the past four months. We talked about kids and kindergarten and babies; topics of conversation parents can never wear out.

I spoke with each of the teachers and told them how pleased I was with the progress Emma and Jonah had made since coming to Noah's Ark. Even the teachers who didn't have one of them in class were responsible for them at least part of the day. I was happy all nine women seemed to dearly love kids, especially my two.

The whole time I kept an eye open for Kyle. Our eyes met occasionally, and we'd wave or smile across the fellowship hall. I couldn't help wondering if he was keeping an eye out for me too.

Since I couldn't seem to stop making goo-goo eyes at Kyle, I was shocked by the nugget of jealousy that wormed its way into my belly when I saw Barry with a pretty redhead about my height who looked smart and chic in a gray tailored jacket and skirt.

I gave myself a mental slap as I tried to stop resenting the woman's perfectly sleek, straight hair cut in a fashionable style my flyaway hair could never pull off. She had high cheekbones and a perfectly chiseled nose. Even her ears were cute. Even without the red hair serving as a dead giveaway, I could tell by the way Caitlyn clung to her and continually climbed in and out of her arms, she was Barry's ex-wife.

I suppose it was a good thing she and Barry were able to put their differences aside for Caitlyn's sake, at least for one night. So many parents couldn't.

I thought about my bargain haircut, poor posture and lack of fashion sense and wondered what Barry saw in me. I looked down at the frilly blouse and straight skirt I thought looked so chic in the store and wondered again why I had even bothered.

I reminded myself this wasn't about me. It was about Caitlyn and two people who obviously loved her. I had no claim to Barry. Every time he asked me out I came up with a reason to put him off. I hadn't decided if I wanted to date anyone, especially a man barely separated from his wife, so why did I care that they were here tonight together? It would be best for Caitlyn if they made amends. At least I assumed it would. Kids needed to be with their parents. Not a mess like me who couldn't decide if she wanted to be someone's mother or go back to an easy life with only a spoiled dog to consider.

Kyle obviously wasn't interested enough to talk about any topics other than the kids and church. Wasn't this what I wanted? To be left alone so I could get back to my life before Jonah and Emma dropped into it and ruined everything?

Emma zeroed in on Caitlyn so I was forced to go over and say hello to the Schilling clan.

"Hi, Barry," I said when I got within speaking range. I turned to the woman at his elbow and extended my hand.

Rats. She was even prettier up close.

"Hi, I'm Michelle Hurley, Emma's aunt. I'm so happy she and Caitlyn became friends."

The woman smiled and displayed a dimple in her left cheek just like Caitlyn's. "I'm Sue," she said as she shook my hand. Her fingers were long and tapered and her nails manicured.

I dropped her hand as quickly as I could without offending her and curled my own stubby, broken fingernails into my fist.

"We hear about Emma all the time."

We? Who was *we?* She and Barry? Or was there someone else in her life? More importantly, why did I care? I needed to get a grip.

Then I noticed she and Barry were staring at me. Even Emma and Caitlyn were gazing up at me like I had a blob of cake icing on the end of my nose.

I resisted the urge to look down to see if a button had come undone on my blouse or if I had lipstick on my teeth.

"So, what do you think?" Sue asked. She cocked her head and light glinted off the diamond studs in her perfect little ears. "We would love it if she could spend the night sometime so we can get to know her better."

We again. Did that mean Barry would be there, too, getting to know Emma? And what was there to know? She wasn't even five yet. Much too young to be a bad influence on their little angel.

Belatedly, my ears latched on to the central theme of the invitation. A sleepover? I didn't know how I felt about Jonah or Emma sleeping anywhere but across the hall from me. They were awfully young. What if one of them got hurt? Or wet the bed? What if they cried to come home or broke something and the adult in charge yelled at them? It was too much pressure. Even if they could handle it, I didn't know if I could.

"Maybe," I said, my lips pulled tight against my teeth. "I'll think about it. Emma's very shy. I don't think she's ready to spend the night away from home."

"Oh." Sue's pretty face looked confused. She glanced at Barry. "I thought Emma was just staying with you until her mom came back. I assumed she was an old hand at spending the night…well…wherever."

It was my turn to glance at Barry. What had he told this woman? I didn't like people thinking Emma had no structure in her life, or that she was a wayward urchin shuffled from one relative to the next. Maybe Nicole sent her to the neighbors to crash whenever she wanted a free night but not me. I took care of Emma and Jonah and didn't pawn them off on whoever was willing. Was that what Barry thought? Was that the impression my words and attitude left on people?

I relaxed my cheeks and managed a genuine smile. "Emma likes routine. She would be very upset sleeping anywhere but her own bed."

I looked down at Emma and hoped she wouldn't contradict me in front of them. Fortunately, her shyness prevented her from speaking up in front of strangers. I would certainly hear her rebuttal when we got in the car.

"I understand," Sue said, though from the look on her face, she clearly didn't. "Maybe at the end of the school year we can plan something. A little celebration for both the girls."

I chastened myself for being too touchy. It was just a sleepover. Kids did that stuff younger and younger all the time. I was sure neither Sue nor Barry planned to kidnap Emma or let her watch R rated movies. "That would be fun," I agreed. "We can talk more about it in a few months. I'm sure Emma would enjoy it. I just don't want to push her into it before she's ready."

Sue's eyes filled with pity. "It's a shame what kids have to deal with at such a young age. People don't seem to care how their actions affect children." She lowered her voice and leaned toward me. "Parents in jail. Doing drugs. Hustling their kids from one relative to the next. It's a real shame. And who suffers for it? The kids." She laid a manicured hand on my arm. "It isn't fair."

I looked again at Barry. He was looking everywhere but at Sue and me. Obviously, he had talked a lot with Sue about Emma and Jonah's situation. What right did they have to feel sorry for *my* kids? They couldn't even hold a marriage together. How much did they care about how their actions affected Caitlyn? Everyone knew children of divorce were screwed up.

I spotted Uncle DeWitt near the door buttoning his coat. "I think everyone's getting ready to go. It was nice meeting you, Sue."

"You, too, Michelle. If you ever need anything, just let me know."

That would be the day.

"Come on, Emma," I called to where she and Caitlyn were trying to pop balloons tied to the back of a chair. "Uncle Dewitt's leaving. Let's go say goodbye."

As I hurried away from Sue and Barry, I saw Kyle watching from the kitchen doorway. When he caught my eye, he turned away and started talking to a group of teens. I was too stirred up about Barry's big mouth to figure out what that meant.

I guess Barry had a right to explain Emma's situation to his ex since she was Caitlyn's best friend, but I didn't like people feeling sorry for me or Emma and Jonah. I especially didn't like it when they discussed my business without knowing the whole story. The kids were fine. Their mother might be a loose cannon, but they had me. I was all they needed.

Chapter Seventeen

“Merry Christmas, Michelle.”

At the sound of Nicole's drunken voice, I pressed the phone into my sweater and swiveled my head to make sure the kids were not within earshot. Then I remembered I was in the car on my way home from work. If Nicole had called twenty minutes later, Jonah and Emma would be strapped in their car seats and exposed to their mother's drunken holiday wishes. The fact that they weren't qualified as a Christmas miracle as far as I was concerned.

I exhaled and loosened my white-knuckle grip on the phone. “Christmas was yesterday,” I reminded her. “Leave it to you to call a day late.”

I wished she hadn't called at all.

“What difference does it make what day it is? I miss my family.”

The slurred speech and sloppy, happy tone told me Nicole was tight. Not to mention the fact we hadn't heard a peep from her since August. Apparently she needed alcoholic inducement to realize she missed her children.

I swallowed my aggravation. I wanted to hang up. I wanted to tell her to please lose my number. The kids were getting along fine without her, and she needed to leave them alone so they could continue enjoying their Christmas break.

Yesterday had been the happiest Christmas of my life. Aunt Wanda and Uncle Jeb got to the farm before the kids woke up so they'd be there watch them unwrap their presents, before hurrying back to their own farm to spend the rest of the morning with Violet and Cliff visiting from Fayetteville. The looks on Emma and Jonah's faces when they came downstairs had made the Black Friday shopping and standing in line for two hours to get pictures with Santa worth every inconvenience.

Aunt Wanda made her special Christmas morning coffee cake, and Uncle Jeb insisted we eat while he read the Christmas story out of the book of Luke before we opened presents. He used to do the same thing with Nicole, Violet and me. I hated it when I was a kid. Now I appreciated the tradition.

I didn't tell Nicole any of that. I needed to keep her happy and cooperative if I wanted to find out where she was and what her plans were.

"We miss you, too. How have you been?"

"I've been fabulous," she said, entirely too perky. "Put the kids on, will you? I want to talk to my babies."

Her voice went from exuberant to pouty in the span of two syllables.

"They're not with me." Thank goodness for that. It would've been a nightmare if she'd left a drunken, rambling message and the kids heard it. For a time after they first arrived, I checked my voicemail when they were safely out of earshot weren't in case she said something I didn't want them to hear. Lately I'd gotten careless. I needed to step up my diligence again.

"I'm on my way to pick them up from the sitter's."

Nicole groaned. "You're not letting Aunt Wanda watch them, are you? She hates me. She'll turn them against me. Don't let her poison my babies against me. I couldn't take it."

She was nearly in tears by the time she finished. Drunken, self-absorbed tears. I wanted to smack her.

"You don't have to worry about Aunt Wanda. She's been wonderful. She and Uncle Jeb love the kids and they love her."

Nicole was immediately placated. "That's good to hear. I miss them sooooo much."

Yet not enough to come home or call on the actual holiday.

"Where are you?" I asked carefully.

Talking to my sister under the best conditions was like walking through a minefield. When she had a few drinks in her it could be disastrous. I didn't want her to see my inquiries as an attack. Nor did I want to sound like I was extending an invitation. I knew she'd come home eventually. I just didn't want it to be today. None of us were ready for that.

"I'm with Dean. Is that what you want to hear? I know you hate him."

I flinched at the venom in her voice. "I don't hate him. I don't even know him."

"Good, because he loves me. That should be all any of you care about. If someone loved you, I would be happy for you. You deserve to be loved, sis. I worry about you. You need someone in your life."

I tuned out the litany of concern for my happiness. Someone did love me. Her children. And I loved them. But I couldn't tell her that.

After she wound down, I tried again. "I appreciate the call. I love you too. So do the kids. They're doing well. Everybody's happy and healthy."

"I'm so glad. I worry about them every minute of the day. Put them on. I need to hear their voices."

It was always about what she needed.

I swallowed my impatience. "I told you they're not with me. I'm on my way home from work. I'll tell them you called."

"What time do you get home? I'll call back then. I want to tell them how much I miss them and love them and can't wait until we can be together again."

When exactly would that be? Didn't we deserve to know that?

Please, please, please don't call back, I prayed.

I prayed she would forget about this call the minute she hung up. The kids didn't need to talk to her, especially when she was drunk and repeating every other word. They were probably used to it, but I didn't want to subject them to it anyway.

"I'm not sure when I'll get home," I hedged. "I have some errands to run. Call first and leave a message. We'll get back to you."

"I miss my babies, Michelle," she blubbered into the phone. "Kids should be with their mom on Christmas."

I didn't bother to remind her again Christmas was yesterday, and the kids hadn't seemed to miss her. After a huge dinner at Aunt Wanda's, they had taken a hike through the fields with Uncle Jeb, Gypsy and Violet's husband Cliff during the unseasonably mild day. Later the whole family played board games and UNO in front of the fireplace in their great room. Cliff turned out to be great with kids. Jonah loved using him as a human jungle gym and wrestling with him on the floor. Cliff listened patiently as Emma pretended to read him a story about her new doll.

"I understand that. I know they miss you too," I said diplomatically.

"Do you think so? No one understands how hard this is on me. Everything's hard for me. I'm not like you. You're so strong. I wish I was more like you."

Even though I was pretty sure she would forget this conversation within five minutes of hanging up, I felt sorry for her. She loved her kids. She probably even missed them in her own way. She might even miss me. I just wished she could see the kids were better off with things staying the way they were for the time being.

"Thanks, Nicole. That means a lot."

I was almost to Angie's. I needed to get her off the phone before she sobered up and decided to come home.

"You're a better person than me, Michelle. You always have been. I mess everything up. Nobody loves me. My kids don't need me. Dean uses me. I need a do-over." She laughed a drunken high-pitched squeal. "Wouldn't that be nice? Start over with no mistakes. Too bad life doesn't work that way."

I gripped the phone tighter. What was she talking about? "It's never too late to make changes, Nicole," I began carefully. "You could go back to school. Find something you really like."

"I'm not talking about that," she snapped. "I'm just tired of the way my life turned out."

I hoped my laugh didn't sound panicked. "You're not even twenty-four. You can do whatever you want. It's not too late."

"It's too late for me."

I wedged my car into a narrow space in front of a little house about two blocks from Angie's. It looked like the whole county had the day off but me. Traffic was light on the highways so that meant there were few parking spaces on the neighborhood streets.

"You make me nervous when you talk like that."

"I can't help it. Something in my life's got to change. I can't take much more of this."

I worked my jaw and squeezed my eyes shut. "Then come home," I said before I could talk myself out of it. "I'll help take care of the kids while you go back to school or whatever you want to do. I can help you get funding. We'll make it work."

I was talking fast and not wanting to follow through with any of the suggestions I was throwing at her. But I couldn't leave her wherever she was, adrift and floating dangerously close to an abyss she might not come out of. She was my baby sister, and I didn't want to see her come to harm, especially at her own hand.

"You think you know what's best for everybody."

I blinked. "What?"

The tears and despair had vanished from her voice. "I don't need you to fix me. You can't control me."

"What…I…that isn't what I'm trying to do. We're family. I want to be here for you, whatever that means."

"You've never been here for me. You want to control me. Stay out of my life."

The call ended. I sat in the idling car and stared out the windshield at the empty street and wondered what I'd done wrong. I wanted to help Nicole. I thought that's what I'd been doing the last few months. I didn't want to control her. I just wanted her to grow up and face her responsibilities.

I sat there a few more minutes. I wish I knew what I could've said or done differently. If I believed in prayer, I'd pray my sister didn't hurt herself. I would pray she'd get her life together. Most of all, I'd pray she stayed as far away from the farm as possible.

Chapter Eighteen

Several extra cars were parked in Angie's driveway and on the street in front of her house. She and her husband, whom I had yet to meet, were probably enjoying a few vacation days with holiday visitors. I hoped Emma and Jonah's presence hadn't spoiled any family plans after I was so careful about not imposing on my own family.

I tried to put my conversation with Nicole out of my head as I squeezed my car into a spot between an SUV and a pickup. Nicole always got maudlin when she was drinking. She would whine about the state of her life or her financial situation and declare she was tired of living that way, and starting tomorrow, she was changing. Then she'd sober up and start the whole process over again.

I didn't need to worry. Still, I couldn't keep from doing exactly that. I didn't want her to hurt herself or do anything stupid. Wherever she was today, I hoped she wasn't behind the wheel of a car and not anywhere near Harrison County.

I rapped gently on Angie's front door and pushed it open without waiting for an answer. Unless she was at the front of the house, Angie didn't answer during daycare hours. If she was in the middle of a feeding or a diaper change, it was inconvenient to stop what she was doing to answer the door.

I called out to make my presence known as I headed to the back where adult voices drowned out the usual childish ones.

"Hello. Where is everybody?"

A voice that didn't belong to Angie called in reply. "In here."

Angie's family room had been converted to her daycare area. The open floor plan made games, using large motor skill toys and naps possible. A bathroom was conveniently located off the room to the left. An open kitchen on the other end was separated by a long bar. Angie could prepare meals and do her housework while keeping her eyes on the children.

An older woman, who bore a striking resemblance to Angie, stepped into the doorway. "Everybody's in here." Adult laughter erupted behind her. She looked over her shoulder at the cause of the noise and then back to me. "Hope you don't mind that nobody got naps today although I'm about ready for one. I'm afraid the big kids kept the little ones awake."

Angie appeared behind her. "Hi, Michelle. Welcome to the nut house. At least for today. Do you know my mom? Mom, this is Michelle Hurley, Emma and Jonah's aunt. This is my mom Carol."

"Nice to meet you, Michelle. Your kids are so sweet. Not like those granddaughters of mine."

Angie smacked her playfully on the shoulder. "Now, Mom, if the girls are spoiled it's because of you and Dad."

Carol grinned and crinkled her nose at me, admitting her guilt.

"Are you in a hurry, Michelle?" Angie asked. "We're having a little impromptu party. Mom and Dad came in for Christmas night before last. As soon as word got out, everyone in town descended on us."

Before I could digest the invitation, Carol added, "We're visiting from Arizona. We retired there a couple years ago. It was the only way we could get out of babysitting grandkids every weekend."

"Mom!" Angie cried. "Michelle's going to think you're awful."

Carol gave me another smile. "You don't think I'm awful, do you, Michelle? I only speak the truth. Ask any grandparent. You can't refuse your grandchildren whatever they ask, so it's easier to move to a different time zone."

She looped her arm through mine and pulled me through the doorway separating the kitchen and daycare room. The daycare area was full of playing, scrambling kids. Sofa cushions had been pulled halfway off the couch and throw pillows littered the floor. The TV was playing an old Pixar movie, though no one was paying attention. Pieces from what looked like a hundred different puzzles were scattered over a Little Tikes tabletop. Coloring books, crayons and Legos lay all over the floor. Angie's standards had apparently gone out the window today.

The other half of the room was filled with adults who were causing more commotion than the children. They leaned against counter tops, perched on barstools and sat around the gigantic table. Soda bottles of every size and variety littered every surface, along with cellophane-wrapped containers, presumably leftovers from Christmas dinner.

"Are you hungry, Michelle?" Angie asked.

"Here, have a buckeye." Carol thrust a plastic plate of the peanut butter and chocolate confections toward me. I never met a buckeye I didn't like but hadn't learned to make them myself. There was no need. Every Christmas at least three different people on staff left them in the break room at the hospital.

"Yo, is that Michelle Hurley?" a voice called out. "I don't believe it."

Angie's older brother sat at the far side of the kitchen table with his hand raised toward me in greeting. Even after fifteen years, a middle-aged paunch and thinning hair, I would've recognized Dave anywhere. He was a year ahead of me in school. There were a few other brothers and sisters in the family, but Dave was the only one I really remembered.

I waved back. I moved into the room and away from the buckeye plate. I'd eaten enough junk in the past three days to last through New Year's. "Where you been keeping yourself?" I asked him.

"I've been around." He put his arm around the smiling, buxom brunette to his left. "This is my wife, Penny. In case you don't know everybody else…"

He went around the room making introductions and stopped at the last person, who was hip-deep in the refrigerator. "I guess you remember this guy," Dave finished with a gleam in his eye.

The man backed out of the refrigerator and turned to face me. Heat rose in my cheeks. Kyle.

Naturally Dave remembered that Kyle and I had been all over each other in high school. I hoped he wouldn't find it necessary to inform the rest of the room.

"I remember," I said. "What brings you out today, Kyle?"

He patted his stomach. "Food. Hey, Angie, I thought you said there were deviled eggs in there."

Angie moved forward. "Oh, get out of my way. I'll find them."

"No, you won't," someone said with a laugh. "John just ate the last one."

Angie turned and glared playfully at the man Dave had introduced as Jenny's husband, though I could no longer remember which woman was Jenny. "John. How could you?"

John raised his hands. "I'm innocent. I didn't even know we had deviled eggs."

Angie reached around Kyle and pushed the refrigerator door shut. "Sorry, Kyle. My gluttonous family has eaten all the deviled eggs. I guess you'll have to go without."

Kyle put a hand on her shoulder. "Don't fret, Sister. I'm sure there's enough other stuff here to keep a man from starving."

"Aunt Shell!"

Jonah jumped over a pile of toys and circled furniture and adult legs to reach me.

I thought of Nicole and her drunken rambling a few minutes ago. I was thankful all over again she had called while the kids weren't within earshot. I had to admit I sort of liked having them to myself.

Jonah hugged my legs and gazed up at me. "We don't gotta leave yet, do we? We wanna stay."

"We really should go," I said thinking of Angie and her family and the fact they hadn't had much time to themselves without the whole town of Winona banging on their door. "I've got to return some things to the store. Remember those pants Aunt Wanda got you that were too short?"

John clapped a large hand on my shoulder. "No need to be in a hurry. You ain't got nothing to return to the stores that can't wait till tomorrow." He shoved a plate at me with his free hand. "If you leave now, you'll just have to fix supper at home. Might as well eat here. We've got plenty."

Angie took my arm and turned me toward the countertop lined with food. "There's no use arguing with him, Michelle. Get something to eat and make yourself at home."

Jonah disappeared into the daycare room, apparently relieved someone had convinced me to stay.

"But you already have so much company, we'll be in the way."

She chuckled. "Are you kidding? If no one came to visit while Mom and Dad were here, they'd think we all forgot them. Fill yourself a plate. I don't want to get stuck with all these leftovers."

It looked as if the others had been eating most of the afternoon. I put a slice of cold ham and a scoop of potato salad on my Styrofoam plate and took a plastic fork out of a bag. A brother-in-law slid off one of the barstools to make room for me to sit down. Kyle sidled up beside me with a soda in his hand. "You still drink nothing but Pepsi?"

Did it mean anything that after fifteen years he remembered what brand of soda I drank? Maybe it was one of those oddball tidbits that stuck in a person's memory. Or maybe it meant he remembered *me*. That he actually thought about me now and then over the years.

I took the can from him and popped the top to get my mind back on track. "How long have you been here?"

"Too long," he said with a grin. He found a depleted stack of plastic cups and removed one. "No, I'm kidding. I hung out with Dave a lot when we were growing up so I know their parents really well. It's nice seeing them again."

As he talked, he went to the refrigerator and filled the cup to the top with ice. I wasn't sure it was for me until he set it down next to my plate. I couldn't get over it. Not only did he remember I drank Pepsi but also that I liked a lot of ice.

"Angie called me on Christmas Eve and told me they were in town," he continued without comment about the soda or the ice. "Nobody had to work today, so we all sort of gravitated here."

"I hope Emma and Jonah didn't get in anyone's way."

"Are you kidding? Everyone loved meeting them."

A flush of maternal pride warmed my cheeks. "I'm glad." I turned to survey the family room. "I'll need to clean up before we leave. I know my two helped create this mess."

Kyle laughed. "I guarantee as soon as everyone leaves, Angie and Carol will have Chris and Pete in there cleaning and restoring order. You'll only insult them if you try to help."

I smiled and cut off a piece of ham with my plastic fork. It was one of those spiral sliced, honey-baked specialties they sell in the grocery store for the holidays. The kind that melts in your mouth. Kyle folded his arms across his chest and leaned against the countertop. We lapsed into a comfortable silence as we watched Angie's family enjoy each other's company.

"Did you have a nice Christmas?" I asked after a few minutes. Immediately I wished I hadn't. Kyle was a single man with little family left in the area. His parents had moved away while he was in the Air Force. I imagined him sitting in his living room Christmas morning staring at a three-foot Christmas tree with no presents to unwrap and no one to talk to. I should have thought to invite him to Christmas dinner. Aunt Wanda would've been thrilled to have an extra mouth to feed. Especially the handsome young pastor.

"It was nice," he was saying. "I drove to Texarkana in the morning to watch my sister's kids open their gifts. I do it every year. Then I came back here and had dinner with the Powell's." At my blank look, he explained. "He's one of the elders of the church, and she runs the ladies' ministry. If you came to church more often, you'd know that."

I wrinkled my nose in response.

"How was your holiday?"

A grin instantly covered my face. "Emma and Jonah had a blast. Aunt Wanda, Uncle Jeb and I went a little overboard in the gift department. Those kids made out like bandits. I don't think their Christmases have been a big deal before now. I probably could have bought them one gift each and they'd have been ecstatic. Putting up the tree and lights and taking pictures with Gypsy in the reindeer antlers I bought her at Hallmark was probably more fun than I think they ever had."

Kyle smiled. "There's nothing wrong with enjoying Christmas."

"I kind of wanted to make it up to them since this has been such a hard year and they haven't heard from their mother since August. I know there's no making up for such thing, but…"

I shrugged. I didn't mention Nicole's phone call. I didn't want to think about it too much myself. I was terrified of what it meant.

Kyle wagged his finger at me. "Don't put all the blame on Nicole. You bought most of those gifts for yourself."

I shrugged again and popped another piece of ham in my mouth. "It was an awful lot of fun watching them tear into those packages," I conceded. "It's going to cost a small fortune developing all the pictures on my phone, if I ever get around to it."

He laughed. "I'm glad you enjoyed yourself."

"Me too." I pushed the plate toward him. "Help me eat this."

He shook his head and laid a hand on his stomach. "Can't. Angie and Carol have been plying me with food for the last hour. For some reason, women always think I'm one meal away from starvation. I don't know if they feel that way about all unmarried men or just pastors. Either way, they're going to fatten me up like a Christmas goose if I don't put a stop to it."

I arched my eyebrows and looked him up and down. "Now that you mention it, you could use a little fattening up."

"Not you too."

We smiled at each other before turning back to watch the crowd. After a while, he asked, "Are you working through New Year's?"

I shook my head in response, my mouth once again full of ham. "Just till the weekend. Then I'm off New Year's Eve and New Year's Day."

He brightened. "You should come to the New Year's Eve church service. It starts at ten that night. We worship for about an hour. I preach a little while and then we go into the fellowship hall for a traditional midnight dinner of cabbage rolls and mashed potatoes."

"You don't pass up an opportunity to preach, do you?"

He grinned. "Not if I can help it. Our church has been doing the New Year's Eve service long before I got there. I'm looking forward to it. What better way to usher in a new year than by honoring the one who's given us so much?"

That's why I couldn't spend a lot of time around Kyle. He always reverted to that religion stuff. It was something I didn't have to worry about when I was around Barry. No real pressure there

I thought of the two little excuses I had to get me out of jams like this. "I would love to, but I have the kids. There's no way I can keep them up till ten o'clock. If I tried, they'd be grouchy as bears."

Kyle just smiled. "No problem. The kids love it. It's such a novelty for them to be up late, they don't realize it's past their bedtime. Most parents bring them in their pajamas. They get into the singing and worship time, then once I start preaching, they fall asleep in the pews."

I laughed at the image. "Must be a real boost to your confidence as a preacher."

"I don't worry as long as the adults don't start dropping off. After the service, a lot of the older kids wake up to go into the fellowship hall to eat, but many of them stay crashed on the pews. I guarantee Emma and Jonah will have fun. They won't give you any trouble."

I winced inwardly. I guess I was stuck. I gave him a half smile and lifted a shoulder in defeat. "Okay, Pastor, you got me. We'll see you at the church around ten, pajamas, fuzzy slippers and all."

Emma and Jonah had never been so excited about anything as they climbed out of the bathtub, into their pajamas and into the car on New Year's Eve. They wouldn't have minded going

to the dentist if they could go in their pajamas in what they saw as the middle of the night.

Nicole hadn't called back. I checked my voicemail with my heart in my throat every time I got a moment to myself. I didn't want the kids to overhear anything. Whether Nicole was drunk or lucid, I knew hearing her voice for the first time in months would only be traumatic and serve no good purpose.

I had called the number several times over the next week, but always got a message her voice mail had not been set up yet. I couldn't decide if it was a good thing or not. I worried Nicole might hurt herself, but I was more concerned how her erratic behavior would affect the kids. So far they seemed okay without her, but I knew this situation couldn't go on like it was forever.

The crowd at the church on New Year's Eve was much smaller than a typical Sunday morning service. Only about a third of the sanctuary was filled. The dress was more casual, too, with no suits or ties and most of the women in pants. Even Kyle wore a polo shirt and jeans.

I led Emma and Jonah to the front of the nearly empty sanctuary and shook hands and greeted the other brave souls who could've been home watching the ball drop in Times Square. I forgot my apprehension about being in church again and caught the spirit of the occasion. The Youth Choir got the ball rolling with a toe-tapping ensemble of songs. Soon everyone was on their feet clapping, singing and smiling at anyone within range. Like Kyle predicted, Emma and Jonah loved it. They raised their hands and belted out songs they knew by heart. It made me wonder about the worship services at preschool. One day I'd have to sneak out of work early and see what went on there.

Nearly an hour later the music stopped, and Kyle took his place behind the pulpit. Jonah got down on the floor at my feet and rolled a little car around in circles until he fell asleep.

Emma stretched out on the pew with her head in my lap. Within minutes she was asleep too.

Kyle assured the congregation his sermon would be brief as he directed us to the tenth chapter of John. I took a Bible out of the slot on the back of the pew in front of me. Hopefully following along with the text would help keep my mind off the man in the pulpit.

Kyle had been a good looking kid in high school, so it was no surprise he turned into a very handsome man. Still I was taken aback every time I looked up in the pulpit and compared him to the boy I thought I loved in high school.

I loved watching the way his mouth lifted on one side when he smiled and how his brown eyes crinkled when he laughed. I thought of how he remembered the way I liked my soda. Had he thought much about me over the last fifteen years? After he went away to the Air Force and I started nursing school, I put Kyle Swann out of my mind as best I could. Surely he had done the same with me. Remembering the way I took my soda was just a piece of information his brain unintentionally filed away.

Still, I sort of hoped…

Kyle was halfway finished with the text by the time I found the passage in John. I pushed away thoughts of high school and what might've been if we had made different choices and tuned in while he read.

"I am the good shepherd, and know my sheep, and am known of mine. As the Father knoweth me, even so know I the Father: And I lay down my life for the sheep. My sheep hear my voice, and I know them, and they follow me: And I give unto them eternal life; and they shall never perish, neither shall any man pluck them out of my hand."

By the time Kyle reached the end of the passage and looked up to survey the small assembly, tears pricked the backs of my eyelids. I found a tissue in my purse and dabbed the end of my nose. This wasn't the first time I'd heard the words of Jesus. I spent more than my share of Sundays next to Grandma Catherine as the pastor droned on and on about Jesus the Good Shepherd. But something about the words tonight pricked my heart.

No longer focused on Kyle and how his large, tanned hands gripped the lectern, I reread the passage myself. I went back to the first of the chapter and read the whole thing. For the first time in my life, the words seemed to come alive. I could almost feel Jesus himself reaching out to me. That couldn't be, my logical brain told my heart. Christianity was for a bunch of do-gooders who lived the way they did in order to make themselves feel better in a rotten world.

Over the past few months I had learned firsthand how good it felt to do something nice for someone less fortunate than myself. I thought of Emma and Jonah opening their presents on Christmas morning.

Kyle was right when he said I bought the presents for myself as much as for them. Doing good for someone else brought a sense of euphoria I had robbed myself of until now. I was already planning Emma's February fourteenth birthday in my head. I wanted to see that expression again. I liked being the hero—the cool aunt who bought exciting gifts in pretty packages and took them to birthday parties in fun locales.

Grandma had puffed herself up through the alleged sacrifices she made on my and Nicole's behalf in the name of Christian charity. Not me. I took care of Emma and Jonah because I enjoyed it, not because some God in heaven forced me into it. It wasn't out of obligation like Uncle Jeb said. It was pleasure on my part.

So why did I feel like Jesus was reaching out to me now?

I always believed if Jesus had existed in human form, he was nothing more than a really nice guy with a knack for teaching and reaching out to people on their level. But if he was just a great teacher and humanitarian, why did I feel his presence so strongly beside me in the pew? Where was it coming from? It wasn't my emotions. They were screaming for me to be reasonable. Why would Jesus—if he was real—bother reaching out to me, of all people? He'd be better off spending his time on people like Angie and Kyle and Billie. I was a lost cause. Surely the Creator of the universe would know that.

I forced my mind back to Kyle. I concentrated on watching his lips move and not the stirring in my heart.

"Like a shepherd is willing to lay down his life for the flock," Kyle said, his eyes aglow with passion, "Jesus was willing to do the same thing for us. He came to earth as a ransom to call people back to God the Father."

"Willing to lay down his life for the flock."

Kyle's words reverberated in my head. I looked down at the Bible page. The words blurred before my eyes.

It couldn't be that simple. Christians were selfish. If they truly followed this man Jesus, they wouldn't make their grandchildren feel like burdens. They would freely open their homes and their hearts to these lost children instead of reminding them every day what an inconvenience they were and what a louse their father was. They would behave with love and compassion the way Jesus taught, not out of obligation laced with resentment.

I closed the Bible and smoothed Emma's hair away from her face. The remaining fifteen minutes or so of the service, I focused on the poinsettia display around the piano and the hairstyles of the women in the pews in front of me.

I had allowed myself to get caught up in the holiday spirit and the notion of a Good Shepherd who knew his sheep and called them by name. If it made these people feel good and helped them face another pointless year of work, heartache and bills, then good for them. I didn't need it. I could handle life on my own strength as I had for the last thirty-three years.

Chapter Nineteen

"I don't wanna go to school," Emma wailed at the top of her voice. "I wanna stay here with you."

I sat back on my haunches and looked at the little girl on the sofa in front of me. I was two seconds away from losing my temper big time. I'd been trying to squeeze her feet into her shoes for the last five minutes. She continued to pull away and curl her toes in resistance.

"That's enough, Emma. You know you have to go to school. If you don't get a move on, you're gonna make me late for work. Do you want me to get in trouble? Do you want my boss to yell at me?"

She sniffed hard and shook her head.

"Then put your foot in this shoe."

She jumped back on the couch and tucked her feet under her bottom. "I wanna stay with you."

I stood up and set my hands on my hips. "All right, that's it. I've had it."

If I could bully a sixty-year-old man into walking down a hallway when he'd just had his chest cracked open, I could certainly put a shoe on one small child. I grabbed her ankle and yanked her foot out from under her. "I guess we'll have to do this the hard way." I jammed her foot into the shoe. She cried and wailed and struggled to pull away from me the whole time.

I couldn't figure out what had gotten into her this morning. I didn't particularly care enough at the moment to pick her brain to find out. I was not a big fan of obstinacy. Open rebellion, I liked even less. When I wanted something done, I wanted it done two minutes ago. I'd lived by my own terms too long to change now simply because I was dealing with children. I had barely enough time to drop her and Jonah off at the preschool and get to the hospital. I didn't have time to deal with a temper tantrum, and I wasn't about to.

Let them get away with it once, and you had big problems on your hands down the road. That was my way of thinking.

After both shoes were secured, I scooped her into my arms and carried her to the front door. "Hurry up, Jonah," I yelled over my shoulder, out of breath and more than a little irritated. "We're going to be late, thanks to your sister."

Emma had stopped crying. She rested her head against my shoulder in weary resignation. Pity swelled inside me. She wasn't a brat. Something was bothering her. But why did she have to let it out right before I had to be at work? I set her down by the front door and kissed her tearstained cheek. I worked her limp arms into her jacket while Jonah bundled up beside us. Whatever was bothering Emma had rubbed off on him. He stared at her face, concern written all over his. My guilt mounted.

"I'm sorry I lost my temper, Emma," I said gently as I zipped her up. "I don't like being late for work. There's no time for tears or temper tantrums in the mornings."

"I'm sorry," she murmured. "I don't want you to get in trouble."

Good going, Michelle. Now she'll worry about it all day.

"I won't get in trouble," I assured her in a soothing voice. "But we have to leave now. Okay?"

She fixed her gaze on her feet and nodded.

I turned to Jonah. "Okay?" I pulled his knitted hat down over his eyes.

He tilted his head back and peered up at me from under the brim. Emma managed a tremulous smile. I sighed and opened the door to let them go out in front of me. Jonah went out, but Emma remained in the doorway. I sighed again and squatted down to pick her up. Regardless of what was bothering her, I'd get to work quicker by giving in and carrying her to the car.

Fifteen minutes later, standing next to the coat pegs that lined the wall along the preschool lobby, the scenario repeated itself. "I wanna go with you," Emma wailed at the top of her voice.

I had carried her inside the building, figuring a little extra attention was all she needed. As I squatted down to set her on the floor, she tightened her arms around my neck and let loose with the tears again.

The last of my patience snapped. "Emma, that's enough. Stop crying this minute or I'll whip you right here in front of everybody. Is that what you want?"

I had never laid a hand on her or Jonah. I doubted I could follow through with my threats now. But if she kept it up, it wouldn't be hardest thing I'd ever done.

Miss Gail bustled out of the play area. "Emma, Emma, Emma. What's the matter, sweetheart?"

She knelt beside us and smoothed Emma's hair behind one ear. Emma tightened her grip on my neck as if she'd been scalded. I pried her hands loose. Not an easy feat since I was bundled against the January wind.

"Come into the play area with me," Miss Gail coaxed. "I need someone to help me with the puzzles. You're so good at that. Don't you want to help me today?"

Emma shook her head and leaned against me. I put my arms around her but kept enough distance between us so she couldn't latch on again. I wanted to get to the bottom of what was bothering her, but the ticking clock inside my head took precedence. Her newfound separation anxiety would need to be addressed later.

"Emma, it's time to stop crying. I'll be here at three-thirty to get you just like always. Now go into the play area with Jonah and Miss Gail and have fun."

Her tears had abated, but her cheeks were flushed and sweaty. Her hair was damp and clinging to her forehead. She shook her head without making eye contact. I felt sick to my stomach, but I didn't have time to give in to whatever was bothering her.

I straightened and put her hand in Miss Gail's. "Go on. Be a good girl. I'll see you at the end of the day."

I reached over and pulled Jonah's cap off his head. My heart sank at the sight of tears glistening in his brown eyes. I pretended not to notice while I unzipped his jacket and helped him out of it. His eyes went from me to Emma. He sucked furiously on his bottom lip in an effort not to cry. I kissed him on top of the head, and then Emma.

"Bye, guys," I said cheerfully as I beat a retreat to the door. "Be good. Learn stuff."

Miss Gail was already turning them toward the play area, talking a mile a minute about all the fun things they would do that day. They never took their eyes off me. I gave them another cheerful wave and exited the building. I cried all the way to work.

I didn't cry when Mom left. For the longest time, I saw no reason to. She would come back. She knew how hard it was on us when Dad left. She experienced Grandma's resentment firsthand. She wasn't strong enough to stand up to Grandma, but she knew how much Nicole and I suffered. Surely she wouldn't leave us there with the same callous disregard as Dad.

Now this thing—this curse or whatever it was—was repeating itself with Nicole in Mom and Dad's place. I wouldn't have imagined it in a million years. Nicole wasn't Mom. Not even close. She wasn't weak. Lazy? Yes. Self-centered? Incredibly so. But she was funny and clever and had a warm heart. How could she put her kids into the very situation that had devastated her?

By the time I realized Mom wasn't coming back, I no longer missed her. Missing her took too much energy. I resigned myself to the way things were and adjusted accordingly. Couldn't Emma do the same? She had to have known her mother couldn't be relied upon to do the right thing. Of course I was almost fifteen when Mom left us, ten years older than Emma was now.

Emma was the same age as Nicole was when Mom left. Was there any significance in that? Were the women in my family only capable of loving and caring for their children until they reached the magical age of four? Mom only lasted longer with me because she had Dad to rely on for the first eleven years.

The summer I graduated from high school was the first time Mom came back to the farm. She'd just divorced a man none of us ever met. She showed up in a red sedan she said she won in the divorce settlement. None of us believed her. We figured the ex was looking harder for the car than he was for Mom.

She hadn't put on an ounce of weight since she left the farm. She talked a lot and laughed too loud and tried to convince us her life was exactly what she wanted. She was up to three packs of cigarettes a day. Underneath the youthful makeup, her age showed terribly.

Nicole, Aunt Wanda and I were politely reserved. Grandma, who didn't have a tactful bone in her body, told Mom she looked like death warmed over. The visit lasted three weeks. Mom got several phone calls late at night that she wouldn't explain. One morning she was up earlier than usual. When I got home that evening from my summer job at the Sack and Save, she was gone. I always assumed the ex—if he was an ex—had tracked her down. Mom was never any good at being without someone to take care of her.

Just like Nicole.

At the hospital I tried to focus on work and forget Emma's morning meltdown. Worrying about it wouldn't change a thing.

I was in Mr. Cho's room checking vitals and making notes in his chart when Aunt Wanda called. Something had to be terribly wrong to warrant a phone call at work. Everyone knew I didn't appreciate interruptions while I was working, even for what most people considered emergencies.

"What's wrong?" I asked without preamble.

"It's Emma."

I swallowed a sigh. "What happened?"

"Nothing," she said in that soothing, condescending tone she used in the old days when explaining why Grandma Catherine had said or done something particularly hurtful. "She's upset, that's all. She's been weepy and pouty all morning. Every time anyone looks at her crossways, she starts bawling. The teachers wanted to know if there was anything they could do to calm her down."

I pinched the bridge of my nose. "I would think they could handle a crying child. I don't see why they had to bother you."

"I think it's more than a few tears. They didn't want to bother you at work if it turned out to be nothing. I told them I'd call and see if you minded if I went in and brought her and Jonah home."

If that didn't beat all. Aunt Wanda was calling to ask my permission about something. I felt oddly touched and flattered. At the same time, this problem was out of my area of expertise.

I chewed my bottom lip. "What do you think? I don't want Emma to get the idea all she has to do is cry and we'll cave and give her what she wants. That's how kids end up spoiled."

"Oh, please. If you buying them every toy they see on TV hasn't spoiled them, a little coddling surely won't do any harm."

"You think that's all it is? She needs some extra coddling."

"Sure it is," Aunt Wanda said with the confidence of someone who'd been doing this motherhood thing a lot longer than me. "The poor thing's only four. Look at everything she's been through in the last year. Besides, Jeb and me love having her and Jonah at the house. It doesn't happen nearly as often as we'd like. I'll go into town and get them and you can pick them up tonight at our house. Plan on staying for dinner. I'll fix up a batch of beef and noodles. It's Emma's favorite."

I heaved a sigh of relief and appreciation for my family. I had always thought of Aunt Wanda as a younger version of Grandma. But she had changed these last few months. Or maybe I was the one who had changed. Either way, I didn't have time to think about it right now.

"Thanks, Aunt Wanda. I hope she won't be any trouble."

"No trouble at all. I'll see you tonight. And, Michelle, don't worry."

I hung up and returned to work feeling much better. Emma would love spending the remainder of the morning helping Aunt Wanda roll out noodles. I didn't dwell on any possible causes of the problem. I liked to believe Aunt Wanda knew what she was talking about and a little attention would have everything back to normal in no time.

Chapter Twenty

The next morning was the same as the one before, and the next and the next. I couldn't let Aunt Wanda pick the kids up from preschool every time Emma decided she wasn't happy, and I let her know it. Our life was too busy for phone calls at work or tears in the middle of the night or temper tantrums when I had somewhere to be. Emma would have to realize she had to go to preschool and Angie's just like always.

Throwing a fit would not get her what she wanted.

Unfortunately, none of my lectures or threats seemed to get through. Emma wouldn't let me out of her sight. She started standing outside the bathroom door when I was taking a shower. While I fixed dinner, she sat at the kitchen table to 'keep me company'. As long as I was within sight, she chattered and laughed and talked about school as if she hadn't spent the whole day crying inconsolably. As soon as I headed toward the pantry or the back porch, she hopped off her chair and followed. She refused to watch TV with Jonah unless I was in the room.

Something was up. Unfortunately I couldn't figure out what. She and Jonah had been here five months. Had it taken all this time for her to develop a fear of being abandoned again?

I knew the awful things that were happening to children out in the real world. I watched the news. Was it possible someone outside the house was abusing her and I was too dense or too busy to recognize the signs?

Whatever it was, she wasn't talking.

I considered calling the caseworker at Children's Services and discussing the matter with her. I hated involving the authorities. The woman would immediately assume I was the cause of Emma's sudden developmental lapse. Whatever was going on would be my fault, and I'd have to defend myself in an investigation.

I needed to take care of the situation alone.

I stopped for pizza on our way home Thursday. I turned down the weekend work at the county hospital so I'd have three days to concentrate on Emma's problem. I hoped pizza would break the ice. There was a gallon of vanilla ice cream in the freezer at home. If it didn't placate Emma, I figured it would go a long way in making me feel better.

I didn't say a word until after we finished our pizza and were seated in front of the TV a couple of hours later. Jonah picked the movie for the evening, and I chose the twenty minutes of upcoming releases to broach the subject.

"Emma, you need to tell me why you've been crying this week every time we go to preschool."

She kept her eyes glued to the TV screen, but I knew I had her attention.

"You like going to preschool, don't you?" I pressed.

Still nothing.

"Come on, Emma. You have to tell me what's bothering you. I have to work on Monday. That means you and Jonah will go back to preschool. I know you like it there. So I don't want any more crying. It doesn't do any good, and it just gets everybody upset for nothing."

There. Who could argue with logic like that?

Emma laughed nervously at something on the TV. She glanced at me out of the corner of her eye. I could see she was hoping I'd stop talking about this uncomfortable topic and pay attention to the movie. I put my arm across the back of the couch and leaned forward so I could look into her face. She leaned to the right to see around me.

"Emma," I warned.

Reluctantly, she brought her face around to mine.

"You're not going to cry again when I take you back to the preschool or to Angie's, are you?" My tone left no room for argument. "You're a big girl. Next month you'll be five. That's too old to be crying like a baby when you don't get your way."

I was coming on too strong and shouldn't resort to name calling, but I couldn't think of any other way to get through to her. I needed to drive the point home, even if it meant a little tough love and manipulation.

"I won't cry no more," she said in a tiny, defeated voice.

I put my arm around her and squeezed her against me. "That's my big girl. How about after the movie, we pop some popcorn and play Old Maid?"

"Yea!" Jonah shouted.

Emma sniffed. "Okay."

Victory didn't taste as sweet as I imagined. I knew I had simply taken care of a symptom and not the disease, but I didn't want to ruin her weekend or mine. Enough talk for one night. She was a good little girl. She'd do whatever she could to please me, even if it meant breaking her own heart in the process.

.... ❀ ....

For Emma's birthday I decided against a huge party at a restaurant or bowling alley. An intimate affair at home with a few friends was more her speed…and mine. I mailed invitations to Angie's daughters, four little girls from the preschool, and one boy for Jonah. Three days before the big day, I called each parent to make sure the invitation had arrived and to see if their child was coming. I sure didn't want to face Sue again so I looked up Barry's number in the church directory to make sure Caitlyn would be in attendance. Emma liked her other preschool friends, but it wouldn't be a party without Caitlyn.

Barry laughed when he recognized my voice. "When I saw your card in the mail, I thought you were inviting me out for Valentine's Day and were too shy to ask in person."

Valentine's Day. Good grief. I hadn't been anyone's sweetheart for so long I hadn't even made the connection with Emma's big day and Valentine's Day.

"The card was addressed to Caitlyn," I reminded him with a laugh.

"I saw your name in the return address before I noticed that. I guess it was just wishful thinking."

I wasn't sure how to respond. He had looked pretty tight with his ex at the Christmas program. He hadn't called to ask me out again. I sort of figured he had given up on pursuing me, if that's what he'd been doing in the first place.

I decided to ignore the comment altogether. "Emma wants Caitlyn at her party more than even Uncle Jeb. I hope you realize what high praise that is."

He laughed. I was beginning to like the sound of it. "Caitlyn's been talking about nothing else since she got the invitation. I couldn't keep her away if I tried."

"Good. It'll be great to see her."

"It'll be great to see you, too."

I swallowed. "Aren't you sweet."

He took a deep breath. "I've been meaning to apologize to you about the Christmas program."

I thought about pretending I didn't know what he was talking about, but I knew exactly what he meant, and he would know I knew.

"You don't need to apologize."

"Yes, I do. I'm sorry for what Sue said. She can come across a little strong. She didn't mean anything against Emma and Jonah personally. She wasn't insinuating your sister did drugs or anything either. As soon as we got out in the parking lot, I pointed out how she had put her foot in her mouth. She wanted to call right away and apologize. I was afraid it would only make things worse, so we didn't do anything."

"It's okay. I wasn't offended by what Sue said."

I took a deep breath to gather my nerve. If I was going to see this guy at Emma's party or spend any amount of time with him in the future, I needed to clear the air.

"I was more offended by you."

"Me?"

"Yes, you. You shouldn't have told Sue or anyone else about Emma and Jonah's situation. It's not like it has any bearing on Emma's friendship with Caitlyn. I'm not embarrassed about my sister. I just don't like people feeling sorry for the kids. Or for me, for that matter"

"Whoa. I'm so sorry. That wasn't my intention."

He sounded sincere.

"I didn't figure it was. I just wanted you to know how I felt."

His end was quiet for a long moment. "Is that a good thing or a bad thing?"

"Is what a good thing or a bad thing?"

"That you want me to know how you feel about stuff."

"I'm not sure I know what you mean. I just didn't want any hard feelings between us."

He chuckled. "That's what I thought. You like me, don't you?"

My cheeks warmed. I imagined my freckles standing out in stark contrast to my pale skin the way they always did when I blushed. "Barry, that's not what I'm talking about."

"Come on, admit it. If you didn't like me, you wouldn't think twice about any insensitive comment I made to my ex."

"I guess you have a point."

Did he? Did I care what Barry thought of Nicole and the kids because I cared about *him*?

He laughed outright. "You just made my day, Michelle. All this time I thought you were giving me the brush-off. But you care what I think."

"I didn't say that."

"Pretty near. I'm going to get a date out of you yet."

I nearly giggled. Good grief, I was acting like a schoolgirl. "You sound awfully sure of yourself."

"Why shouldn't I? You went to all the trouble of setting up a party to get me to your house on Valentine's Day."

"It's Emma's birthday."

"Sure it is."

"I can show you her birth certificate."

"Don't bother. Those things can be forged. But let me put your mind at ease. I'll bring Caitlyn to the party. Then afterwards, I expect you to put some thought into going out with me. Now that I know how much you like me, I'm not taking no for an answer."

I hung up in high spirits. I had to admit Barry had grown on me since the first time I met him at the preschool. Maybe he didn't have Kyle's charisma, but he was funny and nice and a good dad. That had to mean a lot. The most amazing part was he liked me. He was genuinely sorry for making me uncomfortable after the Christmas program, and he wanted to spend an evening in my company.

I almost couldn't recognize myself from the boring woman I had been six months ago. Did I even realize back then how sad and empty my life was? I still wasn't sure I wanted two kids in my life. I wouldn't let myself think beyond the end of the week and the next preschool tuition check. Every time I signed my name I knew we were one week closer to Nicole coming back. Just because I hadn't heard from her since the day after Christmas didn't mean she wasn't out there somewhere plotting how she could knock my world off its axis again.

I wasn't going to waste a minute worrying about Nicole. I wouldn't worry about Sue and what her kind thought of me and the kids. I wouldn't even try to figure out my troublesome thoughts of Kyle and why I couldn't get him out of my head. All that mattered was Barry liked me, and he wanted me to like him back.

Emma wasn't the only one who would enjoy Valentine's Day this year.

Even though we kept Emma's party low key, it still took me out of my comfort zone. With seven little girls, one of Jonah's friends and two tiny siblings tearing through my house and grinding cake crumbs into the carpet, I developed a splitting headache. What if somebody stuck something into my outdated electrical sockets? Or spilled punch behind the couch and didn't tell anyone? Or clogged the circa 1970's toilet? Or stepped on Gypsy's tail and she snapped at them?

Maybe I should've scheduled the party outside the house after all. At least at a restaurant, someone else was liable for accidents and cleaning up messes.

I reminded myself I'd been dealing with chaos in the emergency room for years. This was different. Even though the kids seemed to be running the show, I was responsible should anything go wrong.

Barry smiled encouragingly and lifted his shoulders in surrender every time I looked like I might lose it. I needed to follow his example and relax and enjoy the party. What was the worst a houseful of kids could do? So I'd have to clean cake icing out of the carpet and sweep up a few broken heirlooms from Grandma Catherine's day. Emma looked relaxed and content for the first time in weeks. She didn't even seem to notice when I was out of her sight now and then.

I half expected Nicole to show up just as the party got into full swing and ruin everything. She always had the worst timing. But she didn't show. She didn't even call. It was sort of sad she couldn't be bothered to place a call on her daughter's birthday, but we were all probably better off that she didn't.

After the party I would renew my efforts to track her down. She was obviously unstable. If she was drinking again or in an unsafe relationship with Dean, anything could happen to her and we might never find out. How would I feel then? I didn't want anything bad to happen to her. For the most part, I just worried how her inevitable arrival would affect me.

I gladly relinquished the serving of cake and ice cream to Barry and Aunt Wanda. They seemed better suited for it than me. Afterward Uncle Jeb managed to corral the hyped up group and supervise games. I gladly stepped aside and let the other adults take the lead.

Huddled in a corner of the kitchen as far away from the confusion as I could get while still looking like part of the festivities, I watched Barry deflect a possible argument between Jonah and the girls. He helped one of the toddlers eat a bowl of ice cream and recaptured Caitlyn's flyaway red curls into her hair tie.

I had to admit a guy like him would be handy to have around. It would certainly make my life easier. No more spending half my paycheck on daycare. No more shuttling the kids to Aunt Wanda's when I had to be at work early. Barry was calm, levelheaded and a natural with kids. He could teach Jonah how to throw a fastball and show Emma how a real man was supposed to treat the woman he loved.

Not that I knew for certain Barry knew how to treat a woman. He was divorced after all. I'm sure the demise of his marriage wasn't entirely Sue's fault.

In the confusion of the party he didn't get a chance to ask me out—if he had planned to. I didn't have time to be disappointed until later. I still wasn't sure how I felt about entering the dating pool. Sometimes the thought of sharing the recent changes in my life with someone better suited at handling them was a great relief. Other times, I couldn't stop comparing Barry and every other man on the planet to Kyle. A future with him was impossible, so I needn't even go down that road.

Chapter Twenty-One

At the hospital, Louise Bell was taking her re-certification classes and needed me to cover her shift. For the next two weeks I had to be at work two hours earlier than usual.

With my love life on hold—this time because of a crazy work schedule and not due to my ability to alienate every man who looked at me—I took the kids to Aunt Wanda's and tucked them into bed in Violet's old room every night after dinner and bath time. She got them up around eight and took them to preschool where I picked them up at my usual time.

Emma hadn't shed any tears since her party. She was still clingy at home. She continued to follow me around in the afternoons telling me about her day or something silly Uncle Jeb had done that morning at breakfast. I didn't mind. At least I wasn't getting phone calls at work.

She pouted a little whenever I dropped her and Jonah off at Aunt Wanda's. She clung to my neck until I reassured her a dozen times I'd pick her up the next afternoon at preschool. Uncle Jeb was always there to read her and Jonah a bedtime story and to supervise teeth brushing. My departure wasn't overly traumatic.

At the first of March Louise finished her re-certification classes, and I began dropping the kids off at preschool again. The trees along the driveway were in full bud. Tulips and crocuses had bloomed and died in the flowerbeds almost without my notice. There was a scent of lilac and forsythia in the air, hinting of the beauty and glory to come. Going to work so early meant I hadn't seen my house in the daylight hours for a couple of weeks. Spring was my favorite season, and I hated to miss this one.

I pulled lightweight pants out of the drawer to dress Emma and Jonah my first day back on my regular schedule. Emma stood in the middle of her bedroom floor, an obstinate set to her jaw. She looked so much like her mother.

"I don't wanna go to school. I wanna go with you."

Not this again. It needed to end right here and now. I glared down at her, my expression leaving no room for debate. "Emma, get dressed. You're going to preschool with your brother and I'm going to work. Now dry those tears and let's go."

She crossed her arms over her chest. "No."

I gaped. Open rebellion. From Emma, no less! I recovered quickly. "I said get dressed, young lady. I'm not putting up with any nonsense this morning. I'm not going to let you make us late."

Rather than caving in to my demands like usual, her jaw tightened. She clenched her fists, reared her head back and bellowed, "Nooo! I ain't goin'."

By now I was as angry as she was and only a little more under control.

"Oh, yes you are." I took her by the arm, led her to the bed and sat her on it. "You're in no position to tell me what you are or aren't going to do. I'm the boss around here."

As mad as I was, I realized I sounded just like Grandma Catherine. There was a key difference in us though. I loved Emma and cared about what she was going through. Still, I didn't have the time or patience to deal with a five-year-old who suddenly developed a stubborn streak.

"You get dressed right this minute, little missy, or I'll do it for you."

I winced at Grandma's words coming out of my mouth.

She scowled up at me with no sign of acquiescence on her face.

"Which is it going to be?" I demanded.

The metamorphosis took over her face gradually. The scowl transformed from a pucker into a pout until silent tears slid down her cheeks. She never took her eyes off my face as she blinked rapidly in a valiant but failing effort to keep from crying. My determination crumbled. I tried to keep my serious look in place. The look that said someone who barely reached my belt buckle would not run my house. Looking into that sweet, crestfallen face threatened to snap even my iron will. Before I could say anything, Jonah appeared next to me and climbed onto the bed beside his sister.

"Don't cry, Emmy. She'll come back. She always does."

I ground my teeth as tears pushed at the back of my eyes. I turned away so they wouldn't see.

Nicole.

I should've known.

Wasn't it enough I had given her children a safe home while she was enjoying her respite from motherhood? Must I now argue with her daughter every time I tried to walk out the front door? I thought of calling Aunt Wanda and asking her to come over until Emma calmed down. If possible, she could drive them to preschool later. This was my problem. I couldn't keep letting other people handle things.

Emma shook her head. The tears spilled faster.

After a covert glance at my watch, I lowered myself to the bed between them. I wrapped my arms around them. "I know you guys get scared sometimes, and that's okay. I get scared too. But everything will be all right. I promise."

Jonah pulled away from me so he could look into my face. "You can't get scared, Aunt Shell. You're a grown up."

I smiled and squeezed him against me. "Grown ups get scared all the time, Jonah. We worry that our kids will get picked on at school. We worry about having money to buy you toys and take you to the zoo. We get scared when you're sick. But it's okay. We just have to believe everything will work out all right. We have to trust…"

I wasn't sure how to finish the sentence. Trust. How could I explain such an abstract concept to preschoolers without a bunch of empty platitudes I didn't believe myself?

"God?"

I turned to Emma in surprise. Wouldn't that be an easy way out? Turn all my cares over to a Supreme Being who supposedly loved me and wanted the best for me if only I'd allow it.

Cast your burdens on Jesus for he cares for you.

The line of a song from somewhere in my past rushed unbidden to my mind. I gave up trusting Jesus years ago. I had trusted, or wanted to trust, and it got me nowhere.

I remembered the gentle urging I experienced during the New Year's Eve service at Kyle's church. What if Jesus was up there waiting to take my burdens because he truly did care for me?

"Yes, we can trust God, Emma," I said with more confidence than I felt. "He'll help you when you're scared and worried about…things."

"How?" she asked. She looked around the room. "I don't see him."

I wondered the same thing myself more than once. "Well, um…"

"He lives in your heart, silly," Jonah stated. "That's why you can't see him."

"Yeah, right," I agreed. I tapped her chest with my finger. "He lives right here inside each of us. We just have to believe."

"I believe, Aunt Shell," Jonah said.

I gave him another squeeze. "I'm so happy, Jonah. Maybe you can help Emma be brave when you see she's scared or worried."

He nodded gravely. "I'll try."

Emma worked her bottom lip before she finally answered, "I'll be brave."

"Oh, Emma, we know you will. You're such a brave girl already. You make me proud every day. You know that, don't you?"

She looked doubtful.

I lifted her onto my lap. "You do, and Jonah, too. I'm proud of both of you. Me and Gypsy and Uncle Jeb and Aunt Wanda are so glad you came to live with us."

I was shocked to feel tears sting my eyes. I *was* glad, but it took me actually speaking the words to realize it.

I kissed them goodbye at the preschool, making as small a production of my departure as possible. Miss Gail stood at the ready in case Emma planned to bolt or kick and scream like she had the last time I dropped her off. Miss Gail started chattering about needing a helper and wondering if Emma was up for the job. Emma lowered her head and alternately studied the floor and me. Her lip quivered dangerously. A fat tear glistened in the corner of her eye. My own lip quivered. For the first time in my life, I considered calling in sick.

I couldn't. I had to be strong. The girl had to learn those big tears wouldn't mean she automatically got her way. With fierce resolve, I reached for the door handle. I was needed at work, and I needed my job.

I glanced back one last time and saw Jonah take her hand. "Don't cry, Emmy. She'll come back. She always does."

I hadn't been late for work in three weeks. The distressing phone calls in the middle of a shift stopped. I wasn't naïve enough to think the problem was over. Just temporarily on hold. Still, I was thankful for the respite, however brief.

Barry called once to ask if I saw a free evening on my horizon. I was almost relieved to have the excuse of a busy schedule to turn him down. Going out with him would be nice, but there was so much tension in my life, I wasn't sure I was ready to add something else. Especially with everything going on with Emma.

It didn't help that I couldn't stop thinking of Kyle and hoping I would run into him every time I pulled into the church parking lot to pick up the kids. I wished I could stop torturing myself over him. We had nothing in common anymore. We were high school sweethearts who were never really meant to end up together. Our lives had taken completely different paths. No amount of daydreaming or imagining him curled up beside me on the sofa watching DVDs with the kids would change that.

Emma still dragged her feet and looked close to tears every morning when I dropped her off at preschool, but at least she was getting dressed without threats from me. That was something.

Mondays and Wednesdays when I worked late and picked the kids up at Angie's, she reported Emma was withdrawn and clingy, but there were fortunately no tears. Angie told me what nearly broke her heart was how Emma stared at the door and kept one ear cocked for the sound of my car in the driveway, regardless of what she was doing. Once I arrived, everything was right as rain. A happy, bubbling Emma vied for my attention and wanted to tell me everything she'd done that day all in one breath.

As thanks for me covering for her during her re-certification training, Louise finagled her workload to allow me to leave early one beautiful Thursday afternoon. The unexpected short workday and three-day weekend staring me in the face put me in a better mood than I once thought possible. I used to feel lost when I wasn't at work. Sometime over the last six months, I had turned into one of those people who couldn't wait for the workday to end.

I forgot what it meant to get to the preschool so early in the afternoon until I pulled into the church parking lot and saw the heavy curtains strung across the front doors. It was naptime and would be until three o'clock. I hated to go in and wake Emma and Jonah. They got out of bed so early every morning they were complete bears by evening if they didn't get their daily two-hour naps at preschool. Nor did I want to risk waking another child and making permanent enemies of the staff.

I was sitting there wondering if I had time to run a few errands when I saw the other set of doors farther down the building open and Kyle step outside. I watched as he went to the mailbox and gathered the mail.

I would've thought his secretary could take care of jobs like that until I remembered the position wasn't fulltime. Did that mean the church was having financial difficulties? Was Kyle skimming money from the tithes to hide a gambling problem?

I shook my head at the conspiracy theories rising inside me and scrunched down in my seat so he wouldn't see me. I hadn't seen him since the last Preschool Sunday. That day I had gone out of my way to avoid talking to him. Watching him move around the parking lot in his rumpled khakis and untucked shirt was making my heart do uncomfortable things. It wasn't fair that a human being could look so good without even trying. I sure didn't want him to see me after a long day at work, all sweaty and smelly, my hair doing its own thing and not a shadow of makeup remaining on my face.

Seeing him after all these years and striking up an old friendship shouldn't bother me the way it did. Just like Emma needed to realize her mother would come back when she was good and ready, my heart needed to accept there could never be anything between me and Kyle Swann. I needed to forget he existed, much as I had for the last fifteen years.

He spotted my car, squinted to make sure I was inside and waved. Feeling ridiculous for trying to hide from him in the first place, I straightened up to my full height and waved back.

I groaned as he headed my way. I combed my fingers through my hair and ran my tongue over my teeth. I'd been up since five-thirty and would've done anything for a toothbrush. I didn't bother checking my reflection in the rearview mirror. The less I knew, the better. It was too late anyway to hastily apply lipstick or pinch my cheeks for color. I turned the key in the ignition to lower the window.

"Why are you sitting out here?" he asked when he was close enough to be heard without yelling.

"Naptime." I indicated the door with a nod of my head.

He followed my gaze and then put his finger to his lips. "Must be very quiet," he said in a stage whisper, "or every teacher in there will have your hide."

I laughed. "I learned that the hard way. Back when the kids first started, I didn't even notice the curtains on the door one day and went stomping in during naptime. It was pitch black and I couldn't see where I was going. I walked right into the cubby boxes before Miss Mary caught up with me and saved me from injuring myself."

By now we were laughing out loud. "I tripped over a kid once," he admitted. "I was on my way to Billie's office for some insurance paperwork and was concentrating on the ray of light underneath her door when I banged my shin on this little guy's cot. Fortunately, I caught myself before I fell on top of him."

I laughed even harder as I pictured tall, athletic Kyle hobbling around in a circle trying to regain his balance without falling on and crushing a sleeping child.

"It's not funny. I had a knot on my shin for two weeks." He glanced at his watch. "They won't start waking the kids for another forty-five minutes. Why don't you come inside my office to wait? I promise the lights are on on my end of the building so you won't trip over anything. Besides, I'm freezing."

I hadn't realized he didn't have his coat on. It was February and still much too cold to be outside without a coat. I glanced at the clock on the dash and then the front door. Spending the next forty-five minutes with Kyle sounded more appealing than a quick trip to the supermarket or waiting in line at the bank.

Actually it sounded more appealing than anything else I could think of. I enjoyed his company even if I did find myself stumbling over words and worrying about my appearance way too much. He made me feel like a silly nervous teenager. I needed to remember we were adults. What we had in high school was long gone. I wasn't sure whether or not we had been in love, and it no longer mattered. All that mattered was Kyle was a pastor. If he was looking for a relationship, it surely wouldn't be with someone as hopelessly lost as me.

Chapter Twenty-Two

I got out of the car and followed him to the main entrance of the church. "Want something to drink?" he asked as I settled into an oversized, leather chair in his office. He went to a small refrigerator and opened the door.

"Water would be great if you have it."

He removed two bottles from the refrigerator and handed me one. He sat down in the chair next to mine. The chairs were angled to face the desk and each other. Conducive to open communication, I supposed. Research had probably been done to see which furniture arrangement got couples talking and problems solved in the most time-efficient manner. Our knees nearly touched. Kyle discreetly slid his chair a few inches away from mine to allow more space between us. He had also left the door open, I noted. No impropriety here.

"How's everything going with the kids?" he asked.

Always a first question now that I was playing Mommy.

"Great. Emma recognizes all her letters and numbers, and she can write most of them. Jonah has practically a photographic memory when it comes to new songs and scripture verses. He comes home quoting something new every day."

Kyle rested his elbows on the arms of the chair and leaned toward me. "They're really bright kids. I knew once they got over their awkwardness, they would excel here."

"I wouldn't say that exactly. Emma's going through a rough stretch right now. She hardly lets me out of her sight. It's not so bad at home. But it's murder every morning when I have to go to work. Sometimes I have to get a little rough with her and then I feel like a heel all day."

"She's afraid you're going to leave one day and never come back, just like her mother did."

I shook my head. "No, it's not that. She misses Nicole, and she's displaced her frustration on me. I mean, we aren't that close. Well, we are, but not like mother and daughter or anything. She prefers Aunt Wanda and Uncle Jeb over me any day."

"Michelle, her behavior is classic. She hasn't seen her Mom in what…four months?"

"Five and a half."

"You said yourself neither she nor Jonah has outwardly expressed much concern over Nicole. It's you Emma is worried about. First her Mom disappears without a word. She survives. She and Jonah find out they can get along pretty well without her. They're safe, happy, mentally stimulated for probably the first time in their lives. It's only natural for Emma to start to feel insecure within her new world. What happens if you disappear the way Mommy did? In her mind, there are no guarantees that you won't. What will she do then? Where will they go the next time? What if the new situation isn't as nice as the one they're in now?"

I considered his words. "I guess that makes sense. When I dropped them off at preschool the other morning, Jonah said, 'Don't worry, she always comes back.' He said the same thing at home, but I thought he was talking about Nicole. I've never given them any reason to think I'm leaving. Nothing's changed in our routine. We do the exact same thing every day. They go to preschool and I go to work. Then we go home, go to bed and do it all again the next day. They say kids need routine, structure. Well, they're not getting anything else at my house."

"Then keep it up. Eventually Emma will realize she can trust you. That you're not going to leave her in somebody's yard."

I shuddered. "I guess that is an unimaginable thing for a five-year-old to ponder."

"It's unimaginable at any age. I suggest you talk to her. Tell her you know what she's afraid of and you understand it. Don't tell her she has no reason to worry. In her mind she has every reason to worry. Just be understanding and patient. She'll start to feel secure again if she knows you care about what she's going through."

Tears pricked my eyelids. Poor Emma. No wonder she cried every time I walked away from her. She was scared to death I would get bored or distracted, or worse, that I would decide I didn't love her enough to come back. What a jerk I'd been for yelling at her about it.

I wanted to run into the preschool right now and scoop her into my arms and assure her none of that would ever happen.

Of course an overreaction on my part would make the situation worse.

"You're actually pretty good at this," I said to Kyle with a watery smile.

"It comes with the territory."

"I guess I keep forgetting what your job is."

"Even before God called me, he made me a good listener."

I nodded though I didn't really know what to make of the 'calling' comment. "You were the one everybody went to for advice, even in high school."

"Everybody but you. You were the together one. So aloof and in control. You didn't need anybody."

I snorted. "Was that what everyone thought? I was a mess. I guess there's no harm in admitting it now. Everything about everybody is an act in high school."

Kyle closed the space between us by a small degree. I could feel the warmth from his body though he was still several feet away. The clean spicy scent of his laundry detergent filled my nostrils. I needed to get up and leave right now. I was better off in my car with the heater blasting than sitting here next to him.

"I have to admit I started hanging out with you because you were cool and mysterious," he said. "It didn't take long though to realize you weren't as together as you let everybody believe."

I took a sip of my water. "What was the giveaway?"

"Lots of things. For one, I learned a little bit about your home life. Just what you told me, of course. It was a long time before you actually invited me to your house. I couldn't believe a teenager was almost wholly responsible for taking care of her little sister along with all the other responsibilities you had. And then there was your grandma." He arched his eyebrows. "She was a piece of work. You two treated each other like adversaries, on guard all the time."

I had forgotten that, but he was absolutely right. "You really do pay attention to what goes on around you."

"Only what interests me."

"Does that mean I interested you?"

Easy, Michelle. Do you really want an answer?

He sobered and gave me a piercing look. "You already know. Maybe you still do."

"Still what? Interest you?"

His expression didn't change.

"In what way?" I demanded caustically. "As a hopeless reprobate in need of saving?"

He ignored my cynicism. "Not in the least. Believe me, it'd be easier if those were the only feelings I had for you."

I took another sip of my water and screwed on the lid, my knuckles white against the cap. I wished he wouldn't talk like this. He needed a godly woman. The perfect pastor's wife. Not a heathen like me with no desire to change her life. It was bad enough I couldn't stop thinking about him. He shouldn't waste his time thinking about me.

"I'm not the person I used to be, Kyle. You don't know anything about me except I'm not a Christian."

He sat back in his chair, deflated. "That I do know."

I set the water bottle on his desk and tensed to stand. "Naptime will be over in a little bit. I think I'll wait in the hallway."

He leaned forward and held up his hand. "Michelle, wait, I'm sorry. I didn't mean to upset you."

"You didn't upset me."

He thought he was a good listener? That it came with the territory? I'd give him something to listen to. Something to make him think twice about entertaining an interest in me.

"My whole life I tried to make the people I love, love me back. First it was Dad. He was the coolest person in the world as far as I was concerned. I thought he hung the moon. I was Daddy's little girl. Then, poof, he was gone." I flexed my fingers at him.

"I was lost without him. Mom was devastated, so I tried to be everything for her. Our relationship had never been as close as Dad's and mine, but she needed me and I needed to be needed. I was really into that back then. Needing someone to need me."

With a start, I realized I still needed it. I needed it desperately.

I wasn't sure why it was so important for Kyle to understand. He remained silent.

"Mom moved us back to the farm, and I tried to comfort her as best I could. Grandma seemed to relish tearing her down a peg or two every day, so I became her buffer. I thought she appreciated it. For a year or two, we muddled through. Mom, Nicole, and me against Grandma and Aunt Wanda with their side always winning. But Mom needed me. I tried to be extra good so Grandma wouldn't hate us being here so much. It was already hard to keep the house quiet and un-chaotic with a little kid like Nicole plowing through it. I did what I could to settle things down. I wanted to protect all of them, even Grandma Catherine. I didn't want Mom getting into more trouble than she already was. I thought I was doing a good job of holding things together.

"You should've seen the look on her face when she'd come home from an especially hard day at work and I'd have dinner cooking on the stove or the laundry done or Nicole already bathed and smelling sweet in her pajamas. That look of appreciation from Mom was worth giving up my childhood. I wanted her to love me, to need me, to realize that without me, life would be so difficult. So empty.

"I thought it was working. Then one Friday afternoon my cousin Violet and me got off the school bus and found Grandma and Aunt Wanda sitting at the kitchen table with these grave looks on their faces. Aunt Wanda looked like she'd been crying. Grandma just looked mad. Madder than I'd ever seen her."

I paused, remembering that awful day with absolute clarity. It was a day I seldom allowed myself to relive. It had taken about ten years to get those looks out of my thoughts during the day and out of my dreams at night.

Kyle listened with a look of compassion on his face but no pity. I appreciated that. The time for pity was nearly twenty years too late. I took a deep breath and continued.

"Grandma told me and Violet what happened. I think she actually enjoyed the moment. She had this look of triumph in her eyes behind the aggravation like she always knew her daughter would never amount to anything, and Mom had just gone and proved it.

"'Your Mom's took off,' she said. Just like that. Catherine Boyle didn't believe in sugar coating anything. 'She up and sneaked out this morning after you got on the bus.' My first thought was Nicole. Nicole was Mom's darling, and I thought that meant she took Nicole with her and had left me behind. Grandma must've read my mind because she added real quick, 'Nicole's still here. Your mother up and left, leaving her own baby behind like an old dog you'd leave by the side of the road.'

"I wanted to run upstairs and bawl my eyes out, but their eyes had me rooted to the spot. It was like she and Aunt Wanda were blaming me. My mother was weak and spineless, and because of my failure as a daughter, she couldn't take anymore and had to leave.

"I stood there and listened to the play by play of what they thought drove Mom out. Neither of them said it had anything to do with me, but they didn't have to. I knew what they were thinking. They were furious at Mom and Dad for leaving Grandma saddled with two kids she didn't particularly care for. I was old enough to know I would be the one to pay for it.

"I was pretty well finished with caring for anybody after that. Except for Nicole. She was crazy about me, and I was pretty sure she wasn't going anywhere. But everyone else…" I batted the air with my hand. "Forget it. Apparently, I never mattered to them as much as they mattered to me, and they ended up taking off on me anyway. I was through caring for anybody or anything. No more getting burned. For about a year I was pretty sullen. I tried not to let it show because I knew it gave Grandma some kind of warped satisfaction. I put on a brave face and went on as best I could as if none of it mattered, but anybody with half a brain could see through that façade.

"It was too hard to maintain for any length of time though. For one thing, I was only fourteen. Then there was Nicole. She needed somebody to look after her, to be the buffer between her and Grandma, like I had been between Grandma and Mom. Good ole Michelle stepped up to the plate again. Now when I was fixing dinner and doing laundry and keeping Nicole out from underfoot, it was for Grandma. I wanted her to see what an asset I was to have around. I don't know why I bothered. It hadn't done a lick of good making Mom care about me."

I reached out a shaky hand and twisted the lid off my water. I took a long swallow. I didn't want to cry sitting so close to Kyle. I wasn't sure why I was even bothering with the retelling. I should stop talking, get the kids and go home. Reliving my past wouldn't do anyone any good. But I couldn't stop now if I tried.

I set the water bottle back on the desk and continued, my eyes on the window over the desk instead of on him. "I lived at home while I went to nursing school so I could keep up with housework and keep costs down. I started paying the taxes on the farm as soon as I could afford it. I brought food into the house every payday."

My voice cracked, but I kept going.

"Grandma Catherine never gave me as much as a thank you. After awhile she even started handing me lists on my way out the door on Fridays. I thought for sure all the help around the house and the money would make her love me. If nothing else, at least she would respect me. But she didn't."

I heaved a shuddering sigh, the tears dangerously close to the surface. "Maybe she did a little in spite of herself. She did leave the farm to me. Some of the cousins had the nerve to get mad about it, even though I was the one here taking care of her in her old age and the one who took care of her affairs after she died. They never stopped their busy, important lives for a minute or two to help me out. Not that I blame them," I added with a laugh that sounded more like a croak.

"Grandma wasn't someone whose company you'd seek out on purpose. But they sure balked when the will was read. Now the farm is mine. For as long as I live anyway. Since I don't have any direct heirs, when I die, it'll be split between Uncle DeWitt, if he's still around, and Aunt Wanda or her descendants. Grandma never considered I might have descendants of my own."

I chuckled humorlessly. "Why should she? Like her, I'll live there till I die and then let the family step in and do whatever they want with the place."

"I've spent my life trying to make people love me," I repeated. "I've done everything I could think of to earn their love. No one ever loved me back. I guess I'm not loveable. My own mother and father didn't love me enough to stay, or to even stay in touch after they took off. Grandma didn't love me, period. Even Nicole, who loved me more than anybody, didn't love me enough to take any of my advice.

"As far as God's concerned, obviously I'm not worth his time either. I prayed to him the whole time I sat next to Grandma in that stuffy church of hers, listening to the pastor talk about God's grace and mercy. I asked him to bring my parents back. Then I asked him to make Grandma love me or at least treat me like a person. Finally, I just prayed he would love me since no one else did. Even that didn't happen. I couldn't even be good enough to make God love me."

I threw up my hands in an exaggerated manner and smiled flippantly. "There's no hope for me. Right, Pastor? I'm too old to change. Too much water under the bridge. For the first time in my life, I have two people who love me unconditionally. And I love them back. Yes, they're just kids, and they probably love me for the same reasons I loved at that age— because I pulled them out from under the lilac bushes and took them to Wal-Mart and bought them pretty clothes and took them to birthday parties. They love me because I'm a good aunt. If the good times end tomorrow, they'll stop loving me just like everyone else has."

I shrugged like it didn't matter, though we both knew it did. "What's the difference? It's just the way things are. I'll keep loving them, buying them stuff and taking care of them. Someday they'll grow up and realize I'm not as great as they thought I was. They'll see they can do just as well without me, and they'll stop loving me like everyone before them. So I'll enjoy the feeling while it lasts. Afterwards, I guess I'll be on my own again. It's not like I can't take care of myself.

"But, God—no. He may be in heaven showering his favored few with blessings. I'm just not one of them. Whatever it takes to earn his favor, I haven't done it, and I'm too stubborn to try. I guess I'm too old for games."

I sat back in my chair, too tired to bother any longer with the phony smile. It hadn't been as easy as I thought to be flippant about the pain of my past. It still hurt that my parents disappeared when I needed them. It hurt that my grandmother had never seen me as anything other than a burden. It especially hurt that God chose to bless some while ignoring ones like me. I could play the role of the agnostic all I wanted, but disregard from a God whose existence I couldn't deny no matter how badly I wanted to, was hard to laugh off.

Kyle's hand slid across the desk and covered mine. I pulled it away and nibbled at a cuticle. Neither of us said anything for a long time. Kyle rested his elbows on the chair arms and made a teepee with his fingers. He stared at his hands while I continued to attack the cuticle, making mincemeat of my nails.

Finally, he dropped his hands. "That's the thing about God." His voice was soft and soothing. "You don't have to do one thing to earn his love or his favor. It is a free gift waiting for you to reach out and take it."

I wanted to reach over and slap him. Had he heard a word I said?

"You've been trying to capture the wind in your hands, Michelle."

I brought my eyes up to meet his. Heat from confusion and anger seared my face.

"The reason you haven't found God is not that He's hiding. It's because you tried to earn his favor the same way you tried with everyone else in your life. You can't earn his love, just like you can't push it away. God isn't a person who can fail you. He's your loving heavenly father. He's right here, waiting. The Holy Spirit has been working in your heart for years. That's why you are the way you are. You are a gentle and tender spirit, always trying to please everyone but yourself."

"No, Kyle, I'm not," I spat. "I'm selfish. I never wanted to be saddled with Nicole's kids. Why do you think I never stepped in to help her out before? I knew she was barely holding it together in the city, but I didn't care. Why didn't I just go to Memphis and take the kids? She would've handed them over and been glad to do it. Instead I never let myself think about it at all. I'm not gentle and compassionate. I want my life back. I truly resented those kids messing up my perfectly uncomplicated life just like Grandma Catherine resented me."

At the sound of Grandma's name, my voice cracked again. I covered my face with my hands and gave way to the tears. "Just like Grandma," I sputtered between heaves.

Kyle's hand on the back of my head made the tears flow even harder. I wasn't good with sympathy, but I didn't pull away. I didn't want the contact to end.

He pushed a Kleenex into my hand and smoothed my hair away from my face. "It's all right," he said soothingly.

His chair grated over the low pile carpet as he moved closer. The leather creaked under his weight. I sensed him standing over me. Still crying, I raised my head and wiped my face with the Kleenex. I stood and moved into his open arms.

He kept making soothing sounds in my ear. One hand continued to smooth my hair away from my face. The other cradled my back. His arms tightened around me. I lifted my face at the same time he looked down. He put his hand on my chin so I wouldn't turn away, not that I was considering it. He lowered his face to mine. Our lips met. I leaned into him, grateful for his strong arms around me.

Abruptly, the kiss ended. He pulled back, his face stricken. "Michelle, I..."

A tiny noise of surprise and dismay escaped my throat. Words wouldn't form.

Kyle dropped his arms as if the touch of my skin burned him. He stepped back. His legs bumped against the chair he had been sitting in. "I—I'm sorry." Hastily he moved around the desk and straightened some papers with trembling hands.

My hands shook, too. Every part of me was shaking. I felt cold, disoriented.

"I—no, Kyle, I'm sorry..." I reached for my purse that had slipped onto the floor. "I...um...I'm sure naptime's over. I'll— I better go get the kids."

He nodded while he continued to straighten papers that didn't need straightening. Finally he forced his hands to stop, took a deep breath and looked at me for the first time since going around the desk. "Michelle, you know I care for you. I don't want you to think..."

I raised my hand to cut him off. I couldn't bear to hear another word. The last thing I wanted was an apology for kissing me. "No, Kyle, I understand completely." I turned and hurried to the door.

"I don't think you do," he said from the safety of the other side of the desk.

Chapter Twenty-Three

The next morning while the kids constructed a fort out of sofa cushions in the living room, I sat huddled in the kitchen with my cell phone and hoped they wouldn't walk in until my call was finished.

Kyle was right about a lot of things. I was wasting my time trying to catch the wind in my hands. I couldn't change people into who I wanted them to be. I couldn't make someone love me or need me simply because it was imperative that I be loved and needed. It wasn't a given that husbands loved their wives and parents loved their children. Maybe love and romance and passion weren't in the cards for me, but I could still be happy.

It was a little depressing to think my happiness wouldn't include Kyle. Regardless of whether he was interested or not, there could never be anything between us. Our kiss had been a mistake. I knew it the instant I saw the panicked look on his face. I felt something for him. I probably always would. But he could never reciprocate. Like everyone else in my life, I would never mean as much to him as he meant to me. That didn't mean I didn't want love or need to be needed.

Kyle Swann was out of my life. Period. That didn't mean I didn't have needs. I wasn't going to waste one more day chasing after things I couldn't have. Nor was I going to hide out on the farm or at work the way I'd always done and pretend I was fine.

"Hi, Barry," I said around a painted-on smile when he picked up on the other end as if he could see me in my stretched out t-shirt and the sweats I'd turned into shorts last summer when all my others were in the laundry. "How are you? Long time, no hear."

His end was silent for a moment. He was either trying to identify my voice or come up with a way to let me down gently without hurting my feelings. It hadn't occurred to me until this very minute I could be the last person he wanted to talk to. There was an awful lot of that going around.

"Michelle?" His voice croaked in seeming disbelief. "I'm good. How are you?"

"Good. I'm good." For a moment I couldn't remember what I planned to accomplish with this call. At least he hadn't hung up on me yet. "Hey, um, I was wondering, would you be interested in dinner or something, maybe, tomorrow night? I'm off this weekend and thought we might get together."

"Just the two of us?"

"Sure. You mentioned that Italian restaurant in Genoa a while back."

"Angelino's?"

"Yes, Angelino's. I still haven't been there."

"Me either."

"How about we try it out together? Around seven?" I hoped I didn't sound as pathetic to him as I did to myself.

"Okay. Sounds good."

"Great. Do you want to pick me up here at the house? Or we can meet…" I wasn't sure how dating worked when I was the one to initiate it. Should I pick him up? Did it mean I had to pay for dinner? Would we split everything? Wasn't that what people did now?

I hadn't put enough thought into this.

"No, no. I'll pick you up," he was saying as though he didn't find me pathetic at all. "Seven works for me."

"Okay, great. See you then. Bye."

"Bye."

I hung up the phone and sank into the kitchen chair winded. I wasn't completely sure what I was doing. Barry didn't exactly send my heart into overdrive, but he seemed interested. Maybe that was how all strong relationships started. No fireworks. Just two people who sort of weren't repulsed by each other.

Barry was a nice person, a good provider and a great father who wasn't afraid to get down in the trenches. Good husband material by anyone's standards. And he liked me. What was I saving myself for? There wasn't anyone else beating down my front door. A union between us would make three little kids very happy. Who knew? It might also be what I was looking for. I was tired of living every day one step closer to the grave with nothing to show for it but a healthy bank account and no personal connections.

All I knew was I didn't want to be alone anymore.

The next evening, I fed the kids around five and walked them across the field to Aunt Wanda's. I gave her and Uncle Jeb few details about my plans other than a reminder that they could reach me any time on my cell. The kids knew I was having dinner with Caitlyn's dad. It wouldn't take much prying before one of them blabbed the whole story.

"Aunt Shell's on a date. She's gonna find us a daddy."

Good grief. Was that what I doing? I wanted to go upstairs to my room and hide under the covers for a week or two.

I concentrated on shaking the discomfort of everyone knowing my business and set about making myself beautiful. I managed to tame the frizziness out of my honey blond hair. I was overdue for a trim, but there was no time to do anything about that now. With the help of eyeliner, foundation, mascara and a little blush on my cheekbones—none of which I was completely sure how to apply—I became as beautiful as I was ever going to get. I put an extra layer of powder on my nose to disguise my freckles. I dabbed some lipstick on my lips but decided it wasn't a good shade for me and scrubbed it off. Barry had seen me at my worst during those long, sweaty field trips last summer. He knew what he was getting.

The restaurant was fashionably lit which made me feel better about my lack of cosmetic expertise. The maître d' led us to a secluded table, offered the wine list, which we declined, and made his retreat.

I fingered the crisp stitching on the linen napkin and fiddled with my water glass. Barry clasped his hands in front of him. "I'm glad we're finally doing this, Michelle."

"Me too. I haven't eaten in a restaurant with cloth napkins in a long time."

We both laughed. "You look lovely tonight," he said.

I smiled demurely. I hadn't received many compliments on my appearance before and wasn't sure how to react to one. "Thank you. You're not so bad yourself."

He grinned. "Why are we so much more comfortable together when there are three preschoolers vying for our attention?"

I exhaled with relief. "Oh, good. I thought it was just me."

After that, the evening went much smoother. We found plenty to talk about, most often the kids, sometimes work, and with no uncomfortable lulls in between. After dinner we drove downtown to the renovated historic district. Quaint shops, which probably didn't make much money in a town the size of Genoa, lined the sidewalks. We strolled along in companionable silence and window-shopped. Halfway down one street, Barry took my hand to point out a particular window display and didn't let go. Even as out of practice as I was with men, I knew he had done it on purpose. It felt a little strange but nice. This whole dating/relationship building thing would take some getting used to. We weren't an old married couple who'd been holding hands for years, and we weren't teenagers. I supposed this was how dating worked in your thirties.

All the way home I agonized over the goodnight kiss. Should I or shouldn't I? Would he expect it? I tried to stop worrying. I was a grown woman. A kiss didn't have to mean anything. Practical strangers did it every day.

I thought of the man I had kissed just the other day. My face had been blotchy and tear stained. My knees had been trembling so hard I thought for sure Kyle would hear them knocking together. I hadn't worried about my makeup or frizzy hair or the lack of jewelry to accentuate my long neck. I had just wanted to stay in Kyle's arms forever.

Then he pushed me away and fled to his side of the desk.

I took a deep breath and glanced at Barry out of the corner of my eye. Would he ever make me feel the way Kyle did? I wouldn't know if I didn't give him a chance.

Barry pulled his car into the driveway behind mine. The house was dark except for the porch light. I should've left a light on. The house looked lonely without the kids inside.

"I'm glad you called me, Michelle," he said after a moment's silence.

"So am I. I had a good time."

"We'll have to go back. The food was really good."

"I thought so too."

Was he waiting for me to invite him inside for drinks or something? Didn't a man automatically translate such offers into an invitation to bed? Especially a divorced man anticipating the end of an evening with a woman my age. We weren't kids.

I took hold of the door handle. My fingers were slick with sweat against the cool metal. "Well, thanks a lot, Barry."

I took a deep breath. Still clinging to the door, I turned in the seat and looked back at him. He cupped my chin and leaned toward me. My breath quickened. I let go of the door and moved into his arms. His kiss was nice. Warm and comfortable. No passion or fireworks like I experienced with Kyle but nice, nonetheless.

After the kiss I swallowed my earlier nerves and hitched my purse onto my shoulder.

"I'll call you later," Barry said.

I nodded brightly, his kiss still warm on my lips. "I hope so. Drive carefully."

We shared an affable smile before I hopped out of the car. I gave him a little finger wave and started up the walk. He waited until I unlocked the door, turned on a light and stepped inside before he drove away.

I gave him another wave, though I doubted he could see me and closed the door. I couldn't decide how I felt. I had a nice time. It was fun getting to know Barry better and making it all the way through a meal without having to stop to take someone to the bathroom.

If I'd typed Barry's qualities and my needs into a computer, his picture would've popped up. Two lonely, hard working, generous people with preschoolers. On paper, we were a perfect match.

Kyle and I, on the other hand, had nothing in common unless you counted a minor relationship fifteen years earlier before either of us knew who we were. Kyle was a man after God's own heart. I was a cynical ex-church-goer who doubted God's existence. Anybody could tell we had absolutely no future together. Even if we were perfectly suited, Kyle hadn't asked me out while Barry had sought out my company repeatedly.

I went through the house to the kitchen and dropped my purse on the table. I opened the back door to let Gypsy out and headed upstairs. With the kids spending the night at Aunt Wanda's, I had a rare night to myself. I tried not to spend it comparing Barry to Kyle. It wasn't fair to either of them. They were totally different people. Just like I was different from Barry's ex and every available, single woman in Kyle's congregation.

From this moment on, I would stop gauging every man I met on the Kyle-meter in my head. Kyle was out of my life. Barry wasn't. I touched my fingers to my lips and relived the kiss we had shared. Once again, life had thrown me a curve I hadn't been prepared to catch. So far, it had worked out well with the kids. Who was to say it couldn't do the same with Barry?

Chapter Twenty-Four

There were two texts waiting on my phone from Barry the next morning. He wrote in the first one he'd had a nice time and added a simple; "See you soon." in the next.

I smiled at the warmth that filled my belly. Someone besides the kids and Gypsy wanted to spend time with me. It was a nice sensation.

I enjoyed a brief image of us growing old together. Sitting side by side in the bleachers at one of Jonah's basketball games and again as we watched Emma and Caitlyn receive high school diplomas. The girls would become sisters instead of just friends. Jonah would finally have an attentive, caring father like all boys needed. They would be part of a complete family. Not only the kids. I would be part of one too.

I didn't allow Nicole to intrude into my fantasy. Someday she would come back. Just when the kids and I were getting comfortable with the way things were and settling into our lives, she would barge in and mess everything up.

Not for the first time, I realized my thoughts of Nicole were changing too. For the longest time I resented her staying away and saddling me with her kids. Now, suddenly, I didn't want her to come back. Ever. The kids and I had built a nice life. I had come to love and appreciate my extended family. We were no longer merely neighbors who happened to be related to each other. I looked forward to seeing them when I went to pick up the kids from a long day at work. I liked hearing Aunt Wanda's voice on the other end of the phone telling me she was on her way to the store and did I need milk. Or that Uncle Jeb was making homemade ice cream and we should come over and get some before he ate it all.

Still, I couldn't help thinking something was missing.

I punched into the phone that I enjoyed last night, too, and I looked forward to seeing him again. I studied the screen for a moment before deleting what I'd written. I always put too much in a text. I added a smiley emoji and hit send before I could reconsider. Short and sweet. That's what texts were for. Not sarcasm or witty banter or philosophy.

Smiley emoji.

Send.

Nothing else was required.

I didn't know if anything would develop between Barry and me. All I knew was I didn't need to think about it right now. Just like I didn't need to torture myself over Nicole's imminent return. Sometimes life needed to happen the way it was going to happen, whether I was in charge or not.

I put off talking to the kids about Emma's separation anxiety and any shared fears until Sunday evening. I probably should've done it as soon as I left Kyle's office on Thursday, but it had been a pretty busy weekend. After the success of my date with Barry—which had taken the sting out of Kyle's rebuff—I felt equipped to handle the talk I needed to have with the kids.

Nicole hadn't called again, despite Jonah's assurances to Emma that she would come back. My heart no longer jumped into my throat every time my phone rang or I received a text notification. I hadn't told anyone about her call the day after Christmas. Not even Aunt Wanda. She would just worry and tell me I needed to do something permanent before Nicole showed up shoving her parental rights in our faces.

I wasn't ready for that. I didn't want to hurt the kids, and I didn't want to worry about something that might not happen for a long time. Even if I wanted to risk alienating my sister forever by fighting her for custody of her kids, I wouldn't know where to start. I didn't know where to start looking for Nicole to serve her the papers. I supposed the court had an investigator on payroll to do that for me, but it made me feel like I was stabbing Nicole in the back to demand legal possession of her children. It would open a whole can of worms I wanted to keep firmly closed.

"Guys, we gotta talk," I said that evening over a dinner of corn dogs, baked beans and Aunt Wanda's coleslaw.

Emma licked a dollop of mustard off the side of her corn dog, her eyes fixed on mine. My serious tone did nothing to dim the happiness in her eyes. Jonah and I were in the kitchen with her. Gypsy was under the table, relaxed but ready to pounce on any food that hit the floor. All was comfortable and secure in Emma's world. She sensed no cause for alarm.

I turned my head from her to Jonah to make sure he was listening too. His attitude was much the same as hers. At the moment food was more important than anything their boring old aunt had to say.

I considered letting the matter drop. It had been a wonderful weekend. No tears. No stress, unless you counted me fretting over my goodnight kiss with Barry. Maybe I should wait until morning to see if anyone got upset when they realized I was on my way to work. Maybe Emma had outgrown her anxieties in the last three days and this uncomfortable conversation was unnecessary.

No, I had to do it. Best to jump in with both feet and get it over with.

"Emma, Jonah, do you worry sometimes when I leave for work or go to the store or somewhere that I may not come back?"

Jonah looked across the table at Emma. Emma set her corndog on her plate and stared at it.

I put a hand over each of theirs. Jonah looked at me. Emma continued to study her dinner.

"When I go to work it's because I have to. There are sick people at the hospital who need me to help them feel better. If I weren't there, who would give them their medicine? Who would help them get up and do their exercises so they can go home to their grandkids? Who would help the doctors? I have to go to work. I love my job. I'm good at it. But I also love coming home."

The realization still surprised me. A few months ago I never would've said those words with a straight face. But now I did love coming home. And not just to see Gypsy.

Jonah climbed up on his knees in his chair. "See, Emma. I told you she always comes back."

Emma turned on him. Her blue eyes flashed. "Not always. Mommy didn't come back."

Jonah looked at me. His moist eyes were large and pleading. "You will too come back, won't ya, Aunt Shell? Tell her you'll come back."

I wrapped my arm around Jonah and pulled him against me. "Of course, I'll come back. Don't I come back every night when I say I will? This is my home. It's where I belong. Right here with you and Emma and Gypsy."

Emma set her jaw and glared at Jonah as if I wasn't in the room. "What if she's lying? Mommy lied. She said she'd always take care of us. But she didn't. She let Dean put us in the car, and she didn't even try to stop him." She jerked her hand out from under mine and pulled her knees into the chair like Jonah had done a moment ago. She wrapped her arms around her legs, dropped her head onto them and began to cry.

I jumped out of my chair and hurried around the table to her. Jonah was right behind me.

"Emma, Emma. Honey, please, look at me."

She thrust her face deeper into her arms and shrugged me away. I scooted her chair around so it was facing me and not the table. I knelt in front of her and pulled her long hair away from her face.

"Emma, is this why you started crying over my leaving? Are you afraid I won't come home from work?"

She mumbled something into her knees.

"I can't understand you, Emma. If you want me to make it better, you have to tell me what's wrong."

She lifted her head enough for me to make out her next words. "I don't want you to go."

I picked her up and set her on my lap. She still wouldn't look at me. I pulled a strand of white-blond hair out of her face and wiped away a trail of tears with my thumb. "I have to go to work. Sometimes I have to go to the grocery store or the bank or take Gypsy to the vet. I always come back. You have to trust me and believe me when I tell you something. I'm not lying to you."

She wiped her wet face on her shirtsleeve. "Mommy said the same thing every time I cried."

Jonah nodded beside me in solemn agreement. How could I dispute history? They had no reason to believe me when they couldn't believe their own mother. I pulled Emma closer. I wrapped my other arm around Jonah and hugged him against me.

"Your Mommy loves both of you," I began, though I wondered if it was true. "You know how I know? Because she's my sister and I took care of her when she was your age. She has a big heart, and I know that's where she's holding both of you right now. I just don't think she can come back yet. She loves you and she'll come back as soon as she's able."

"Dean won't let her," Jonah piped up.

I hated to make Dean, whom I'd never met, the bad guy, but things would be a lot simpler on everyone if the kids could blame him instead of Nicole and me.

"Whatever the reason, Mommy decided you needed to stay here awhile longer. I think we're getting along really well, don't you?"

Jonah nodded. I nudged Emma on my lap. She nodded too.

"We've been having a lot of fun. You like preschool. Everybody says you're doing great there. Uncle Jeb finally has somebody to take fishing. Aunt Wanda's teaching you how to cook."

"We never had a dog before," Emma added with a sniff.

"Hey, that's right. Now you've got a dog and your own rooms just like big kids." I hugged them again and kissed the tops of their heads.

"Aunt Shell?"

I looked at Jonah.

"When Mommy comes back, are you gonna tell her we want to keep living here?"

I swallowed hard. They'd asked this question before, and I promised I'd make everything all right with Nicole, whatever that meant. I had hoped by this time they would want to go back with their mother—in the event she wanted them. No matter how hard it would be on me, I still believed children belonged with their mother.

"Are you sure that's what you want?"

He and Emma exchanged solemn looks. They nodded.

I tightened my arms around them. "All right, then. I'll talk to her."

"You promise?" Emma asked.

"She might be pretty mad," Jonah pointed out.

"That's okay." I squared my shoulders with a confidence I didn't feel. "I'm the big sister. She has to do what I say."

They looked at each other. I could almost visualize the weight lifting off their tiny shoulders.

Kyle had been right.

Emma wasn't worried about Nicole. She was worried I would leave and not come back. She feared I was a liar-liar-pants-on-fire just like her mother. I didn't know why it took so long for her worries to manifest. That was a concern for another day. Maybe she had finally begun to feel secure in her new family and was afraid it would fall apart. A family that included me.

I kissed them both, set them back in their chairs and reheated the remainder of our dinner in the microwave.

For the first time in my life, I was part of a real family—Emma and Jonah's family. They needed me. They hurt when I wasn't around.

Crazier than that, I hurt too. The day I found them in the front yard under the lilac bushes all those months ago I never dreamed it would come to this. What happened to the independence I prized so highly? What about fulfilling my obligation and doing my part until Nicole got her head on straight and came after her kids so I could get back to my life?

Now I dreaded the day it would happen.

The microwave dinged. I set the plates in front of the kids. I wouldn't think about that right now. Especially after promising I'd make Nicole understand they wanted to stay here instead of leaving with her. No matter how confident I sounded about being the big sister, Nicole would not appreciate the kids choosing me over her. She would see it as betrayal on their part and brainwashing on mine. As always, she would accept none of the responsibility over the changes in her kids' allegiance during the last few months.

I should prepare Emma and Jonah for the firestorm to come. They needed to know that someday, when they were least prepared to see her, Nicole would waltz in and open her arms and expect the kids to run into them as if she'd stepped out twenty minutes ago.

How could I explain that to preschoolers? How could I heap more weight on their shoulders when they were already worried I would disappear in the night the way Mommy had. They deserved to run and play and chase Gypsy and ride the tractor around the fields and go to bed at night without worrying that the next morning everything they knew and loved could be gone. Life was tough. Bad things happened no matter how much we tried to protect children from them. As long as I could keep those bad things at bay, I would.

I watched as they finished their dinner and half listened to them laugh and tease each other. What had begun as a major imposition and aggravation to my comfortable existence had turned into a greater blessing than I ever imagined.

Grandma Catherine hadn't known what she was missing. Her rejection of Nicole and me didn't sting the way it used to. Happiness and contentment were a choice. Grandma made her choices. I made mine.

I still wasn't ready to give credit to some omniscient being for the love swelling my Grinchy heart to three times its original size. It could very well be nothing more than my baby sister's selfishness that forced me out of my cocoon. Whether I had changed, Nicole was still selfish, or there was a God in heaven working on the way I perceived things, I was thankful. That was enough for now.

After the kids helped put away the dinner dishes, they dashed out the back door before it got too dark to play outside. It would be time for baths and bed soon. A little outside time to burn off the corndogs would help all of us sleep better tonight. I watched them lope around the yard for a few moments, Gypsy at their heels, barking and bouncing as they alternately chased her or she chased them.

I smiled at the sight, a lump in my throat and my eyes heavy with tears. They deserved so much. While they might belong to Nicole, I wanted to be the one to provide a life worthy of them.

Before my nerves could talk me out of it, I snatched my phone off the counter. I nearly started a text before I decided this occasion warranted an actual call.

"Barry, hi," I said as soon as he picked up. "Sorry I didn't get back with you this weekend."

"Hey, no problem." The shock was evident in his voice, as well as delight at hearing my voice. "It's been a busy weekend for me too."

"No, really, I'm sorry I didn't call sooner. To be honest, I didn't know what to say."

"Oh, yeah?"

I snagged my lower lip with my teeth. He was waiting to hear what it was I couldn't put into words. The problem was, I didn't know what to say since I wasn't sure how I felt. The only thing I did know was my heart still yearned for Kyle. I expected it always would. But he made it crystal clear he wasn't interested in a mess like me in his life. Who could blame him? I wouldn't choose me either.

Barry apparently had. He was interested. I had a feeling he was as big of a mess as I was. I didn't want to wait forever for something that might never happen. I wanted my life to start.

It never would as long as I remained unyielding like Grandma had been and paralyzed with fear of opening my heart to rejection. Sometimes you just had to take a chance. Barry seemed in the same place. We could take our chances together.

"I wanted to tell you again I had a really nice time the other night," I blurted out in one breath.

He laughed. The tension broken, I laughed with him.

"Did that sound as pathetic to you as it did to me?" I asked.

"Not pathetic. More like you're really out of practice hearing a man tell you how beautiful you are and how much he wants to spend time with you."

"I don't remember you telling me I was beautiful."

"Sorry. I must've been thinking that part."

We laughed again. I was glad he couldn't see my face, which was blazing hot all the way up to my strawberry-blond roots.

"Next time you'll have to tell me what you're thinking." I hoped I hadn't asked for more than I was ready to hear.

"Next time I will."

He wanted there to be a next time. Surprisingly, so did I. More than I thought I would.

The back door banged open. The kids charged in ahead of Gypsy. "Aunt Shell, Gypsy got in the sticker bush."

I groaned at the twig of briers tangled in Emma's hair. "Looks like you did too." I hoped I could get it out without calling Aunt Wanda.

"Nuh, uh. Jonah did."

More laughter on Barry's end. "Sounds like you have a slight emergency to respond to before bed."

"A nurse's work is never done."

Or a mother's.

Jonah took hold of the brier twig in his sister's hair and yanked. "Jonah, don't!" I exclaimed as Emma let out a yowl.

"I'll call you later," Barry said over her cries of protest.

"You'd better," I said and ended the call before I could embarrass myself further.

I rummaged in the junk drawer for a comb. I hoped I wouldn't need the scissors as well. This was my life now. Untangling hair. Foraging under the couch for lost toys and socks. Making sure everyone had a bath before bed. Sneaking a moment on the phone like a teenager. It felt strange, but nice.

Was this what I'd been missing my whole life and hadn't even known it? For a moment, I missed Grandma Catherine. I wish I could've loved her like I realized I loved Aunt Wanda and Uncle Jeb, even if she never loved me back. Maybe if I had, I could've helped soften her grinchy heart.

Or not. Before a person could change, they had to want to change. There was nothing I could do the help Grandma. Or Mom. Or Nicole.

There was something, however, I could do for me.

I wasn't looking forward to the day Nicole came back, but when it came, I didn't want my life to go back to the way it had been when it was only Gypsy and me rattling around the farm by ourselves.

It was disheartening to think my life wouldn't include Kyle. I loved him; it was time I stopped pretending I didn't. But some things weren't meant to be. I'd survive. I had gotten good at accepting my life wasn't an endless parade of rainbows and smiley emojis.

Kyle wasn't here, but Barry was. He didn't set my heart to racing, but he was funny and interesting and a great dad. Best of all, he liked me and wanted to get to know me better. I wouldn't end up like Grandma. Being right all the time was overrated. I was tired of being right. I'd rather be happy. And loved. Maybe Barry could take Kyle's place in my stubborn heart. If God was truly in charge of the universe, only He knew for sure. For tonight, that was enough.

The End

Before You Go

If you enjoyed Michelle's story—or any of my books—please take a moment and leave a review on Amazon or any other marketplace or blog that allows reviews. Even a short review proves to Amazon there is interest in the book, and they will display it to more readers.

The best way to support any author is still the old-fashioned method of recommending the book to a friend. Share my links on social media outlets. Follow me on Amazon, BookBub and GoodReads. Sign up for my newsletter if you haven't already and receive a free western romance *A Promise for Josie: A Willow Wood Brides Prequel.*

Give the books a thumbs up and leave a comment whenever you see them posted somewhere. No greater compliment can be paid to any author of stories you love.

I love hearing from readers. Email me at teresa@teresaslack.com anytime with your thoughts and input about my stories and series ideas you would love to read.

Next in the Series

A Little Goodbye. Book Two of the Tender Blessings Series

When her sister abandoned her two kids in Michelle Hurley's front yard, she never dreamed it would be the best thing that ever happened to her.

The kids aren't the only changes in Michelle's life. Barry Schilling has made her realize she may have been too hasty in shutting the world out of her life. Still, she can't forget the love she once shared with Kyle Swann.

As if she doesn't have enough daily drama going on, Nicole breezes back onto the farm, making demands and upsetting Michelle's well-ordered life. Again.

As the kids are pulled from her arms, Michelle must make a decision to follow her heart, regardless of what direction that is. She may lose more than the children as she prepares her heart for a little goodbye.

Check out--

Runaway Heart: A Sweet & Clean Contemporary Romance

Kyla Parrish has never held onto a relationship for more than a few months. She's quit more jobs than most people have applied for. Until Will Lachland. He's the first man who ever made her think of getting serious about something, about putting down roots.

What if she's wrong? What if Will's wrong for her? To avoid a decision, Kyla does what she always does. She runs. Back to the one place where life was simple—the family farm. But no matter how far she goes, she can't outrun her heart. Can she find peace and the love she longs for? Or is something else, something greater, calling her heart toward home?

Joy Redefined: A Novel of Suspense

"An unlikely hero..."

When Joy Kessler's neighbor and best friend Dorothea Westlake disappears and a long-lost nephew takes over her house, Joy's suspicions go into full

alert. Where is Dorothea, and why is no one else suspicious? As days turn into weeks with no sign of her friend, Joy must become the woman of courage she always wanted to be to uncover the truth to save Dorothea—and herself.

The Ultimate Guide to Darcy Carter: A Sweet, Small-Town Romance

Comfort food and romance. Ultimate Guide guru Darcy Carter has no time for either until she meets the subject of her next book.

Darcy is an expert at everything--except her own life. She has written over twenty how-to books on every subject under the sun, but she can't guide herself out of a paper bag, especially when it comes to romance.

When her editor suggests a new book idea, *The Ultimate Guide to Finding Mr. Right*, Darcy wants no part of it. She heads south to research an idea of her own. She soon discovers Mr. Right might be hiding in the last place she thought to look.

Don't miss this contemporary Christian romance, a feel-good, laugh-out-loud story that reminds us how fun--and complicated-- falling in love can be.

About the Author

Teresa Slack's down-to-earth writing style and endearing, true-to-life characters can be attributed to her upbringing in rural Ohio. Writing from her home in the southern Ohio hills, she is thankful for the opportunity to do what she loves while sharing her faith with readers.

"I write stories to entertain first. Reading should be fun— an escape. Secondly, I want my stories to inspire and edify the reader. If we're breathing, we're going to face challenges in our daily lives. I strive to create characters my readers can identify with and learn from. Life isn't easy. But it's good to know we don't have to go it alone."

Check out her website www.teresaslack.com or her author page on FaceBook & Twitter to stay abreast of what's coming next. Readers can contact her at teresa@teresaslack.com